The BEST *of*
SPORTS FICTION

REX LARDNER

Selects

The BEST *of*

SPORTS FICTION

Edited with an introduction by

REX LARDNER

Grosset & Dunlap

PUBLISHERS   NEW YORK

Acknowledgments

A MATTER OF SECONDS by ELLERY QUEEN
Copyright © 1953 by United Newspapers Magazine Corporation.
Reprinted by permission of the author and the author's represent-
atives, Scott Meredith Literary Agency, Inc.

UNCLE JIMBO'S MARBLES by EVAN HUNTER
Copyright © 1963 by Evan Hunter. Reprinted by permission of the
author and the author's agents, Scott Meredith Literary Agency,
Inc.

THE LAST RODEO by ERNEST HAYCOX
Copyright 1933 by P. F. Collier & Co. Copyright renewed 1960 by
Jill Marie Haycox. Reprinted by permission of Jill Marie Haycox
and agents for the Ernest Haycox estate, Scott Meredith Literary
Agency, Inc.

A CADDY'S DIARY by RING LARDNER
Copyright 1922 by Curtis Publishing Company; renewal copyright
1950 by Ellis A. Lardner. Reprinted with the permission of Charles
Scribner's Sons from HOW TO WRITE SHORT STORIES by
RING LARDNER.

Contents

Introduction

SPORT has as many meanings as there are people involved in its various forms. It is fun, it is deadly serious, it is relaxation, it burns off hostility and creates it, it is a source of personal pride, it is adventure. Sport can be the means of making a living, of accepting a challenge, of reinforcing the ego. It can be brutal and cruel, it can inspire feelings of poetry. It can inflame spectators to the pitch where an incident will cause a riot. It can cause rancor between nations.

The sports hero is loved and hated, admired and imitated, even immortalized. His feats thrill us in a way that no other activity can match, for sport is life in microcosm. The athlete trains to develop his skills, makes sacrifices and takes risks, suffers and fights discouragement, rises to elation or sinks into despair, ultimately wins or loses.

Sport is also like war. There is an enemy the athlete must outthink, outmaneuver, outperform and outlast, sometimes under conditions least favorable to himself. Surely no mounted general, watching his troops stream by in retreat, feels more anguish than the golfer who misses a six-inch putt on the eighteenth hole—losing a five-dollar bet, a thousand-dollar purse, a goodly amount of prestige, or confidence in his legendary ability to stand firm under pressure. In the same manner, no bombardier who has smuggled a live bomb inside the smokestack of an enemy carrier can know the ecstasy of a golfer who sinks an impossible four-foot putt in a championship match with the wind whipping his clothing off his back and his competitor barely restraining a skeptical smile.

For the spectator, sport invites intense emotional involvement. It satisfies his Walter Mitty dreams and makes him believe in the rags-to-riches story of Cinderella. It furnishes a drama whose main titillation is that of a whodunit—no one knows in advance how it will come out. For the participant, it blows the cobwebs out of the mind, tones up the body, and holds out the expectation of a winning struggle against odds and a feeling of being something more than mortal when he has triumphed. It affords, in fact, a total rejuvenation.

Sport makes us all kin. Any sandlot baseball player who has struck out at the end of an inning with the bases full sympathizes with the major-leaguer who does the same with a great deal more at stake. Any amateur yachtsman who has been knocked out by a captious boom can almost taste the feeling of a professional boxer being kayoed by a Joe Louis or a Jack Dempsey.

In the area of factual reporting, the world of sport has been the source of more yarns about colorful, eccentric and uninhibited personalities than any other activity of modern times —not excluding politics and the cinema. In sports fiction, however, this has not always been the case. Sports stories tend to be cast in standard images and cliches—the unsung hero who remains without recognition until, by a fluke of fate or a desperate decision by a coach, he is thrust into the game when all seems lost and rallies the team to triumph, thereby getting the girl and saving the college. There is a moral to be drawn from all this, and the author usually spells it out in capital letters.

Sport is not that pat, of course. Bad guys often win and 99-pound weaklings, no matter how courageous, usually lose. Adrenalin is not reserved for the virtuous. But whatever the outcome, the nature of all games is such that there is drama and excitement and humor enough for everyone.

Sport brings out the worst and the best in its participants, and sometimes the most poignant and the most amusing as well. People are notorious self-deceivers, and no other field, except perhaps the performing arts, lends itself more to this type of illusion. Fishermen talk about the ones that got away, infielders complain about bad hops, ten-count boxers insist that their opponents barely touched them. Without this healing fantasy, life would be insupportable. Man not only needs to play: he needs to believe that, at least when he is up at bat, he is the best player around.

In this collection of sports fiction, sport is approached from many points of view. There are humorous stories of overriding ambition and preoccupation with success, tales of fakery and fixes, a sporting mystery, a glimpse of an intriguing sport of the future, and a saga of sport used as a tool of pride and breadwinning. The sports covered run the gamut from baseball, prizefighting and golf, to hunting, polo and marble-shooting. And more.

Many of the authors have illustrious names. Some are more noted for their writing in other areas, which makes them, in my opinion, more inventive and cogent when they turn their hands to creating sporting figures in provocative situations. They include, among others, short storyist William Saroyan, mystery writer Ellery Queen, poet Rudyard Kipling, humorists

James Thurber and Irvin S. Cobb, science-fiction author
Arthur C. Clarke, novelist and screenwriter Evan Hunter, and
P. G. Wodehouse, creator of the hilarious butler, Jeeves.

It is hoped that these stories will provide solid mental
nourishment and some chuckles for anyone who has enjoyed
the zest of competitive sport and is also a student of human
frailty. It is hoped, too, if any morals are drawn by the authors,
they will be morals you've never heard before.

Rex Lardner

ELLERY QUEEN

A Matter
of Seconds

You don't have to be a fight expert to recall what happened in the ring that wild night the Champ fought Billy (the Kid) Bolo. Fans are still talking about how it put Wickiup, Colorado, on the map. But the odds are you've never heard how close that fight came to not being fought.

You remember how Wickiup got the match in the first place. The deputation from the Wickiup Chamber of Commerce, headed by millionaire cattleman Sam Pugh, trooped into the promoter's New York office, plunked down a seating plan of the new Wickiup Natural Amphitheater—capacity 75,000—and a satchel containing a guarantee of $250,000 cash money, and flew back home with a contract for what turned out to be—figuring the TV, radio, and movie take— the first million-dollar gate west of Chicago in the history of boxing.

It promised to be a real whingding, too, well worth any sport's investment. Both fighters were rough, tough and inde-

15

structible, their orthodox style carrying no surprises except in the sudden-death department. Anything could happen from a one-round knockout to a hospital bed for two.

The Champ trained at the Wickiup Country Club, and Billy the Kid at the big Pugh ranch, and days before the fight every hotel, motel, trailer camp and tepee within three hundred miles was hanging out the *No Vacancy* sign. Wickiup became the Eldorado of every fight fan, sportswriter, gambler and grifter between Key West and Puget Sound who could scare up a grubstake.

Ellery was in Wickiup to see the contest as the guest of old Sam Pugh, who owed him something for a reason that's another story.

The fight was scheduled for 8 P.M. Mountain Time, to make the 10 P.M. TV date for the Eastern fans. Ellery first heard that something was wrong exactly an hour and a half before ringtime.

He was hanging around the Comanche Bar of the Redman Hotel, waiting for his host to pick him up for the drive out to the Amphitheater, when he was paged by a bellboy.

"Mr. Queen? Mr. Pugh wants you to come up to Suite 101. Urgent."

The cattleman himself answered Ellery's knock. His purple-sage complexion looked moldy. "Come in, son!"

In the suite Ellery found the State Boxing Commissioner, nine leading citizens of Wickiup, and Tootsie Cogan, Billy the Kid's bald little manager. Tootsie was crying, and the other gentlemen looked half inclined to join him.

"What's the matter?" asked Ellery.

"The Kid," growled Sam Pugh, "has been kidnaped."

"Snatched," wept Cogan. "At three o'clock I feed him a rare steak at Mr. Pugh's ranch and I make him lay down for a snooze. I run over for a last-minute yak with Chick Kraus, the Champ's manager, about the rules, and while I'm gone—"

"Four masked men with guns snatched the Kid," said the

cattleman. "We've been negotiating with them by phone ever since. They want a hundred thousand dollars' ransom."

"Or no fight," snarled the Boxing Commissioner. "Eastern gangsters!"

"It'll ruin us," groaned one of the local elite. "The business-men of this town put up a quarter of a million guarantee. Not to mention the lawsuits—"

"I think I get the picture, gentlemen," said Ellery. "With the fight less than ninety minutes off, there's no time to climb a high horse. I take it you're paying?"

"We've managed to raise the cash among us," said the old cattleman, nodding toward a bloated briefcase on the table, "and, Ellery, we've told 'em that you're going to deliver it. Will you?"

"You know I will, Sam," said Ellery. "Maybe I can get a line on them at the same time—"

"No, you'll put the whammy on it!" shrieked the Kid's manager. "Just get my boy back, in shape to climb into that ring!"

"You couldn't anyway. They're not showing their dirty faces," rasped Sam Pugh. "They've named a neutral party, too, and he's agreed to act for them."

"What you might call a matter of seconds, eh? Who is he, Sam?"

"Know Sime Jackman, the newspaperman?"

"The dean of West Coast sportswriters? By reputation only; it's tops. Maybe if Jackman and I work together—"

"Sime's had to promise he'd keep his mouth shut," said the Boxing Commissioner, "and in the forty years I've known him, damn it, he's never broken his word. Forget the sleuthing, Mr. Queen. Just see that Billy Bolo gets back in time."

"All right," sighed Ellery. "Sam, what can I do?"

"At seven o'clock sharp," said the cattleman, "you're to be in Sime Jackman's room at the Western Hotel—Room 442. Jackman will then notify the kidnapers some way that you're there with the ransom, and Billy Bolo will be released. They've promised that the Kid will walk into this room by seven-fifteen, unharmed and ready to climb into the ring, if we keep our word."

"How do you know they'll keep theirs?"

"You're not to leave the money with Jackman till I phone you, in his room, that the Kid's back safe."

"Then you'd better give me a password, Sam—voices can be imitated. In my ear . . . if you gentlemen don't mind?"

A stocky man with white hair and keen blue eyes opened the door of Room 442 in the Western Hotel at Ellery's rap.

"You're Queen, I take it. Come on in. I'm Sime Jackman."

Ellery looked around while the newspaperman shut the door. On the telephone table stood a battered portable typewriter and a bottle of Scotch. There was no one else in the room.

"I think," said Ellery, "I'd like some identification."

The whitehaired man stared. Then he grinned and fished in his pockets. "Driver's license—press card—you'll find my name engraved on the back of this presentation watch from the National Sportswriters' Association—"

"I'm sold." Ellery opened the briefcase and dumped its contents on the bed. The money was in $1,000 bundles, marked on the bank wrappers—tens, twenties, and fifties. "Are you going to take the time to count it?"

"Hell, no. I want to see that fight tonight!" The sportswriter went to the window.

"I was told you'd immediately notify the kidnapers—"

"That's what I'm doing." Jackman raised and lowered the windowshade rapidly several times. "You don't think those lice gave me any phone numbers, do you? This is the signal I was told to give—they must have a man watching my window. I suppose he'll phone them it's okay. Well, that's that."

"Have you actually seen any of them?" Ellery asked.

"Have a heart, Queen," grinned the newspaperman. "I gave my word I wouldn't answer any questions. Well, now all we can do is wait for Sam Pugh's phone call. How about a drink?"

"I'll take a raincheck." Ellery sat down on the bed beside the ransom money. "What's the *modus operandi,* Jackman? How do you get the money to them?"

But the whitehaired man merely poured himself a drink. "Ought to be a pretty good scrap," he murmured.

"You win," said Ellery ruefully. "Yes, it should. How do you rate Bolo's chances? After all this, his nerves will be shot higher than Pike's Peak."

"The Kid? He was born without any. And when he gets mad, the way he must be right now—"

"Then you think he's got a chance to take the Champ?"

"If those punks didn't sap him, I make it the Kid by a K.O."

"You're the expert. You figure he's got the punch to put a bull like the Champ away?"

"Did you see the Kid's last fight?" smiled the sportswriter. "Artie Starr's nobody's setup. Yet Bolo hit him three right hooks so fast and murderous, the second and third exploded on Starr's chin while he was still on his way to the canvas. It took his handlers ten minutes to bring him to—"

The phone made them both jump.

"They must have had the Kid around the corner!" Ellery said.

"You better answer it."

Ellery raced to the phone. "Queen speaking. Who is this?"

"It's me—Sam!" roared Sam Pugh's voice. "Listen, son—"

"Hold it. What's the password?"

"Oh! Solar plexus." Ellery nodded, relieved. "The Kid's back, Ellery," the cattleman exulted, "and he's all riled up and r'arin' to go. Release the money. See you at ringside!" His phone clicked.

"Okay?" smiled the whitehaired man.

"Yes," Ellery smiled back, "so now I can let you have it." And, swinging the telephone receiver, Ellery clubbed him neatly above the left ear. He was over at the clothes closet yanking the door open even before the whitehaired man bounced on the carpet. "So it *was* the closet he parked you in," Ellery said cheerfully to the trussed, gagged figure on the closet floor. "Well, we'll have you out of these ropes in a jiffy, Mr. Jackman, and then we'll settle the hash of this double-crossing road agent!"

While the real Sime Jackson stood guard over the prostrate man, Ellery stuffed the money back into the briefcase. "Hijacker?" asked the newspaperman without rancor.

"No, indeed," said Ellery. "He couldn't have been a hijacker, because the gang released the Kid after this man gave the signal. So I knew he was one of them. When they told you I was to be the contact man, you said something about you and me not knowing each other, didn't you? I thought so. That's what gave this operator his big idea. He'd put you on ice, and when I handed him the ransom thinking he was you, he'd run out on his pals."

"But how," demanded the sportswriter, "did you know he wasn't me?"

"He said in the Bolo-Starr fight the Kid flattened Starr with three right hooks. You could hardly have become the dean of West Coast sportswriters and a national fight expert, Jackman, without learning that in the lexicon of boxing there's no such blow as a right hook for a fighter with the orthodox stance. The righthand equivalent of a left hook in a righthanded fighter is a right cross."

"Why, the palooka," scowled the newspaperman, taking a fresh grip on the unconscious gangster's gun as the man stirred. "But about this ransom, Queen. I don't know what to do. After all, the rest of the gang did keep their word and return the Kid. Do I keep mine and deliver the dough to them, or does this bum's doublecross take me off the hook?"

"Hm. Nice problem in ethics." Ellery glanced at his watch and frowned. "We'll miss the fight unless we hurry! Tell you what, Sime."

"What?"

"We'll pass the buck—or should I say bucks?—to a higher authority." Ellery grinned and picked up the bruised phone. "Desk? Two reliable cops for immediate guard duty, please, and meanwhile get me the nearest office of the FBI—rush!"

EVAN HUNTER

Uncle Jimbo's Marbles

LAST summer they quarantined the camp two weeks after we'd arrived.

Uncle Marvin called all us counselors into the dining room one July night and announced briefly that there was a polio scare at a nearby camp. He went on to say that whereas all of *our* campers had of course been vaccinated, he nonetheless felt it would be in the best interests of public safety if we voluntarily agreed not to leave the campgrounds until the threat had subsided. The words "public safety" were Uncle Marvin's own. He was the principal of a junior high school in the Bronx, and he also happened to own Camp Marvin, which is why it was called Camp Marvin and not Camp Chippewa or Manetoga or Hiawatha. He could have called it "Camp Levine," I suppose, Levine being his last name, but I somehow feel his choice was judicious. Besides, the name Marvin seemed to fit a camp whose owner was a man given to saying things like "public safety," especially when he became *Uncle* Marvin for the summer.

I was Uncle Don for the summer.

The kids in my bunk had never heard of Uncle Don on the radio, so they never made any jokes about my name. To tell the truth, I'd barely heard of him myself. Besides, they were a nice bunch of kids, and we were getting along fine until the voluntary quarantine in the best interests of public safety was declared by Marvin, and then things got a little strained and eventually led to a sort of hysteria.

Marvin's wife was named Lydia, and so the girls' camp across the lake from Camp Marvin was called Camp Lydia, and the entire complex was called Camp Lydia-Marvin, which was possibly one of the most exciting names in the annals of American camp history. I was Uncle Don last summer, and I was nineteen years old. Across the lake in Camp Lydia was a girl named Aunt Rebecca, who was also nineteen years old and whom I loved ferociously. When the quarantine began, I started writing notes to her, and I would have them smuggled across the lake, tied to the handles of the big milk cans. *I love you, Aunt Rebecca,* my notes would say. And I would look across the still waters of the lake and try to imagine Becky opening my note, her dark eyes lowered as she read the words, her quick smile flashing over her face. I imagined she would look up hastily, she moved hastily, her eyes would dart, the smile would widen, she would stare into the distance at the pine trees towering over the boys' cabins, and maybe her heart would skip a beat, and maybe she would murmur softly under her breath, *I love you, too, Uncle Don.*

I hated Camp Marvin.

I will tell you what I loved.

I loved Rebecca Goldblatt, that's all. I had loved Rebecca Goldblatt long before I met her. I had loved her, to tell the truth, from the day I was twelve years old and was allowed to join the adult section of the public library. I had clutched my new card in my hand that bright October day, the card unmarked, every space on it empty, and wandered among the shelves. It was very warm inside the library, warm and hushed, and as I walked past the big windows I could hear the wind outside, and I could see the huge tree out front with its leaves shaking loose every time there was a new gust, and beyond that on the other side of the street some smaller trees, bare already, bending a little in the wind. It was very cold outside, but I was warm as I walked through the aisles with a smile on my face, holding my new library card, and wondering if everyone could tell I was an adult now, it said so on my card.

I found the book on one of the open shelves. The cover was red, tooled in gold. The title was *Ivanhoe*.

And that night I fell in love with Rebecca, not Rebecca Goldblatt, but the girl in *Ivanhoe*. And then when they re-released the movie, I fell in love with her all over again, not Elizabeth Taylor, but Rebecca, the girl in *Ivanhoe*. I can still remember one of the lines in the movie. It had nothing to do with either Ivanhoe's Rebecca or my own Rebecca Goldblatt, but I will never forget it anyway. It was when Robert Taylor was standing horseless, without a shield, trying to fend off the mace blows of the mounted Norman knight. And the judge or the referee, or whatever he was called in those days, looked at Robert Taylor, who had almost hit the Norman's horse with his sword, and shouted, "Beware, Saxon, lest you strike horse!" That was a rule, you see. You weren't allowed to strike the horse.

Oh, how I loved Rebecca Goldblatt!

I loved everything about her, her eyes, her nose, her mouth, her eyes. Her eyes were black. I know a lot of girls claim to have really black eyes, but Rebecca is the only person I have ever known in my entire life whose eyes were truly black and

not simply a very dark brown. Sometimes, when she was in a
sulky, brooding mood, her eyes got so mysterious and menac-
ing they scared me half to death. Girls' eyes always do that to
me when they're in that very dramatic solitary mood, as if
they're pondering all the female secrets of the world. But
usually her eyes were very bright and glowing, like a black
purey. I shouldn't talk about marbles, I suppose, since marbles
started all the trouble that summer—but that was how her
eyes looked, the way a black purey looks when you hold it up
to the sun.

I loved her eyes and I loved her smile, which was fast and
open and yet somehow secretive, as if she'd been amused by
something for a very long time before allowing it to burst onto
her mouth. And I loved her figure which was very slender with
sort of small breasts and very long legs that carried her in a
strange sort of lope, especially when she was wearing a
trenchcoat, don't ask me why. I loved her name and the way
she looked. I loved her walk, and I loved the way she talked,
too, a sort of combination of middle-class Bronx Jewish girl
with a touch of City College Speech One thrown in, which is
where she went to school and which is where I met her.

I think I should tell you now that I'm Italian.

That's how I happened to be at Camp Marvin in Stockbridge, Massachusetts, with a girl named Rebecca Goldblatt
across the lake in Camp Lydia.

I know that's not much of a problem these days, what with
new nations clamoring for freedom, and Federal troops
crawling all over the South, and discrimination of all sorts
every place you look. It's not much of a problem unless you
happen to be nineteen years old and involved in it, and then it
seems like a pretty big problem. I'm too young to have seen
Abie's Irish Rose, but I honestly don't think I will ever
understand what was so funny about *that* situation, believe
me. I didn't think it was so funny last summer, and I still don't

think it's funny, but maybe what happened with Uncle Jimbo's marbles had something to do with that. I don't really know. I just know for certain now that you can get so involved in something you don't really see the truth of it any more. And the simple truth of Becky and me was that we loved each other. The rest of it was all hysteria, like with the marbles.

I have to tell you that I didn't want to go to Camp Marvin in the first place. It was all Becky's idea, and she presented it with that straightforward solemn look she always gets on her face when she discusses things like sending food to the starving people in China or disarmament or thalidomide or pesticides. She gets so deep and so involved sometimes that I feel like kissing her. Anyway, it was her idea, and I didn't like it because I said it sounded to me like hiding.

"It's not hiding," Becky said.

"Then what is it if not hiding?" I answered. "I don't *want* to be a counselor this summer. I want to go to the beach and listen to records and hold your hand."

"They have a beach at Camp Marvin," Becky said.

"And I don't like the name of the camp."

"Why not?"

"It's unimaginative. Anybody who would name a place Camp Marvin must be a very unimaginative person."

"He's a junior high school principal," Becky said.

"That only proves my point." She was looking very very solemn just about then, the way she gets when we discuss the Cuban situation, so I said, "Give me one good reason why we should go to Stockbridge, Massachusetts, to a camp named *Marvin*, of all things, would you please?"

"Yes."

"Well, go ahead."

"We would be together all summer," Becky said simply, "and we wouldn't have to hide from my father."

"That's the craziest thing I ever heard in my life," I said.

"You want to go away and hide from him just so we won't have to hide from him."

"That's not what I'm saying," Becky said.

"Then what is it, if not hiding from him?"

"It's not my fault he's a bigoted jerk!" Becky said angrily, and I didn't realize how much this meant to her until that minute, because tears suddenly sprang into her eyes. I never know what to do when a girl starts crying, especially someone you love.

"Becky," I said, "if we run away this summer, we're only confirming his . . ."

"He doesn't even know you, Donald," she said. "He doesn't know how sweet you are."

"Yes, but if we hide from him . . ."

"If he'd only meet you, if he'd only talk to you . . ."

"Yes, but if we run away to hide, then all we're doing is joining in with his lunacy, honey. Can't you see that?"

"My father is not a lunatic," Becky said. "My father is a dentist and a prejudiced ass, but he's not a lunatic. And anyway, you have to remember that *his* father can still remember pogroms in Russia."

"All right, but this isn't Russia," I said.

"I know."

"And I'm not about to ride into the town and rape all the women and kill all the men."

"You don't even know *how* to ride," Becky said.

"That's right," I said, "but even if I *did* know how to ride, I wouldn't do it."

"I know, you're so sweet," Becky said.

"Okay. Now if your father believes that I'm some kind of assassin with a stiletto, that's *his* fantasy, you see, Beck? And if I sneak away with you this summer, then I'm *joining* his fantasy, I'm becoming as crazy as he is. How can you ask me to do that?"

"I can ask you because I love you and I want to be alone with you without having to sneak and skulk all the time. It isn't fair."

"What isn't fair?"

"Sneaking and skulking all the time."

"That's right."

"When I love you so much."

"I love you, too, Beck," I said. "But . . ."

"Well, if you love me so much, it seems like a very simple thing to do to simply say you'll come with me to Camp Lydia-Marvin this summer."

I didn't say anything.

"Donald?" Becky said.

"This is a mistake," I said, shaking my head.

"We'll be alone."

"We'll be surrounded by eight thousand screaming kids!"

"The kids go to sleep early."

"We'll be hiding, we'll be—"

"We'll be alone."

"Damn it, Becky, sometimes . . ."

"Will you come, Donald?"

"Well, what else can I do? Let you go alone?"

"I think that's what scares my father," Becky said, the smile coming onto her mouth, her black eyes glowing.

"What are you talking about?"

"That fiery Italian temper."

"Yeah, go to hell, you *and* your father," I said smiling, and then I kissed her because what else can you do with a girl like that whom you love so terribly much?

That's how we came to be at Camp Lydia-Marvin last summer.

The quarantine was very ironic in an O. Henry way because we had gone to camp to be *together,* you see, and when Uncle Marvin had his bright quarantine idea, he really meant *quarantine,* the girls with the girls and the boys with the boys. So there was Rebecca clear the hell over on the other side of the lake, and here was I with a bunch of counselors named Uncle Bud and Uncle Jimbo and Uncle Dave and Uncle Ronnie and even Uncle Emil, who was a gym teacher at Benjamin Franklin High School in Manhattan. All the uncles took the quarantine in high good spirits for the first week, I guess. I must admit that even I found a sense of adventure in tying my love notes to the handles of the milk cans. I never once questioned the validity of a quarantine that allowed milk to be passed from one side of the lake to the other. In fact, if it hadn't been for the milk cans, I would have gone out of my mind immediately. As it was, I *almost* went out of my mind, but not until much later. And by that time everybody was a little nutty.

I think it all started with the kids. Everything usually starts with kids. I once read a Ray Bradbury story called "Invasion" or something, about these Martians, or aliens, anyway, I don't remember which planet, who are planning an invasion of Earth, and they're doing it through the kids. Boy, that story scared me, I can tell you, since I have a kid brother who gets a very fanatical gleam in his eye every now and then. I wouldn't be at all surprised.

The thing that started with the kids was the marbles. Now every kid who goes to camp for the summer takes marbles with him. There's usually what they call Free Play or Unassigned, and that's when the kids go to ping-pong or tether ball or marbles. Marbles were very big at Camp Marvin, especially after the quarantine started, though I'm still not sure whether the quarantine really had anything to do with the craze. Maybe there was just an unusual number of marbles at camp that summer, I don't know. At the end there, it sure *seemed* like a lot of marbles. The most marbles I had ever seen in my life before that was when I was eight years old and still living in Manhattan, before we moved up to the Bronx. My mother and father gave me a *hundred* marbles for my birthday, and they also gave me a leather pouch with drawstrings to put the marbles in. I went downstairs with the hundred marbles, and I lost them all in a two-hour game. I almost lost the pouch, too, because a kid on the block wanted to trade me forty immies and a steelie for it, but I had the wisdom to refuse the offer. I'll never forget my mother's face when I went upstairs and told her I'd been wiped out.

"You lost *all* the marbles?" she asked incredulously.

"Yeah, all the immies," I said.

"How?"

"Just playing immies," I said.

They didn't play immies at Camp Marvin; they played marbles. They used to draw a circle in the dirt, and each kid would put five or six marbles in the circle and try to hit them out with his shooter. I didn't know how to play marbles because all I played as a kid was immies, which is played by the curb, in the gutter. In fact, it was best to play immies after a rainstorm because then there would be puddles all over the street, and you never knew where the other guy's immie was. You just shot and prayed and felt around in the dirty water with your hand spread, trying to span the immies. It used to be fun when I was a kid. A city street is something like a summer camp all year round, you see. There are always a thousand kids on the block and a hundred games to choose from: stickball, stoopball, skullies, Johnny-on-a-Pony, Kick the Can, Statues, Salugi, Ring-a-Leavio, hundreds of games. I sometimes wonder why the *Herald Tribune* sends slum kids to the country. I think somebody ought to start sending country kids to the slums. In a way, when the marble craze started at Camp Marvin, it was very much like a craze starting on a city street, where one day a kid will come down with his roller skates, and the next day the roller-skating season has started. It was the same thing with the marbles at Camp Marvin. A couple of kids started a game, and before any of us were really completely aware of it, there were marble games being played all over the camp.

It would have been all right if the craze had restricted itself to the kids. But you have to remember that we were quarantined, which meant that we worked with the kids all day long, and then were not permitted to leave the grounds at night, on our time off. Children are very nice and all that, and someday I hope to have a dozen of my own, but that summer it was important to get away from them every now and then. I mean, physically and geographically *away* from them. It was important to have other interests. It was important to have an emotional and mental respite. What it was important to do, in fact, was to hold Becky in my arms and kiss her, but Marvin of course had made that impossible with his stupid quarantine. The funny thing was he didn't seem to miss his wife Lydia at all. Maybe that's because they'd been married for fourteen years. But most of the rest of us began to feel the strain of the quarantine by the end of the second week, and I think it was then that Uncle Jimbo ventured into his first game of marbles.

Jimbo, like the rest of us, was beginning to crave a little action. He was a very tall man who taught science at a high school someplace in Brooklyn. His real name was James McFarland, but in the family structure of Camp Marvin he immediately became Uncle Jim. And then, because it is fatal to have a name like Jim at any camp, he was naturally renamed Jimbo. He seemed like a very serious fellow, this Jimbo, about thirty-eight years old, with a wife and two kids at home. He wore eyeglasses, and he had sandy-colored hair that was always falling onto his forehead. The forehead itself bore a perpetual frown, even when he was playing marbles, as if he were constantly trying to figure out one of Einstein's theories. He always wore sneakers and Bermuda shorts that had been made by cutting down a pair of dungarees. When the quarantine started, one of the kids in his bunk painted a big PW on

Jimbo's dungaree Bermuda shorts, the PW standing for prisoner of war—a joke Jimbo didn't think was very comical. I knew how he felt. I wasn't married, of course, but I knew what it was like to be separated from someone you loved, and Jimbo's wife and kids were away the hell out there in Brooklyn while we were locked up in Stockbridge.

I happened to be there the day he joined one of the games, thereby starting the madness that followed. He had found a single marble near the tennis courts and then had gone foraging on his free time until he'd come up with half a dozen more. It was just after dinner, and three kids were playing in front of my bunk when Jimbo strolled over and asked if he could get in the game. If there's one thing a kid can spot at fifty paces, it's a sucker. They took one look at the tall science teacher from Brooklyn and fairly leaped on him in their anxiety to get him in the game. Well, that was the last leaping any of them did for the rest of the evening. Jimbo had seven marbles. He put six of them in the ring, and he kept the biggest one for his shooter. The kids, bowing graciously to their guest, allowed him to shoot first. Standing ten feet from the circle in the dust, Jimbo took careful aim and let his shooter go. It sprang out of his hand with the speed of sound, almost cracking a marble in the dead center of the ring and sending it flying out onto the surrounding dirt.

The kids weren't terribly impressed because they were very hip and knew all about beginner's luck. They didn't begin to realize they were playing with a pro until they saw Jimbo squat down on one knee and proceed to knock every single marble out of the ring without missing a shot. Then, because there's no sucker like a sucker who thinks he knows one, the kids decided they could take Jimbo *anyway*, and they spent the rest of the evening disproving the theory by losing marble after marble to him. Jimbo told me later that he'd been raised in Plainfield, New Jersey, and had played marbles practically every day of his childhood. But the kids didn't know that at the time, and by the end of that first evening Jimbo had won perhaps two hundred marbles.

I wasn't sure I liked what Jimbo had done. He was, after all, a grown man, and he was playing with kids, and one of the kids he'd beaten happened to be a kid in my bunk. I watched that kid walk away from the game after Jimbo collected all the marbles. His name was Max, which is a funny name for a kid anyway, and he was walking with his head bent, his hands in the pockets of his shorts, his sneakers scuffing the ground.

"What's the matter, Max?" I asked.

"Nothing," he said.

"Come here, sit down," I said. He came over and sat on the bunk steps with me. I knew better than to talk about the marbles he had lost. I talked about the baseball game that afternoon and about the volleyball tournament, and all the while I was thinking of those hundred marbles I had got for my eighth birthday, and the leather pouch, and the look on my mother's face when I climbed to the third floor and told her I'd lost them all. It was getting on about dusk, and I said to Max, "Something very important is going to happen in just a few minutes, Max. Do you know what it is?"

"No," Max said.

"Well, can you guess?"

"I don't know. Is it the boxing matches tonight?" he asked.

"No, this is before the boxing matches."

"Well, what is it?" he asked.

"It happens every day at about this time," I said, "and we hardly ever stop to look at it." Max turned his puzzled face up to mine. "Look out there, Max," I said. "Look out there over the lake."

Together, Max and I sat and serenely watched the sunset.

The madness started the next day.

It started when Uncle Emil, the gym teacher from Benjamin Franklin, decided that marbles was essentially a game of athletic skill. Being a gym teacher and also being in charge of the camp's entire sports program, he naturally decided that in order to uphold his honor and his title, he would have to defeat Uncle Jimbo. He didn't declare a formal match or anything like that. He simply wandered up to Jimbo during the noon rest hour and said, "Hey, Jimbo, want to shoot some marbles?"

Jimbo looked at him with the slow steady gaze of a renowned gunslick and then said, "Sure. Why not?" Lazily he went back to his own bunk. In a few minutes he returned with a cigar box containing his winnings of the night before. They drew a circle in the dust, and each put twelve marbles in the circle. I was only sitting there writing a letter to Becky, and I guess they decided I wasn't doing anything important, so they made me referee. Jimbo was wearing a yellow short-sleeved sports shirt and his sawed-off dungarees. Emil was wearing spotless white shorts and a spotless white T-shirt, as if he were about to settle the Davis Cup at Wimbledon or someplace. They flipped a coin to see who would shoot first. Emil won the toss.

Standing behind the line they had drawn in the dust some ten feet from the ring, Emil held his shooter out and sighted along the length of his arm. Jimbo stood watching him with a faintly amused look on his face. I looked up from my letter because I was supposed to be referee, even though I'd been in the middle of telling Becky I loved her, which I always seemed to be in the middle of doing whenever I got the chance. Emil licked his lips with his tongue, cocked his thumb against the big marble in his fist, and then triggered his shot. The marble leaped from his hand, spinning across the open air in a direct, unwavering, deadly accurate line toward the middle of the circle. It collided with one of the marbles in the ring, which richocheted off onto another marble, which struck two more marbles, which knocked out yet another marble for a total of five marbles knocked out of the circle on the first shot. I must admit I felt a slight thrill of pleasure. I can remember thinking, *All right, Jimbo, this time you're not playing with kids.* But I can also remember looking over at Jimbo and noticing that he didn't seem at all disturbed, that he was still wearing that same faintly amused expression on his long face.

Emil walked to the ring and, grinning, turned to Jimbo and said, "Want to forfeit?"

"Shoot," Jimbo said.

Emil grinned again, crouched in the dust, picked up his big marble, and shot. He knocked two more marbles out of the ring in succession and then missed the third by a hair, and that was the end of the game. I say that was the end of the game only because Jimbo then shot and knocked out all the remaining marbles in the circle. And then, because he had won this round, it was his turn to shoot first in the next round. He shot first, and he knocked four marbles out with his opening blast, and then proceeded to clean up the ring again. And then, because he'd won this round as well, he shot first again, and again cleaned up the ring, and he kept doing that all through the rest period until he'd won seventy-five marbles from Uncle Emil.

Uncle Emil muttered something about having a little rheumatism in his fingers, throwing his game off, and Jimbo listened sympathetically while he added the seventy-five marbles to the collection in his bulging cigar box. That afternoon Emil came back with a hundred marbles he had scrounged from the kids, and Jimbo won them all in a matter of a half hour. That evening Jimbo went to the mess hall to pick up a cardboard carton for his marble winnings. And, also that evening, he became a celebrity.

I guess I was the only person, man or boy, in that camp who didn't want to try beating Uncle Jimbo in the hectic weeks that followed. To begin with, I am not a very competitive fellow, and besides, I only knew how to play immies, not marbles. Marbles required a strong thumb and a fast eye, Jimbo explained to me. My thumbs were pretty weak and my eyes were tired from staring across the lake trying to catch a glimpse of a distant figure I could identify as Becky. But everyone else in camp seemed to possess powerful thumbs and 20/20 vision, and they were all anxious to pit these assets against the champion. When you come to think of it, I suppose, champions exist *only* to be challenged, anyway. The challengers in this case included *everybody*, and all for different reasons.

Uncle Ronnie was a counselor whom everyone, including the kids, called Horizontal Ronnie because his two favorite pursuits both required a bed and a horizontal position. He wanted to beat Jimbo because the quarantine had deprived him of the satisfying company of a girl named Laura in Camp Lydia. Jimbo won two hundred marbles from Ronnie in an hour of play.

Uncle Dave taught mathematics at Evander Childs High School, and he thought he had figured out a foolproof system that he wanted to try in practice. The system worked for fifteen minutes, at the end of which time Jimbo blasted the game from its hinges and then barged on through to win a hundred and fifty marbles.

Uncle Marvin, too, had his own reason for wanting to beat Jimbo. Before the season had begun, when Marvin was still hiring counselors, he had offered Jimbo twelve hundred dollars for the job. Jimbo had held out for thirteen hundred, which Marvin eventually and grudgingly paid him. But the extra hundred dollars rankled, and Marvin was determined to get it back somehow.

You may think it odd that he decided to get back his hundred dollars by winning *marbles* from Jimbo. After all, marbles are marbles, and money is money. But a very strange thing had happened in the second week of the madness. Marbles, which up to that time had only been round pieces of colored glass, suddenly became the hottest item of currency in the camp's vast and complicated trading system. Before then, dimes were very hot property because the Coke machine in the counselors' shack took only dimes. The kids weren't allowed to enter the counselors' shack, nor were they allowed to drink Cokes, all of which made it absolutely necessary for them to have dimes so they could sneak into the counselors' shack and drink Cokes. Almost every letter home, before the marble madness began, started with the words, "Dear Mom and Dad, I am fine. Please send me some dimes." But suddenly, because Jimbo kept winning marbles with such frequency, there was a shortage of marbles in the camp. Marbles became a precious commodity, like gold or silver, and the basis of the camp economy. If you had marbles, you could trade them for all the dimes you needed. You could, in fact, get almost anything you wanted, if you only had marbles. Uncle Jimbo had a lot of marbles. Uncle Jimbo had a whole damn suitcase full of them, which he kept locked and on a shelf over his bed. He was surely the richest man in camp.

He became even richer the afternoon he played Uncle Marvin and won five hundred marbles from him, a blow from which Marvin never recovered. By this time, beating Jimbo had become an obsession. Jimbo was the sole topic of camp discussion, overshadowing the approaching Color War, eclipsing the visit of a famous football player who talked about the ways and means of forward passing while nobody listened. The counselors, the kids, even the camp doctor, were interested only in the ways and means of amassing more marbles to pit against Jimbo's growing empire. They discussed shooting techniques, and whether or not they should play with the sun facing them or behind their backs. They discussed the potency of the mass shot as against a slow deliberate one-at-a-time sort of game. They discussed different kinds of shooters, the illegality of using steelies, the current exchange rate of pureys. The kids loved every minute of it. They awoke each morning brimming with plans for Jimbo's ultimate downfall. To them, beating him was important only because it would give them an opportunity to prove that adults, especially adult counselors, were all a bunch of no-good finks.

On Monday of the third week of the madness, the smart money entered the marbles business—and the gambling element began taking over.

But before that, on Sunday night, I broke quarantine.

I am usually a law-abiding fellow, and I might never have broken quarantine were it not for Horizontal Ronnie, who, I later came to learn, had very definite criminal leanings.

"Look," he said to me, "what's to stop us from taking one of the canoes and paddling over to the other side?"

"Well," I said, "there's a polio scare."

"Don't you want to see What's-her-name?"

"Rebecca."

"Yeah, don't you want to see her?"

"Sure I do."

"Has every kid in this camp and also in Camp Lydia, by Marvin's own admission, in his very own words, been inoculated against polio?"

"Well, yes," I said.

"Then would you mind telling me how there is a polio scare?"

"I don't know," I said.

"Fine. I'll meet you at the boat dock tonight at nine o'clock. I'll take care of getting word to the girls."

I guess I didn't trust him even then, because I took care of getting word to Becky myself that afternoon, by sending over one of my notes tied to an empty milk can. That night, at nine o'clock on the dot, Ronnie and I met at the boat dock and silently slipped one of the canoes into the water. We didn't talk at all until we were in the middle of the lake, and then Ronnie said, "We'll come back around eleven. Is that all right with you?"

"Sure," I said.

"Boy, that Laura," he said, and fell silent again, apparently contemplating what was ahead. Laura, whom I had only seen once or twice before the quarantine, was a very pretty blond girl who always wore white sweaters and tight white shorts. She also wore a perfume that was very hard to avoid smelling, and the few times I had seen her was in the counselors' shack where she kept playing the "Malaguena" over and over again on the piano. She was a very mysterious girl, what with her sweater and shorts and her perfume and her "Malaguena." She was eighteen years old.

"I think I know how to beat him," Ronnie said suddenly.

"Huh?"

"Jimbo. I think I know how to beat the bastard."

"How?" I asked.

"Never mind," Ronnie said, and then he fell silent again, but it seemed to me he was paddling more furiously.

I met Rebecca under the pines bordering the lake. She was wearing black slacks and a black bulky sweater, and she rushed into my arms and didn't say anything for the longest time, just held herself close to me, and then lifted her head and stared into my face, and then smiled that fast-breaking smile, and fleetingly kissed me on the cheek, and pulled away and looked into my face again.

We skirted the edge of the pine forest, the night was still, I could feel her hand tight in my own. We sat with our backs to one of the huge boulders overlooking the lake, and I held her in my arms and told her how miserable I'd been without her, and she kept kissing my closed eyes as I spoke, tiny little punctuating kisses that made me weak.

The night was very dark. Somewhere across the lake a dog began barking, and then the barking stopped and the night was still again.

"I can barely see you, Becky," I whispered.

I held her close, I held her slender body close to mine. She was Becky, she was trembling, she was joy and sadness together, echoing inside me. If I held her a moment longer my heart would burst, I knew my heart would burst and shower trailing sparks on the night. And yet I held her, wanting to cry in my happiness, dizzy with the smell of her hair, loving everything about her in that timeless, brimming moment, still knowing my heart would burst, loving her closed eyes and the whispery touch of her lashes, and the rough wool of her sweater, and the delicate motion of her hands on my face. I kissed her, I died, I smiled, I listened to thunder, for oh, the kiss of Rebecca Goldblatt, the kiss, the heart-stopping kiss of my girl.

The world was dark and still.

"I love you," she said.

"I love you," I said.

And then she threw her arms around my neck and put her face against mine, tight, I could feel her cheekbone hard against mine, and suddenly she was crying.

"Hey," I said. "What . . . honey, what is it?"

"Oh, Donald," she said, "what are we going to do? I love you so much."

"I think we ought to tell him," I said, "when we get back."

"How can we do that?" Becky said.

"I can go to him. I can say we're in love with each other."

"Oh yes, *yes*," Becky said breathlessly. "I *do* love you, Donald."

"Then that's what we'll do."

"He . . ." She shook her head in the darkness. I knew that her eyes were very solemn, even though I couldn't see them. "He won't listen," Becky said. "He'll try to break us up."

"Nobody will ever break us up," I said. "Ever."

"What—what will you tell him?"

"That we love each other. That when we finish school we're going to get married."

"He won't let us."

"The hell with him."

"He doesn't *know* you. He thinks Italians are terrible."

"I can't help what he thinks," I said.

"Donald . . ." She paused. She was shaking her head again, and she began to tremble. "Donald, you can't do it."

"Why not?"

"Because he *believes* it, don't you see? He really believes you *are* some—some terrible sort of person."

"I know, but that doesn't make it true. And simply because *he* believes it is no reason for me to behave as if *I* believe it." I nodded my head in the darkness. I felt pretty convinced by what I was saying, but at the same time I was scared to death of facing her father. "I'll tell him when we get back," I said.

Becky was quiet for a long long time.

Then she said, "If only I was Italian."

I held her very close to me, and I kissed the top of her head very gently. Right then I knew everything was going to be all right. I knew it because Becky had said, "If only I was Italian," when she could just as easily have said, "If only you were Jewish."

Horizontal Ronnie swung into action the very next day.

He had been inordinately silent the night before on the trip back across the lake, and I hadn't disturbed his thoughts because I assumed he was working out his system for beating Jimbo. Besides, I was working out what I would tell Becky's father when we got back to the city.

The course of action Ronnie decided upon was really the only one that offered the slightest opportunity of defeating Jimbo and destroying his empire. He had correctly concluded that Jimbo was the best marble player in camp, if not in the entire world, and had further reasoned it would be impossible to beat him through skill alone. So, discounting skill, Ronnie had decided to try his hand at luck. At eight o'clock that Monday morning, as the kids lined up for muster, Ronnie came over with his fist clenched. He held out his hand to one of the senior boys and said, "Odds or evens?"

"Huh?" the senior said. The senior boys at Camp Marvin weren't exactly the brightest kids in the world. In fact, the junior boys had written a song about them which went something like "We've got seen-yuh boys, dumpy, lumpy seen-yuh boys, we've got seen-yuh boys, the worst!" Besides, it was only eight o'clock in the morning, and when someone thrusts his fist in your face at eight o'clock in the morning and says, "Odds or evens?" what else can you reply but "Huh?"

"My fist is full of marbles," Ronnie explained.

"Yeah?" the senior boy said. Mention of marbles seemed to have awakened him suddenly. His eyes gleamed.

"They're either an odd number of marbles or an even number," Ronnie went on. "You guess odds or evens. If you're right, I give you the marbles in my hand. If you're wrong, you match the marbles in my hand."

"You mean if I'm wrong I give you the number of marbles you're holding?"

"That's right."

The senior boy thought this over carefully for a moment, then nodded and said, "Odds."

Ronnie opened his fist. There were four marbles in his hand.

"You pay me," he said, and that was the beginning of the Las Vegas phase of the marble madness.

If Uncle Marvin saw what was going on, he made no comment upon it. The common opinion was that he was still smarting from his loss of five hundred marbles to Jimbo and deliberately avoided contact with everyone in the camp. It is doubtful that he could have stopped the frenzy even if he'd wanted to. The kids, presented with a new and exciting activity, took to it immediately. Here was a sport that required no skill. Here was a game that promised and delivered immediate action: the closed fist, the simple question, the guess, the payoff. Kids who were hopeless washouts on the baseball diamond suddenly discovered a sport in which they could excel. Kids who couldn't sing a note in a camp musical set the grounds reverberating with their shouted "Odds or evens?" A large shipment of marbles from home to a kid named Irwin in bunk nine only increased the feverish tempo of the gambling activity. The simple guessing game started at reveille each morning, before a kid's feet had barely touched the wooden floor of his bunk. It did not end until lights out, and even after that there were the whispered familiar words, and the surreptitious glow of flashlights.

Uncle Jimbo, startled by this new development, stayed fastidiously away from the gambling in the first few days. Ronnie, meanwhile, exhibiting his true gambler's instincts, began by slowly winning a handful of marbles from every kid he could challenge, and then became more and more reckless with his bets, clenching his fists around as many marbles as they could hold. Before too long, a bookie system became necessary, with counselors and campers writing down a number on a slip of paper and then folding the slip, so that a challenger had only to guess odds or evens on a written figure rather than on an actual fistful of marbles. That week, Ronnie successfully and infallibly called bets ranging from a low of three marbles to a high of a hundred and fifty-two marbles. It became clear almost immediately that if Jimbo were to defend his title, he would have to enter this new phase of the sport or lose by default.

I think he was beginning to like his title by then. Or perhaps he was only beginning to like his wealth. Whatever it was, he could not afford to drop out of the race. He studied the new rules, and learned them. They were really quite simple. If someone challenged you, you could either accept or decline the challenge. But once you had accepted, once the question "Odds or evens?" was asked in earnest, you either called immediately or lost the bet by default. In the beginning, Jimbo took no chances. He deliberately sought out only those campers whose luck had been running incredibly bad. His bets were small, four marbles, seven marbles, a dozen marbles. If he won a bet, he immediately pocketed a portion of his initial investment and then began playing on his winnings alone. And then, because he thought of himself as a blood-smelling champion closing in for the kill, he began to bet more heavily, taking on all comers, swinging freely through the camp, challenging campers and counselors alike. Eventually he wrote a bookie slip for five hundred and seven marbles and won the bet from a kid in bunk seven, knocking him completely out of the competition. Jimbo's luck was turning out to be almost as incredible as his skill had been. He lost occasionally, oh yes, but his winnings kept mounting, and marble after marble poured into the locked suitcase on the shelf over his bed. It was becoming apparent to almost everyone in the camp —except Uncle Marvin, who still didn't know what the hell was going on—that an elimination match was taking place, and that the chief contenders for Jimbo's as yet unchallenged title were Ronnie and the *nouveau riche* kid in bunk nine, who had parlayed his shipment from home into a sizable fortune.

Irwin, the kid in bunk nine, was a tiny little kid whom everybody called Irwin the Vermin. He wore glasses, and he always had a runny nose and a disposition to match. Ronnie, correctly figuring he would have to collar every loose marble in the camp before a showdown with Jimbo, went over to bunk nine one afternoon and promptly challenged Irwin the Vermin. The number of marbles being wagered on a single bet had by this time reached fairly astronomical proportions. It was rumored that Irwin owned one thousand seven hundred and fifty marbles. Ronnie, whose number of marbles now totaled nine hundred and four, sat on the edge of Irwin's bed and wrote out a slip of paper with the number 903 on it.

He folded the slip of paper and then looked Irwin directly in the eye.

"Odds or evens?" he said.

Irwin blinked behind his glasses, grinned maliciously, licked his lips with his tongue and said, "Odds."

Ronnie swallowed. "What?"

"Odds," Irwin repeated.

"Yeah," Ronnie said. He unfolded the slip, and together they walked back to his bunk where he made payment. "I've got a few marbles left," he lied; he had only one marble to his name. "Do you want to play some more?"

Irwin looked at him steadily and then, true to his nature, said, "Find yourself another sucker, jerk."

Ronnie watched Irwin as he left the bunk loaded down with his winnings. He must have seen in that tiny figure retreating across the grounds a symbol of all his frustration, the quarantine that kept him from the mysterious Laura, the defeat of his system to beat Jimbo. It was late afternoon, and the cries of the boys at Free Play sounded from the ball diamonds and the basketball courts far off in the camp hills. Ronnie must have watched little Irwin walking away with his shattered hopes and dreams in a brown cardboard carton, and it must have been then that he made his final decision, the decision that brought the marble madness to its peak of insanity.

I was coming back from the tennis courts, where I was trying to help little Max with his backhand, when I saw Ronnie striding across the grounds towards Jimbo's bunk. He was carrying an old battered suitcase, and there was something odd about his walk, a purposeful, angry stride which was at the same time somewhat surreptitious. I looked at him curiously and then followed him past the flagpole and watched as he entered the bunk. I stood outside for a few minutes, wondering, and then I quietly climbed the front steps.

Ronnie was in the middle of forcing the lock on Jimbo's suitcase. He looked up when I entered the bunk and then went right back to work.

"What are you doing?" I said.

"What does it look like I'm doing?" he answered.

"It looks like you're trying to break open Jimbo's suitcase."

"That's right," Ronnie said, and in that moment he broke the lock and opened the lid. "Give me a hand here," he said.

"No."

"Come on, don't be a jerk."

"You're stealing his marbles," I said.

"That's just what I'm doing. It's a gag. Come on, give me a hand here."

The next second was when I almost lost my own sanity because I said, I actually heard myself say, "You can go to jail for that!" as if even *I* had begun to believe there was a fortune in that suitcase instead of hunks of colored glass.

"For stealing marbles?" Ronnie asked incredulously. "Don't be a jackass."

His answer startled me back to reality, but at the same time it puzzled me. Because here he was, a grown man, twenty years old, and he was telling me these were only marbles, and yet he was thoroughly involved in all this frantic nuttiness, so involved that he was in Jimbo's bunk actually *stealing* marbles which he claimed he *knew* were only marbles. He opened his own suitcase and then, seeing I was staring at him with a dumfounded expression, and knowing I wasn't about to help him, he lifted Jimbo's bag himself and tilted it. The marbles spilled from one bag to the other, bright shining marbles, yellow and red and striped and black and green; glass marbles and steelies and glistening pureys, marbles of every size and hue, thousands and thousands of marbles, spilling from Jimbo's bag to Ronnie's in a dazzling, glittering heap.

I shook my head and said, "I think you're all nuts," and then I walked out of the bunk. Ronnie came out after me a minute later, carrying his own full suitcase, bending over with the weight of it. I watched him as he struggled across to the flagpole in the center of the camp. He put the bag down at his feet and then, his eyes gleaming, he cupped his hands to his mouth and shouted, "Where's Jimbo McFarland?"

There was no answer.

"Where's Jimbo McFarland?" he shouted again.

"Stop yelling," I called from the steps of the bunk. "He's up at the handball courts."

"Jimbo McFarland!" Ronnie screamed. "Jimbo McFarland!" and the camp voice-telephone system picked up the name, shouting it across behind the bunks and down by the gully and through the nature shack, "Jimbo McFarland!" and over to the lake where some kids were taking their Red Cross tests, and then up into the hills by the mess hall, and across the upper-camp baseball diamond, and the volleyball court, and finally reaching Jimbo where he was playing handball with one of the counselors.

Jimbo came striding down into the camp proper. He walked out of the hills like the gunslick he was, his back to the sun, crossing the dusty grounds for a final showdown, stopping some twenty feet from where Ronnie stood near the flagpole.

"You calling me?" he said.

"You want to play marbles?" Ronnie answered.

"Have you *got* any marbles?" Jimbo said.

"Will you match whatever I've got?"

Jimbo hesitated a moment, weighing his luck, and then said, "Sure," tentatively accepting the challenge.

"Whatever's in this bag?" Ronnie asked.

Again Jimbo hesitated. A crowd of kids had begun to gather, some of whom had followed Jimbo down out of the hills, the rest of whom had felt an excitement in the air, had felt that the moment of truth had finally arrived. They milled around the flagpole, waiting for Jimbo's decision. The gauntlet was in the dust, the challenge had been delivered, and now they waited for the undisputed champion to decide whether or not he would defend his title. Jimbo nodded.

"However much you want to bet," he said slowly, "is all right with me." He had irrevocably accepted the challenge. He now had to call or lose the bet by default.

"Okay, then," Ronnie said. He stooped down beside his suitcase. Slowly, nonchalantly, he unclasped the latches on either side. He put one hand gently on the lid, and then he looked up at Jimbo, grinned, quietly said, "Odds or evens, Jimbo?" and snapped open the lid of the bag.

From where I sat, I saw Jimbo's face go white. I don't know what crossed his mind in those few terrible moments as he stared into the bag at those thousands and thousands of marbles. I don't know whether or not he even made a mental stab at calculating the number of glistening spheres in the suitcase. I only know that he staggered back a pace and his jaw fell slack. The kids were silent now, watching him. Ronnie kept squatting beside the suitcase, his hand resting on the opened lid, the sun glowing on the marbles.

"Well, Jimbo?" he said. "Odds or evens?"

"I . . ."

"Odds or evens, Jimbo?"

Perhaps Jimbo was feverishly calculating in those breathless moments. Perhaps he was realizing he had walked into a trap from which there was no return: he would either call correctly and become the marble king of the entire world; or he would call incorrectly or not at all, and lose his fortune and his fame.

"Odds or evens?" Ronnie demanded.

Odds or evens, but how to call? How many thousands of marbles were in that suitcase, and really what difference did it make when it all narrowed down to a single marble, the real difference between odds and evens, one solitary marble, call wrong and the empire would come crashing down. Jimbo took a deep breath. The sweat was standing out on his face, his eyes were blinking. The kids around the flagpole stood silently awaiting his decision. Ronnie squatted by the suitcase with his hand on the lid.

"Odds or evens?" he asked again.

Jimbo shrugged. Honestly, because it was what he was really thinking, he said, "I . . . I don't know."

"Did you hear him?" Ronnie said immediately. "He loses by default!"

"Wait a minute, I . . ."

"You refused to call, you said you didn't know! I win by default!" Ronnie said, and he snapped the lid of the bag shut, latched it and immediately lifted it from the ground.

"Now just a second," Jimbo protested, but Ronnie was already walking away from him. He stopped some five paces from the flagpole, turned abruptly, put the bag down, grinned, and said, "You stupid jerk! They were your own marbles!"

For a moment, his announcement hung on the dust-laden air. Jimbo blinked, not understanding him at first. The kids were silent and puzzled in the circle around the flagpole. Ronnie picked up the bag of marbles again and began walking toward his bunk with it, a triumphant grin on his face. And then the meaning of what he had said registered on Jimbo's face, his eyes first, intelligence sparking there, his nose next, the nostrils flaring, his mouth then, the lips pulling back to show his teeth, and then his voice, bursting from his mouth in a wounded roar. "You thief!"

His words, too, hung on the silent air, and then one of the kids said, "Did he steal them from you, Uncle Jimbo?" and another kid shouted, "He's a crook!" and then suddenly the word "Thief!" was shouted by one of the senior boys and picked up by a junior, "Thief!" and the air rang with the word, "Thief!" and then it was shouted in unison, "Thief! Thief!" and all at once there was a bloodthirsty mob. A kid who had come down from the ball diamond waved his bat in the air and began running after Ronnie. Another kid seized a fallen branch and rushed past the flagpole with it. The others bellowed screams of anger and rage, hysterically racing toward Ronnie, who had dropped the suitcase and turned to face them. There was a pale, sickly smile on his mouth, as though he hadn't expected this kind of backfire. "Look," he said, but his voice was drowned out in the roar of the kids as they rushed forward with Jimbo. Ronnie turned and tried to run for his bunk, but Jimbo caught his collar from behind, and pulled him backward to the ground. I saw the kid raise his baseball bat and I leaped to my feet and yelled, "Stop it! Goddamn you, stop it!"

The bat hung in midair. Slowly they turned toward me.

"It's only marbles," I said.

The camp was silent.

"It's only marbles," I repeated. "Don't you see?"

And then, because I had intruded upon a fantasy and threatened to shatter it, because the entire spiraling marbles structure was suddenly in danger, they turned from Ronnie, who was lying on the ground, and they ran toward me, shouting and screaming. Jimbo, the champion, struck me on the jaw with his fist, and when I fell to the ground, the kids began kicking me and pummeling me. There was more than anger in their blows and their whispered curses. There was conviction and an overriding necessity to convince the unbeliever as well. I refused to be convinced. I felt each deliberate blow, yes, each fierce kick, but I would not be convinced because I knew, even if they didn't, that it was only marbles.

I quit Camp Marvin early the next morning. Not because of the beating. That wasn't important. I carried my two suitcases all around the lake to Camp Lydia. It was raining, and I got soaking wet. I waited at the gate while one of the girl campers ran to get Rebecca. She came walking through the rain wearing her dirty trenchcoat, walking with that peculiar sideward lope, her hair wet and clinging to her face.

"Come on, Beck," I said. "We're going home."

She looked at me for a long time, searching my face with her dark solemn eyes while the rain came down around us. I knew that word of the beating had traveled across the lake, but I didn't know whether she was looking for cuts and bruises or for something else.

"Are you all right?" she said at last.

"Yes, I'm fine," I said. "Becky, please go pack your things." And then, as she turned to go, I said, "Becky?"

She stopped in the center of the road with the rain streaming on her face and she looked at me curiously, her eyebrows raised, waiting.

"As soon as we get back," I said, "today, this afternoon, I'm going to talk to your father."

She stared at me a moment longer, her eyes very serious, and then she gave a small nod, and a smile began forming on her face, not the usual fast-breaking smile, but a slow steady smile that was somehow very sad and very old, even though she was only nineteen.

"All right, Donald," she said.

That afternoon I went to see her father at his dental office on Fordham Road in the Bronx. It was still raining. When he heard who was calling, he told his receptionist he didn't want to see me, so I marched right in and stood beside his chair while he was working on a patient, and I said, "Dr. Goldblatt, you had better see me, because you're going to see a lot of me from now on."

He didn't want to make a very big fuss because a patient was sitting in the chair with her mouth open, so he walked over to his receptionist and quietly asked her to get the police, but I just kept standing by the chair very calmly. He didn't know it, but I had been through the hysteria bit before, in spades, and this mild case didn't faze me at all. Finally, when he realized I wasn't going to leave, he again left his patient sitting in the chair, and he told his receptionist to never mind the police, and he led me to a private little office where we sat on opposite sides of a desk.

He looked at me with dark solemn eyes, almost as black as Rebecca's, and he said, "What the hell do you want from my life?"

"Dr. Goldblatt," I said, "I don't want anything from your life."

"Except my daughter," he said sourly.

"Yes, but that's not from *your* life, that's from *hers.*"

"No," Dr. Goldblatt said.

"Dr. Goldblatt," I said politely, "I didn't come here to ask your permission to see her. I came here to tell you that we're getting engaged, and as soon as we graduate we're going to get married."

"No," Dr. Goldblatt said. "You're a Gentile, she's a Jewish girl, it would never work. Don't you know the trouble you're asking for? Different religions, different cultures, how will you raise the children, what will you . . . ?"

"Dr. Goldblatt," I said, "that's only marbles."

"What?"

"I said it's only marbles."

The office went very silent, just the way the camp had when I'd shouted those words the day before. Dr. Goldblatt looked at me for a long time, his face expressionless. Then, all he said was "Marbles."

"Yes," I said, "marbles. Dr. Goldblatt, I'm going to pick up Becky at the house tonight at eight o'clock. At the *house,* Dr. Goldblatt. I'm not going to meet her in some dark alley any more."

Dr. Goldblatt said nothing.

"Because she's too nice to be meeting in dark alleys," I said, "and I love her."

Dr. Goldblatt still said nothing.

"Well," I said, "it was nice talking to you."

I got up and offered my hand to him, which he refused. I shrugged and started for the door. I had my hand on the knob when I heard him say behind me, "Marbles. *This* is what my daughter picked. Marbles."

I didn't let him see me smile. I walked downstairs to the street. The rain had tapered off to a fine drizzle. The gutters ran with water, and large puddles had formed in the hollows near the curb. I could remember sticking my hand into puddles just like those long ago when I was a kid, when the loss of a hundred immies had meant a great deal to me.

I called Becky from a telephone booth in the corner drugstore.

The nut—she cried.

ERNEST HAYCOX

The
Last Rodeo

THE pickup men galloped forward, after the judge's gun, and wedged Smoky Joe between them. Jim Cherburg left Smoky Joe's saddle, vaulted across the rump of the left pickup man's pony and struck the ground with a little springing of muscles. He stood there a moment, waiting for the chugging sensation in his stomach to subside, quiet eyes watching the late afternoon's shadows reach into a high, bright sunlight. Applause washed down the grandstand's slope and the announcer's voice, without color or personality, swelled from the field loudspeakers, announcing the day's end. Cherburg retrieved his hat and turned through the thinning dust to where Buck Merrilies waited on the edge of the field.

"It will do for a ride," said Merrilies.

"Another day, another dollar," drawled Cherburg.

They were the sort that alone survived the grueling drudgery of the game; tall, flat-muscled and heavy-boned men, now gone slack with ease. Jim Cherburg lit a cigarette, impersonally scanning the dissolving crowd. Sweat beaded a broad, tanned brow, and he drew in the smoke with a quick relish. The frontal ligaments along his neck tightened against bronzed flesh and went loose.

"Anything about Red?"

Merrilies said taciturnly: "He died ten minutes ago in the hospital."

Cherburg held his partner's glance a moment, then looked down. He dropped his cigarette, ground it beneath a boot. When his head rose again one strong flash of feeling had been covered and his eyes were a little grim. "I guess," he said without inflection, "we might as well amble on."

They swung abreast and walked through the arena's wide arch into a stream of people flowing along the street toward the town's center. Cherburg collided with a slim girl in a green dress and turned aside, murmuring an apology; the girl's sudden attention lifted obliquely across a hat brim's tilted horizon, quick and alert—and then smiling.

"I don't understand," puzzled Merrilies. "He was an old hand, a careful one."

"That steer broke from the chute fast. Red undoubtedly figured he had to cut corners to make any decent time. I saw him reach for the brute's horns. He was taking a chance. When he left the saddle his body began to twist. He must have tripped the steer, for the next thing it was eight hundred pounds of beef somersaultin' on top of him."

Merrilies said, oddly moody: "The time gets faster, the brutes tougher."

They went on, heels clicking the pavement together, big bodies rolling, both staring inscrutably into a world turning pale violet beneath the heavy-branched locusts. Jim Cherburg laid the flat of his big hand gently against the shoulder of a man backing into him. He passed around. "He left a widow in Green River. In his time he had plenty, but it was a free and easy world to Red. Now what's left but a woman waitin' and a pile of fresh dirt a long ways from home? He should've quit last year when he meant to. Ten years is too long for competition. A lot of us ought to quit."

"Quit," grunted Merrilies ironically. "Then what? You've salted your money away. Me, I ain't. It'd be back to ridin' fences or a five-dollar job around flicker-flicker cowboys in Hollywood. After ridin' up where the world's your oyster? Try it!" He stopped beside a poolroom door and he looked thoughtfully at it. "This is your home town, ain't it, kid?"

"Yes. Where you going? Careful."

"No," said Merrilies, dryly grinning. "No liquor."

Jim Cherburg went on alone, thinking of the day's tragedy. There was a lot of hurt in the game, though you took it straight and never let it get you. All the same, it was hell to think of a woman in Green River getting a printed slip of paper that would cut the solid earth from beneath her feet. It only strengthened a belief he had held since his first sight of a rodeo death: as long as he rode in competition he rode alone.

He reached an intersection, plowed into a denser current of tourists, ranchers, reservation Indians and street peddlers. Somebody spoke to him and he answered with the detached courtesy fashioned from so much casual acquaintance. Then another voice, definitely arresting, brought him about. Old Isom Gay stood in the swirl like a rooted tree resisting upheaval. Beside Isom Gay were his daughter Judith and young Dave Blackby, and another man Cherburg did not know. Cherburg beat his way over to them, frankly grinning. Isom Gay pumped his hand and swore cheerfully. Judith, smiling out of straight, gray eyes, said: "Why haven't we seen you earlier in the week?"

"Didn't get into town till this morning," he explained, reaching for Dave Blackby's fist. Blackby—and Cherburg's ceaseless attention got this instantly—showed a definite constraint. The man was nearly as tall as Cherburg, a flat and supple-bodied chap who had a fine record as a university athlete behind him and the beginnings of a wheat-milling business in town. Meanwhile the stranger was looking on politely. Isom Gay spoke up.

"This is Richey Knight, visitin' us from the East. You expressed a desire, Richey, to meet a real buckaroo. Well, here's Jim Cherburg, probably the best rider in the game today. His ranch is next ours, over in the valley, but that's only a hide-out for him in winter. Summertime he's on the long rodeo circle, from Fort Worth to Calgary."

"You seem," Knight said with the direct curiosity of the well-bred, "young for it."

Judith Gay cut in, lightly provocative: "But he's ancient. His record goes clear back to when he turned eighteen. Before that he and I used to ride the hills, roping out poor old cows. I knew him when, Mr. Knight."

Isom Gay watched his daughter indulgently. Dave Blackby's manner showed greater self-isolation. "It seems like a lot of punishment," pondered Knight.

Judith slanted a searching, speculative glance at Cherburg. "There's always another year of it. He's made of unbreakable material."

"You've lost tallow," announced Isom Gay critically.

"He always comes home lean and hungry," interposed Judith. "Season over now, Jim?"

Cherburg studied the color of the girl's eyes a measurable interval. "Two more shows," he told her, then drawled at Isom Gay: "Your daughter's grown up."

"It's a kind of vaudeville circuit, then?" said Knight.

Isom Gay opened and closed his mouth and stared at Knight with faint irritation. But Cherburg's reply was suavely quiet: "Yes, I guess that's about it."

"Ain't gone to see your ranch yet?" asked Isom Gay.

"Johnny Pipal's driving me out tomorrow, if there's time."

"A fine foreman—and he's making money for you."

"What," broke in Knight, "happened to that Conroy who had the accident today?"

"He died in the hospital a little while ago," said Cherburg gently.

"So that's what happens to them," Knight mused, quite regretful.

"That's what happens to them," repeated Judith Gay, and tipped her yellow head till Cherburg saw the old resentment in her eyes—as he had seen it long ago when his first fall had brought a cry from her. The rodeo band was parading toward the intersection, making a vast racket. Cherburg wished suddenly to be away.

"I shall see you all later," he told them, and turned into the crowd. But not before Judith's eyes had reached him with a swift, definite message. He had known her so long that he understood it; she had known him so long that she knew he did. Half a block on he went into the telegraph office.

Coming out of the dining room that evening, he saw her waiting in a lobby corner. She had on a long orchid evening dress, with a scarf thrown loosely about slim, military shoulders; and she came toward him with a free and graceful striding that stopped him in his tracks. A faint swagger was there, a memory of that reckless, boyish Judith from the earlier years. Her smile, for him alone, held the mobile corners of her lips momentarily quiet.

"You're dancing with Dave tonight?" he asked.

"Not for an hour. That's your hour, Jim."

Not looking at her, he said: "We can walk."

Her quick, free laughter was a flash of silver across darkness. "We always quarreled best in motion, didn't we?"

He opened the door and they went along the hotel wall, northward to the quieter side of town. At the next corner they turned down a long, dim street beside which a creek, trapped by concrete walls, made a minor melody in the gathered dusk. "You put all that in the past, I observe."

"Is there any present for us, Jim? I hadn't known it."

"There's this."

"One hour out of a summer's night—such as it is—such as it may mean."

An auto screamed around the corner, skewered them with its lights and passed on. Somebody whooped. Somebody else said: "That's Jim Cherburg. You know—Cherburg."

Judith's murmur was touched with amused mockery. "The king is discovered flirting with the peasant girl." She turned, her face a softened oval in the warm shadows. "You are thinner than usual. Hard season?"

"A steady grind."

"Listen, Jim. You always had ambition. No man ever fought harder to get what he wanted. Here you are at twenty-eight with a ranch the rodeo game has bought you, with a riding record they say will not be beaten for years. What is there now to keep you with it? When is the end?"

"It's—it's hard to quit," he said, slowly.

Her hand moved palely through the dark; her voice flattened. "So I was right. There is always another year."

"It isn't the money now," he added quickly.

"I know."

They crossed a park block to a building flooded with light. "I want to see what I've drawn for tomorrow," he told her. They went up a queasy flight of stairs into a hall full of smoke and confusion. It was strictly a riding crowd gathered here for its own amusement, its own hour of let-down after a hard day. There was a dice game going and a little stud was being played. Talk boiled up in endless pattern while solid and fluid and bronzed figures moved restlessly around. Merrilies came out of a small side office, silent laughter in his careless eyes. It meant something.

"You're ridin' Feather Bed," he told Cherburg.

"Who got Midnight?"

Merrilies's grin played into his broad lips. "Me," he said, as if it were a joke on him. He looked at Judith Gay, adding: "What are you so blamed selfish for?"

"Why should I be generous?" retorted Cherburg, and introduced Merrilies to the girl. Merrilies bowed. He had fine manners and his speech held that silken effortlessness which was a complete expression of his gallant self. Over in a corner Troy Watts leaned against a wall and chuckled at something Hilton Ring was telling him. Tomorrow Watts and Ring—and all of them—would be fighting in the arena for the winning time, but tonight they were at ease. Cherburg lit a cigarette, suddenly relaxed by a feeling of comfort, a feeling of belonging to this scene. It was a part of the game; it was a part of his life.

Merrilies was saying, half amused, half serious: "Jim and I hit this business together ten years ago. We were wild then. We're ancient now. We've seen 'em come and we've seen 'em go. Old ones die, new ones ride along—and here we still are, a couple of relics that can't quit. It gets in your blood."

"What big teeth you have, parson," jeered Cherburg, and escorted Judith down the stairs. They idled through the park block, strolling in time, the silence riding on. Judith's slippers made a tapping rhythm; the scent of her hair was one more call from the past. His thoughts kept working onward, demanding expression, and because this was so the transitory ease of the evening went away.

"There is always some horse a man can't stay on. There is always some youngster better than you are. Just say I'm near the top after ten years of trying. It's a hard place to be, Judith. If I'm leaner in the flanks that is why."

"The king," said Judith, "must live up to his crown. Nothing else matters—to a king."

"Put it this way: The higher a man goes the more is expected of him, the fewer mistakes he dares make, the better ride he must put on."

"It is an old story." Her voice changed and she seemed to

slide away from him. "You work to possess something. Then it
possesses you. I won't ask you to come in and dance with me."

"I lead a monk's life," he drawled. "It has been a long time
since I played, which is another penalty for being at the top of
the pile."

She spoke with a swiftness and an energy: "There are more
penalties than that, Jim, though you may not realize it now."
Then they were at the hotel again and Dave Blackby was
coming forward to claim her, agreeable yet unsmiling. His
eyes searched her face. "If you'd rather stay longer with Jim,
we can let the dance wait a while."

Judith took his arm. "I know better than to interfere with a
buckaroo's sleep." It wasn't malicious; it was wistful. Her
glance touched Cherburg as she turned and she said: "Good
luck for tomorrow." A party of men, mostly strangers, surrounded him, and he got only a brief glance of her sturdy
shoulders swinging through the crowd. But, abruptly old and
tired, he observed Dave Blackby look down at her in a way
that was as clear as a pronouncement. As soon as he could he
broke away and went to his room.

He scrubbed up, undressed and snapped out the light. He
tried to sleep and found his mind too clear and too rebellious
for it. Twice today he had been asked a question he seldom
had cared to ask himself. What kept him on? There was
nothing now in the game he needed and no future but a harder
and harder fight to keep the reputation that was a shining
mark for all the world to shoot at. The ending was inevitable
as fate. He knew that. What kept him on?

Well, he knew. He was at the top of the heap and it was
hard to quit. It was a feeling of power you couldn't surrender.
It was the pride a man had before his fellows.

The steer broke fast from the chute—a tawny mass of
wildness bolting across the white starting line. Cherburg's
pony exploded into pursuit, knowing exactly what was ex-

pected of him. Dust raveled up from the steer's churning feet, his body faded down the field. Bent low, Cherburg let his reins hang over the pommel; he slipped down as the pony drew abreast the steer and he reached out and got a secure grip on the wide, bobbing horns. Instantly he kicked clear of the stirrups, the pony veering off. Cherburg's legs swooped in a pendulum swing and bit the ground ahead; and a series of long, hard shocks ran up his bones and jolted his vitals. But his feet remained forward, braking the steer's speed, and finally stopping the run altogether.

Buried in the thickness of the rising yellow dust he advanced his right arm under the steer's right horn and surged his strength into a wringing pull. Sudden sweat cracked through his skin; and it was like an old pattern, so often repeated that he had no need of thinking. His steady twisting met elastic resistance as the neck of the beast slowly gave and slowly stiffened. Cold energy played through him at the thought of the seconds passing. He walked his lower body under the steer's head. He bounced his weight upward, gathered a momentum and heaved down.

The steer, its neck twisted into the horizontal plane, teetered and capsized on its side, echoing like a soaked drum, muzzle half cushioned on Cherburg's lap. Cherburg shot his free arm into the air. That was it. The judges closed in and a field man sat on the steer's neck while Cherburg pulled himself free and walked stiffly away. Getting on his horse he rode out of the arena with the loud-speakers' barking noise following: "Time for Cherburg, 17.2 seconds. That's all the bulldogging. Buckers coming out!"

His legs felt slightly numb from the jamming and a little finger of uneasiness went searching through his stomach. Out in the stable area he found Buck Merrilies idly casting loops around two pegs stuck in the corners of a hay bale. Merrilies's eyes came up, crowded with a tense, rain-blue brightness. It was, Cherburg knew, an old signal of battle. He went on, stabled his pony, and came back. A gust of cheering rolled over the grandstand's rear wall.

"The dumb brutes know when they've killed a man," grunted Merrilies. "They feel it."

"You'll ride that horse?"

They returned to the arena. The buckers were being saddled and the loud-speakers fed their hollow articulations into a tightening silence: "Merrilies on Midnight. Watch out!" Merrilies slanted a look at Cherburg, the old grin breaking long and thin across the reckless face. He said: "And the condemned ate a hearty breakfast," and strode for Midnight, high legs straddling the air.

He got to the horse and swung quickly into the leather. The field hands slipped the blind, unsnapped the snubbing rope. Midnight pivoted on all four feet, leaped high into the air, for that fractional second as rigid as carved marble. He came down with a wrench that threw Merrilies far over and he rose again, shuddering.

Cherburg, staring into that smolder of dust, swore under his breath. Merrilies was loose. Merrilies was off Midnight, spread in the air like a swimmer. He struck hard, rolled over and, still rolling, fought himself to his knees and to his feet, at once striking blindly across the field. Midnight plunged off, still bucking.

Cherburg cut rapidly over his partner's path. "Watch it, kid." But Merrilies stared at him without recognition, fury shaking him, and hurried by. The loud-speakers carried a monumental indifference across the arena: "Cherburg on Feather Bed."

The field hands were ready for him and he rose to the saddle. Feather Bed stood still, wasting no energy.

"All right," he said. The field hands whipped away the blind and the snubbing rope and faded. Feather Bed took two waltzing paces and dropped his canny head.

Cherburg went off the earth in one great lunge; and at that

instant the tightness left him and the old exultance returned. Feather Bed crashed down, not solidly but two legs at a time, the second shock twisting Cherburg from buttocks to neck. Feather Bed pivoted and shrewdly broke up the attack. He fell into little fiddling plunges, he went storming about, and he rose on his hind feet.

Cherburg scratched automatically, seeing the ground vanish behind dust. Then a hammer seemed to beat into his neck and the wings of his chaps cracked like rifle bullets. Feather Bed's big barrel swelled and he took to the sky again, not straight-forwardly but at an angling leap; and as he came down he lifted his back quarters in one mighty kick. Cherburg weathered it. He said: "That's it," out loud, and the ride was done.

When he left the field he found Buck Merrilies smoking on a hay bale, serene again.

"A ride?"

"A ride," said Cherburg. They were through for the day and they went into the street and walked downtown, heels clicking sharply on the paving.

"Well," reflected Merrilies, "I'm out of it now. And you're in, as usual. It'll be you and Watts and Hilton Ring for a finish tomorrow." He let the silence drag a moment. Afterward his talk ran into a shaded thoughtfulness. "Kid, I've often wondered what Sonora looked like. Maybe I better go see."

"It was Midnight?"

Merrilies snapped his cigarette away. "I can't ride that horse. Not today or any day. And when I get to feelin' that way about a horse it's time to wind up the clock. One of you three will get him. He's a killer, Jim. The same sort of a brute that killed Sam Flagg in Tucson four years ago."

They parted at the hotel corner. Cherburg went up to his room. He got under a shower. When he had dressed, he went down the elevator. Judith Gay waited in a corner.

"I'm running off from a dinner," she said. "Is it your desire to feed me?"

He made a gesture of consent with his big, bronzed hands—as an Indian would have made it—and took her across the dining room to his table. Seated, he said: "Why, Judith?"

"Does there have to be a reason for everything? Jim, you *do* look tired."

"Tomorrow's the last of it."

"Until next week. After that, until next year."

"How do you know?"

Her manner changed. The warmth went away. She was retreating—he felt it keenly. "Kings," she murmured, "don't quit. They die."

There was little to be said, little that had not been said somewhere along the years of their companionship. The mood of silence held them, as so frequently, and they ate through the meal with that feeling lying between. Kelly, of a Portland paper, stopped by. "We'll want a new picture of you. At the field at ten in the morning?" He smiled at Judith and went away. Judith bent forward. "So you sent a thousand dollars of your money to Mrs. Red Conroy of Green River."

"Who told you that?" challenged Cherburg.

Judith's smile was very gentle. "The king has his traditions to keep—and the king has no secrets."

He stirred his coffee, a pair of heavy lines thickening across his forehead. "A married man has got no place in this game. I saw my first rodeo death six years ago and I knew then I had no right to drag a girl into it. Not as long as I rode. Mrs. Red is a widow—that's her reward."

"Why explain? Don't you suppose I *know* you? Here comes your friend."

Merrilies threaded his way between the tables, came to them and halted. The storm signals of deviltry were in his eye corners and he was drunk—though Cherburg alone saw it. Merrilies bowed to Judith, stared at Cherburg. "Kid," he said, "the bad news is all yours. You got Midnight."

"That horse?" breathed Judith.

"As clearly as I can recall," reflected Merrilies, "it was three or four horses. But I wouldn't be sure, now." He bowed and stalked away.

Judith Gay laid her interlocked fingers before her, looked at them and raised an odd, bright glance to Cherburg. "Swan song, Jim."

"A little more clearly, Judith."

"Well, this is the end of this. I remember the beginning of it very well—me sitting on a rock so long ago, watching you bulldog that white-faced steer. I was your audience then. Now you've got a bigger one and you'll not miss my withdrawal. This week I am twenty-five. It has been nice. Later I may cry about that." She got up abruptly, looking away; and her voice was hurried: "I think Dave's waiting."

Blackby was in the lobby. He nodded at Cherburg, but it was brief recognition, for his serious eyes searched Judith Gay's face. Some older woman came along to draw Judith away, and Blackby transferred his attention back to Cherburg. Something stirred him and made him bitter. "You've had a swell time going up in the world, Cherburg," he said with a curtness barely inside civility. "A lot of people have stood by and watched you climb. But maybe some of these people get weary of just standing and watching. Ever think of that?"

He faced about. Judith came along and took his arm and he drew her toward the door. Judith's smile, fixed and brilliant, touched Cherburg. He heard her say: "So long." It wasn't very strong.

The buckers were ready and the crowd's silence went keying up toward suspense. Troy Watts ambled toward Cherburg, his square, white teeth dazzling against a brown skin. "Bite his ears off, Jim," he called, and wheeled away. Cherburg walked toward Midnight and stopped, waiting.

Infrequently along his riding years he had come to some such moment as this, a bad horse saddled and the high point of the show at his command for the space of a few brief seconds while the thought of battle moved like smoke and fire through him. All that the game meant was crowded in this small point of time; and the demand of pride was strongly on him.

He got the field hands' signal, ducked in beside Midnight and lightly reached leather. Nor did he waste time, knowing the horse beneath would not endure it. His free arm lifted and he said: "All right," gently. It was all in a pattern, something so long done that it belonged to his blood and not to his brain.

The field hands loosed Midnight and started to fade, but it wasn't quickly enough done. Midnight, gone mad, sprang to his hind quarters whistling, and laid the fore part of his body across the nearest hand's pony, fighting it backward. The field hand lashed at Midnight's nose with the snubbing rope, and Cherburg, realizing the quality of his ride lay endangered in this snarl, slashed his spurs into Midnight's hide. The bucker whistled again, bit at the other pony and lunged to the sky.

There was nothing like this in Cherburg's memory, nothing to equal the savagery of attack. This small Midnight was willing to tear his own vitals out from the insensate urge to destroy. He went up, a grunting, malevolent mass against the sun, and he came terrifically down. The impact to Cherburg was like the shattering of bone. It mauled his spine and surged against his reason; it trembled the fragile sense of balance aloof in his head. Then Midnight rushed again, whipped his body and dropped stiff-legged, snapping Cherburg's neck with a dangerous violence.

Cherburg saw opalescent flakes float across his vision. A rank taste of blood reached his palate and the smell of it was in his nostrils. Midnight's mane whipped flat from a straining twist; he heaved himself off the ground, descended in screaming jolts. All the day dimmed for Cherburg then. His teeth were grinding together, with flesh between, and a ball of fire burned hotter and hotter in his stomach. Racked and lonely on this crucifying seat he heard a dim report streak through the roar of his ears, and into the edges of his vision appeared the pickup men, blurred and distant. The pleasure he felt then was bitter beyond the bounds of reason. It was a ride. He said that to himself the moment before a cowled, woolly blackness fell about his head. . . .

He smelled ether and heard the murmuring of voices. But there was no dust and no arena noise; and when he opened his eyes the corners of a white-walled room moved out of mist and became definite. His own bronzed hands were lying atop sheets and on one of them slim, small fingers rested. Judith was beside the bed. Behind Judith stood Merrilies, with no visible expression, and a doctor. Disappointment sliced through Cherburg.

"I thought," he said, laboring to get the words expelled, "I made that ride."

Merrilies's drawl was ironic, hiding a tremendous emotion: "It was a ride. It's in the books as a ride. You fell after the gun."

"Fell?" said Cherburg. He moved a leg and got the bite of a binding force about his stomach. It hardened him; he spoke sharply to the doctor: "What's the matter with me?"

"Nothing, in a few months. But you're through with the tough ones, Jim. This is your last rodeo. I put your liver approximately back where it belonged."

Judith's gray eyes were narrowed against tears. "The king is dead, Jim."

Cherburg's lids came together. The long silence was here, but somewhere a familiar sound flowed dimly—of a rodeo crowd tramping down the streets. They had, he thought, their ride, and this was the last of the ten-year trail. One more man gone and room for a newer one at the top. He opened his eyes, looking at Judith.

"No more time for Cherburg," he said. "No more time for that rider."

"Jim, I'm sorry!"

But he was already looking back on another time and on

another man, coolly and critically. "No, the thing's complete. I can hang up my saddle, knowing there's nothing left undone, nothing to call me back. The trail ends here. The game gave me a great deal—and now that bill is settled." He stopped, stared more somberly at the girl. "I wish it had come sooner. I have lost what I really wanted."

Judith's answer was swift: "Why am I here, then?" And her supple hands moved gracefully before him, making that sign of consent as the Indians would have made it.

Merrilies's voice was like the off-key pitch of some reed instrument: "Well, they claim the grass grows sweet down there in Sonora."

RING LARDNER

A
Caddy's Diary

Wed. Apr. 12.

I AM 16 of age and am a caddy at the Pleasant View Golf Club but only temporary as I expect to soon land a job some wheres as asst pro as my game is good enough now to be a pro but to young looking. My pal Joe Bean also says I have not got enough swell head to make a good pro but suppose that will come in time, Joe is a wise cracker.

But first will put down how I come to be writeing this diary, we have got a member name Mr Colby who writes articles in the newspapers and I hope for his sakes that he is a better writer then he plays golf but any way I cadded for him a good many times last yr and today he was out for the first time this yr and I cadded for him and we got talking about this in that and something was mentioned in regards to the golf articles by Alex Laird that comes out every Sun in the paper Mr Colby writes his articles for so I asked Mr Colby did he know how much Laird got paid for the articles and he said he did not know but supposed that Laird had to split 50–50 with who

77

ever wrote the articles for him. So I said don't he write the articles himself and Mr Colby said why no he guessed not. Laird may be a master mind in regards to golf he said, but that is no sign he can write about it as very few men can write decent let alone a pro. Writeing is a nag.

How do you learn it I asked him.

Well he said read what other people writes and study them and write things yourself, and maybe you will get on to the nag and maybe you wont.

Well Mr Colby I said do you think I could get on to it?

Why he said smileing I did not know that was your ambition to be a writer.

Not exactly was my reply, but I am going to be a golf pro myself and maybe some day I will get good enough so as the papers will want I should write them articles and if I can learn to write them myself why I will not have to hire another writer and split with them.

Well said Mr Colby smileing you have certainly got the right temperament for a pro, they are all big hearted fellows.

But listen Mr Colby I said if I want to learn it would not do me no good to copy down what other writers have wrote, what I would have to do would be write things out of my own head.

That is true said Mr. Colby.

Well I said what could I write about?

Well said Mr Colby why don't you keep a diary and every night after your supper set down and write what happened that day and write who you cadded for and what they done only leave me out of it. And you can write down what people say and what you think and etc., it will be the best kind of practice for you, and once in a wile you can bring me your writeings and I will tell you the truth if they are good or rotten.

So that is how I come to be writeing this diary is so as I can get some practice writeing and maybe if I keep at it long enough I can get on to the nag.

Friday, Apr. 14.

We been haveing Apr. showers for a couple days and nobody out on the course so they has been nothing happen that I could write down in my diary but dont want to leave it go to long or will never learn the trick so will try and write a few lines about a caddys life and some of our members and etc.

Well I and Joe Bean is the 2 oldest caddys in the club and I been caddying now for 5 yrs and quit school 3 yrs ago tho my mother did not like it for me to quit but my father said he can read and write and figure so what is the use in keeping him there any longer as greek and latin dont get you no credit at the grocer, so they lied about my age to the trunce officer and I been caddying every yr from March till Nov and the rest of the winter I work around Heismans store in the village.

Dureing the time I am cadding I genally always manage to play at lease 9 holes a day myself on wk days and some times 18 and am never more then 2 or 3 over par figures on our course but it is a cinch.

I played the engineers course 1 day last summer in 75 which is some golf and some of our members who has been playing 20 yrs would give their right eye to play as good as myself.

I use to play around with our pro Jack Andrews till I got so as I could beat him pretty near every time we played and now he wont play with me no more, he is not a very good player for a pro but they claim he is a good teacher. Personly I think golf teachers is a joke tho I am glad people is suckers enough to fall for it as I expect to make my liveing that way. We have got a member Mr Dunham who must of took 500 lessons in the past 3 yrs and when he starts to shoot he trys to remember all the junk Andrews has learned him and he gets dizzy and they is no telling where the ball will go and about the safest place to stand when he is shooting is between he and the hole.

I dont beleive the club pays Andrews much salery but of course he makes pretty fair money giveing lessons but his best graft is a 3 some which he plays 2 and 3 times a wk with Mr Perdue and Mr Lewis and he gives Mr Lewis a stroke a hole and they genally break some wheres near even but Mr Perdue made a 83 one time so he thinks that is his game so he insists on playing Jack even, well they always play for $5.00 a hole and Andrews makes $20.00 to $30.00 per round and if he wanted to cut loose and play his best he could make $50.00 to $60.00 per round but a couple of wallops like that and Mr Perdue might get cured so Jack figures a small stedy income is safer.

I have got a pal name Joe Bean and we pal around together as he is about my age and he says some comical things and some times will wisper some thing comical to me wile we are cadding and it is all I can do to help from laughing out loud, that is one of the first things a caddy has got to learn is never laugh out loud only when a member makes a joke. How ever on the days when theys ladies on the course I dont get a chance to caddy with Joe because for some reason another the woman folks dont like Joe to caddy for them wile on the other hand they are always after me tho I am no Othello for looks or do I seek their flavors, in fact it is just the opp and I try to keep in the back ground when the fair sex appears on the seen as cadding for ladies means you will get just so much money and no more as theys no chance of them loosning up. As Joe says the rule against tipping is the only rule the woman folks keeps.

Theys one lady how ever who I like to caddy for as she looks like Lillian Gish and it is a pleasure to just look at her and I would caddy for her for nothing tho it is hard to keep your eye on the ball when you are cadding for this lady, her name is Mrs Doane.

Sat. Apr. 15.

This was a long day and am pretty well wore out but must not get behind in my writeing practice. I and Joe carried all day for Mr Thomas and Mr Blake. Mr Thomas is the vice president of one of the big banks down town and he always slips you a $1.00 extra per round but beleive me you earn it cadding for Mr Thomas, there is just 16 clubs in his bag includeing 5 wood clubs tho he has not used the wood in 3 yrs but says he has got to have them along in case his irons goes wrong on him. I don't know how bad his irons will have to get before he will think they have went wrong on him but personly if I made some of the tee shots he made today I would certainly considder some kind of a change of weppons.

Mr Thomas is one of the kind of players that when it has took him more than 6 shots to get on the green he will turn to you and say how many have I had caddy and then you are suppose to pretend like you was thinking a minute and then say 4, then he will say to the man he is playing with well I did not know if I had shot 4 or 5 but the caddy says it is 4. You see in this way it is not him that is cheating but the caddy but he makes it up to the caddy afterwards with a $1.00 tip.

Mr Blake gives Mr Thomas a stroke a hole and they play a $10.00 nassua and neither one of them wins much money from the other one but even if they did why $10.00 is chickens food to men like they. But the way they crab and squak about different things you would think their last $1.00 was at stake. Mr Thomas started out this A. M. with a 8 and a 7 and of course that spoilt the day for him and me to. Theys lots of men that if they dont make a good score on the first 2 holes they will founder all the rest of the way around and raze H with their caddy and if I was laying out a golf course I would make the first 2 holes so darn easy that you could not

help from getting a 4 or better on them and in that way
everybody would start off good natured and it would be a few
holes at lease before they begun to turn sour.

Mr Thomas was beat both in the A. M. and P. M. in spite of
my help as Mr Blake is a pretty fair counter himself and I
heard him say he got a 88 in the P. M. which is about a 94 but
any way it was good enough to win. Mr Blakes regular game is
about a 90 takeing his own figures and he is one of these cocky
guys that takes his own game serious and snears at men that
cant break 100 and if you was to ask him if he had ever been
over 100 himself he would say not since the first yr he begun
to play. Well I have watched a lot of those guys like he and I
will tell you how they keep from going over 100 namely by
doing just what he done this A. M. when he come to the 13th
hole. Well he missed his tee shot and dubbed along and finely
he got in a trap on his 4th shot and I seen him take 6 wallops
in the trap and when he had took the 6th one his ball was
worse off then when he started so he picked it up and marked
a X down on his score card. Well if he had of played out the
hole why the best he could of got was a 11 by holeing his next
niblick shot but he would of probly got about 20 which would
of made him around 108 as he admitted takeing a 88 for the
other 17 holes. But I bet if you was to ask him what score he
had made he would say O I was terrible and I picked up on
one hole but if I had of played them all out I guess I would of
had about a 92.

These is the kind of men that laughs themselfs horse when
they hear of some dub takeing 10 strokes for a hole but if they
was made to play out every hole and mark down their real
score their card would be decorated with many a big casino.

Well as I say I had a hard day and was pretty sore along
towards the finish but still I had to laugh at Joe Bean on the
15th hole which is a par 3 and you can get there with a fair
drive and personly I am genally hole high with a midiron, but

Mr Thomas topped his tee shot and dubbed a couple with his mashie and was still quiet a ways off the green and he stood studing the situation a minute and said to Mr Blake well I wonder what I better take here. So Joe Bean was standing by me and he said under his breath take my advice and quit you old rascal.

Mon. Apr. 17.

Yesterday was Sun and I was to wore out last night to write as I cadded 45 holes. I cadded for Mr Colby in the A. M. and Mr Langley in the P. M. Mr Thomas thinks golf is wrong on the sabath tho as Joe Bean says it is wrong any day the way he plays it.

This A. M. they was nobody on the course and I played 18 holes by myself and had a 5 for a 76 on the 18th hole but the wind got a hold of my drive and it went out of bounds. This P. M. they was 3 of us had a game of rummy started but Miss Rennie and Mrs Thomas come out to play and asked for me to caddy for them, they are both terrible.

Mrs Thomas is Mr Thomas wife and she is big and fat and shakes like jell and she always says she plays golf just to make her skinny and she dont care how rotten she plays as long as she is getting the exercise, well maybe so but when we find her ball in a bad lie she aint never sure it is hers till she picks it up and smells it and when she puts it back beleive me she don't cram it down no gopher hole.

Miss Rennie is a good looker and young and they say she is engaged to Chas Crane, he is one of our members and is the best player in the club and dont cheat hardly at all and he has got a job in the bank where Mr Thomas is the vice president. Well I have cadded for Miss Rennie when she was playing with Mr Crane and I have cadded for her when she was playing alone or with another lady and I often think if Mr

Crane could hear her talk when he was not around he would not be so stuck on her. You would be surprised at some of the words that falls from those fare lips.

Well the 2 ladies played for 2 bits a hole and Miss Rennie was haveing a terrible time wile Mrs Thomas was shot with luck on the greens and sunk 3 or 4 putts that was murder. Well Miss Rennie used some expressions which was best not repeated but towards the last the luck changed around and it was Miss Rennie that was sinking the long ones and when they got to the 18th tee Mrs Thomas was only 1 up.

Well we had started pretty late and when we left the 17th green Miss Rennie made the remark that we would have to hurry to get the last hole played, well it was her honor and she got the best drive she made all day about 120 yds down the fair way. Well Mrs Thomas got nervous and looked up and missed her ball a ft and then done the same thing right over and when she finely hit it she only knocked it about 20 yds and this made her lay 3. Well her 4th went wild and lit over in the rough in the apple trees. It was a cinch Miss Rennie would win the hole unless she dropped dead.

Well we all went over to hunt for Mrs Thomas ball but we would of been lucky to find it even in day light but now you could not hardly see under the trees, so Miss Rennie said drop another ball and we will not count no penalty. Well it is some job any time to make a woman give up hunting for a lost ball and all the more so when it is going to cost her 2 bits to play the hole out so there we stayed for at lease 10 minutes till it was so dark we could not see each other let alone a lost ball and finely Mrs Thomas said well it looks like we could not finish, how do we stand? Just like she did not know how they stood.

You had me one down up to this hole said Miss Rennie.

Well that is finishing pretty close said Mrs Thomas.

I will have to give Miss Rennie credit that what ever word she thought of for this occasion she did not say it out loud but when she was paying me she said I might of give you a quarter tip only I have to give Mrs Thomas a quarter she dont deserve so you dont get it.

Fat chance I would of had any way.

Thurs. Apr. 20.

Well we have been haveing some more bad weather but today the weather was all right but that was the only thing that was all right. This P. M. I cadded double for Mr Thomas and Chas Crane the club champion who is stuck on Miss Rennie. It was a 4 some with he and Mr Thomas against Mr Blake and Jack Andrews the pro, they was only playing best ball so it was really just a match between Mr Crane and Jack Andrews and Mr Crane win by 1 up. Joe Bean cadded for Jack and Mr Blake. Mr Thomas was terrible and I put in a swell P. M. lugging that heavy bag of his besides Mr Cranes bag.

Mr Thomas did not go off of the course as much as usual but he kept hitting behind the ball and he run me ragged replaceing his divots but still I had to laugh when we was playing the 4th hole which you have to drive over a ravine and every time Mr Thomas misses his tee shot on this hole why he makes a squak about the ravine and says it ought not to be there and etc.

Today he had a terrible time getting over it and afterwards he said to Jack Andrews this is a joke hole and ought to be changed. So Joe Bean wispered to me that if Mr Thomas kept on playing like he was the whole course would be changed.

Then a little wile later when we come to the long 9th hole Mr Thomas got a fair tee shot but then he whiffed twice missing the ball by a ft and the 3d time he hit it but it only went a little ways and Joe Bean said that is 3 trys and no gain, he will have to punt.

But I must write down about my tough luck, well we finely got through the 18 holes and Mr Thomas reached down in his

pocket for the money to pay me and he genally pays for Mr
Crane to when they play together as Mr Crane is just a employ
in the bank and dont have much money but this time all Mr
Thomas had was a $20.00 bill so he said to Mr Crane I guess
you will have to pay the boy Charley so Charley dug down and
got the money to pay me and he paid just what it was and not
a dime over, where if Mr Thomas had of had the change I
would of got a $1.00 extra at lease and maybe I was not sore
and Joe Bean to because of course Andrews never gives you
nothing and Mr Blake dont tip his caddy unless he wins.

They are a fine bunch of tight wads said Joe and I said well
Crane is all right only he just has not got no money.

He aint all right no more than the rest of them said Joe.

Well at lease he dont cheat on his score I said.

And you know why that is said Joe, neither does Jack Andrews cheat on his score but that is because they play to good.
Players like Crane and Andrews that goes around in 80 or better cant cheat on their score because they make the most of the
holes in around 4 strokes and the 4 strokes includes their tee
shot and a couple of putts which everybody is right there to
watch them when they make them and count them right along
with them. So if they make a 4 and claim a 3 why people would
just laugh in their face and say how did the ball get from the fair
way on to the green, did it fly? But the boys that takes 7 and 8
strokes to a hole can shave their score and you know they are
shaveing it but you have to let them get away with it because
you cant prove nothing. But that is one of the penaltys for
being a good player, you cant cheat.

To hear Joe tell it pretty near everybody are born crooks,
well maybe he is right.

Wed. Apr. 26.

Today Mrs Doane was out for the first time this yr and
asked for me to caddy for her and you bet I was on the job.

Well how are you Dick she said, she always calls me by name. She asked me what had I been doing all winter and was I glad to see her and etc.

She said she had been down south all winter and played golf pretty near every day and would I watch her and notice how much she had improved.

Well to tell the truth she was no better then last yr and wont never be no better and I guess she is just to pretty to be a golf player but of course when she asked me did I think her game was improved I had to reply yes indeed as I would not hurt her feelings and she laughed like my reply pleased her. She played with Mr and Mrs Carter and I carried the 2 ladies bags wile Joe Bean cadded for Mr Carter. Mrs Carter is a ugly dame with things on her face and it must make Mr Carter feel sore when he looks at Mrs Doane to think he married Mrs Carter but I suppose they could not all marry the same one and besides Mrs Doane would not be a sucker enough to marry a man like he who drinks all the time and is pretty near always stood, tho Mr Doane who she did marry aint such a H of a man himself tho dirty with money.

They all gave me the laugh on the 3d hole when Mrs Doane was makeing her 2d shot and the ball was in the fair way but laid kind of bad and she just ticked it and then she asked me if winter rules was in force and I said yes so we teed her ball up so as she could get a good shot at it and they gave me the laugh for saying winter rules was in force.

You have got the caddys bribed Mr Carter said to her.

But she just smiled and put her hand on my sholder and said Dick is my pal. That is enough of a bribe to just have her touch you and I would caddy all day for her and never ask for a cent only to have her smile at me and call me her pal.

Sat. Apr. 29.

Today they had the first club tournament of the yr and they

have a monthly tournament every month and today was the first one, it is a handicap tournament and everybody plays in it and they have prizes for low net score and low gross score and etc. I cadded for Mr Thomas today and will tell what happened.

They played a 4 some and besides Mr Thomas we had Mr Blake and Mr Carter and Mr Dunham. Mr Dunham is the worst man player in the club and the other men would not play with him a specialy on a Saturday only him and Mr Blake is partners together in business. Mr Dunham has got the highest handicap in the club which is 50 but it would have to be 150 for him to win a prize. Mr Blake and Mr Carter has got a handicap of about 15 a piece I think and Mr Thomas is 30, the first prize for the low net score for the day was a dozen golf balls and the second low score a ½ dozen golf balls and etc.

Well we had a great battle and Mr Colby ought to been along to write it up or some good writer. Mr Carter and Mr Dunham played partners against Mr Thomas and Mr Blake which ment that Mr Carter was playing Thomas and Blakes best ball, well Mr Dunham took the honor and the first ball he hit went strate off to the right and over the fence outside of the grounds, well he done the same thing 3 times. Well when he finely did hit one in the course why Mr Carter said why not let us not count them 3 first shots of Mr Dunham as they was just practice. Like H we wont count them said Mr Thomas we must count every shot and keep our scores correct for the tournament.

All right said Mr Carter.

Well we got down to the green and Mr Dunham had about 11 and Mr Carter sunk a long putt for a par 5, Mr Blake all ready had 5 strokes and so did Mr Thomas and when Mr Carter sunk his putt why Mr Thomas picked his ball up and said Carter wins the hole and I and Blake will take 6s. Like H you will said Mr Carter, this is a tournament and we must play every hole out and keep our scores correct. So Mr Dunham putted and went down in 13 and Mr Blake got a 6 and Mr Thomas missed 2 easy putts and took a 8 and maybe he was not boiling.

Well it was still their honor and Mr Dunham had one of his dizzy spells on the 2d tee and he missed the ball twice before he hit it and then Mr Carter drove the green which is only a midiron shot and then Mr Thomas stepped up and missed the ball just like Mr Dunham. He was wild and yelled at Mr Dunham no man could play golf playing with a man like you, you would spoil anybodys game.

Your game was all ready spoiled said Mr Dunham, it turned sour on the 1st green.

You would turn anybody sour said Mr Thomas.

Well Mr Thomas finely took a 8 for the hole which is a par 3 and it certainly looked bad for him winning a prize when he started out with 2 8s, and he and Mr Dunham had another terrible time on No 3 and wile they was messing things up a 2 some come up behind us and hollered fore and we left them go through tho it was Mr Clayton and Mr Joyce and as Joe Bean said they was probly dissapointed when we left them go through as they are the kind that feels like the day is lost if they cant write to some committee and preffer charges.

Well Mr Thomas got a 7 on the 3d and he said well it is no wonder I am off of my game today as I was up ½ the night with my teeth.

Well said Mr Carter if I had your money why on the night before a big tournament like this I would hire somebody else to set up with my teeth.

Well I wished I could remember all that was said and done but any way Mr Thomas kept getting sore and sore and we got to the 7th tee and he had not made a decent tee shot all day so Mr Blake said to him why dont you try the wood as you cant do no worse?

By Geo I beleive I will said Mr Thomas and took his driver out of the bag which he had not used it for 3 yrs.

Well he swang and zowie away went the ball pretty near 8 inchs distants wile the head of the club broke off clean and saled 50 yds down the course. Well I have got a hold on myself so as I dont never laugh out loud and I beleive the other men was scarred to laugh or he would of killed them so we all stood there in silents waiting for what would happen.

Well without saying a word he come to where I was standing and took his other 4 wood clubs out of the bag and took them to a tree which stands a little ways from the tee box and one by one he swang them with all his strength against the trunk of the tree and smashed them to H and gone, all right gentlemen that is over he said.

Well to cut it short Mr Thomas score for the first 9 was a even 60 and then we started out on the 2d 9 and you would not think it was the same man playing, on the first 3 holes he made 2 4s and a 5 and beat Mr Carter even and followed up with a 6 and a 5 and that is how he kept going up to the 17th hole.

What has got in to you Thomas said Mr Carter.

Nothing said Mr Thomas only I broke my hoodoo when I broke them 5 wood clubs.

Yes I said to myself and if you had broke them 5 wood clubs 3 yrs ago I would not of broke my back lugging them around.

Well we come to the 18th tee and Mr Thomas had a 39 which give him a 99 for 17 holes, well everybody drove off and as we was following along why Mr Klabor come walking down the course from the club house on his way to the 17th green to join some friends and Mr Thomas asked him what he made and he said he had turned in a 93 but his handicap is only 12 so that give him a 81.

That wont get me no wheres he said as Charley Crane made a 75.

Well said Mr Thomas I can tie Crane for low net if I get a 6 on this hole.

Well it come his turn to make his 2d and zowie he hit the ball pretty good but they was a hook on it and away she went in to the woods on the left, the ball laid in behind a tree so as they was only one thing to do and that was waste a shot getting it back on the fair so that is what Mr Thomas done and it took him 2 more to reach the green.

How many have you had Thomas said Mr Carter when we was all on the green.

Let me see said Mr Thomas and then turned to me, how many have I had caddy?

I dont know I said.

Well it is either 4 or 5 said Mr Thomas.

I think it is 5 said Mr Carter.

I think it is 4 said Mr Thomas and turned to me again and said how many have I had caddy?

So I said 4.

Well said Mr Thomas personly I was not sure myself but my caddy says 4 and I guess he is right.

Well the other men looked at each other and I and Joe Bean looked at each other but Mr Thomas went ahead and putted and was down in 2 putts.

Well he said I certainly come to life on them last 9 holes.

So he turned in his score as 105 and with his handicap of 30 why that give him a net of 75 which was the same as Mr Crane so instead of Mr Crane getting 1 dozen golf balls and Mr Thomas getting ½ a dozen golf balls why they will split the 1st and 2d prize makeing 9 golf balls a piece.

Tues. May 2.

This was the first ladies day of the season and even Joe Bean had to carry for the fair sex. We cadded for a 4 some which was Miss Rennie and Mrs Thomas against Mrs Doane and Mrs Carter. I guess if they had of kept their score right the total for the 4 of them would of ran well over a 1000.

Our course has a great many trees and they seemed to have a traction for our 4 ladies today and we was in amongst the trees more then we was on the fair way.

Well said Joe Bean theys one thing about cadding for these dames, it keeps you out of the hot sun.

And another time he said he felt like a boy scout studing wood craft.

These dames is always up against a stump he said.

And another time he said that it was not fair to charge these dames regular ladies dues in the club as they hardly ever used the course.

Well it seems like they was a party in the village last night and of course the ladies was talking about it and Mrs Doane said what a lovely dress Miss Rennie wore to the party and Miss Rennie said she did not care for the dress herself.

Well said Mrs Doane if you want to get rid of it just hand it over to me.

I wont give it to you said Miss Rennie but I will sell it to you at ½ what it cost me and it was a bargain at that as it only cost me a $100.00 and I will sell it to you for $50.00.

I have not got $50.00 just now to spend said Mrs Doane and besides I dont know would it fit me.

Sure it would fit you said Miss Rennie, you and I are exactly the same size and figure, I tell you what I will do with you I will play you golf for it and if you beat me you can have the gown for nothing and if I beat you why you will give me $50.00 for it.

All right but if I loose you may have to wait for your money said Mrs Doane.

So this was on the 4th hole and they started from there to play for the dress and they was both terrible and worse then usual on acct of being nervous as this was the biggest stakes they had either of them ever played for tho the Doanes has got a bbl of money and $50.00 is chickens food.

Well we was on the 16th hole and Mrs Doane was 1 up and Miss Rennie sliced her tee shot off in the rough and Mrs Doane landed in some rough over on the left so they was clear across the course from each other. Well I and Mrs Doane went over to her ball and as luck would have it it had come to rest in a kind of a groove where a good player could not hardly make a good shot of it let alone Mrs Doane. Well Mrs Thomas was out in the middle of the course for once in her life and the other 2 ladies was over on the right side and Joe Bean with them so they was nobody near Mrs Doane and I.

Do I have to play it from there she said. I guess you do was my reply.

Why Dick have you went back on me she said and give me one of her looks.

Well I looked to see if the others was looking and then I kind of give the ball a shove with my toe and it come out of the groove and laid where she could get a swipe at it.

This was the 16th hole and Mrs Doane win it by 11 strokes to 10 and that made her 2 up and 2 to go. Miss Rennie win the 17th but they both took a 10 for the 18th and that give Mrs Doane the match.

Well I wont never have a chance to see her in Miss Rennies dress but if I did I aint sure that I would like it on her.

Fri. May 5.

Well I never thought we would have so much excitement in the club and so much to write down in my diary but I guess I better get busy writeing it down as here it is Friday and it was Wed. A. M. when the excitement broke loose and I was getting ready to play around when Harry Lear the caddy master come running out with the paper in his hand and showed it to me on the first page.

It told how Chas Crane our club champion had went south
with $8000 which he had stole out of Mr Thomas bank and a
swell looking dame that was a stenograpfher in the bank had
elloped with him and they had her picture in the paper and I
will say she is a pip but who would of thought a nice quiet
young man like Mr Crane was going to prove himself a gay
Romeo and a specialy as he was engaged to Miss Rennie tho
she now says she broke their engagement a month ago but any
way the whole affair has certainly give everybody something to
talk about and one of the caddys Lou Crowell busted Fat
Brunner in the nose because Fat claimed to of been the last
one that cadded for Crane. Lou was really the last one and
cadded for him last Sunday which was the last time Crane was
at the club.

Well everybody was thinking how sore Mr Thomas would
be and they would better not mention the affair around him
and etc. but who should show up to play yesterday but Mr
Thomas himself and he played with Mr Blake and all they
talked about the whole P. M. was Crane and what he had
pulled.

Well Thomas said Mr Blake I am curious to know if the
thing come as a surprise to you or if you ever had a hunch that
he was libel to do a thing like this.

Well Blake said Mr Thomas I will admit that the whole
thing come as a complete surprise to me as Crane was all most
like my son you might say and I was going to see that he got
along all right and that is what makes me sore is not only that
he has proved himself dishonest but that he could be such a
sucker as to give up a bright future for a sum of money like
$8000 and a doll face girl that cant be no good or she would
not of let him do it. When you think how young he was and
the carreer he might of had why it certainly seems like he sold
his soul pretty cheap.

That is what Mr Thomas had to say or at lease part of it as I
cant remember a ½ of all he said but any way this P. M. I

cadded for Mrs Thomas and Mrs Doane and that is all they
talked about to, and Mrs Thomas talked along the same lines
like her husband and said she had always thought Crane was
to smart a young man to pull a thing like that and ruin his
whole future.

He was geting $4000 a yr said Mrs Thomas and everybody
liked him and said he was bound to get ahead so that is what
makes it such a silly thing for him to of done, sell his soul for
$8000 and a pretty face.

Yes indeed said Mrs Doane.

Well all the time I was listening to Mr Thomas and Mr
Blake and Mrs Thomas and Mrs Doane why I was thinking
about something which I wanted to say to them but it would of
ment me looseing my job so I kept it to myself but I sprung it
on my pal Joe Bean on the way home tonight.

Joe I said what do these people mean when they talk about
Crane selling his soul?

Why you know what they mean said Joe, they mean that a
person that does something dishonest for a bunch of money or
a gal or any kind of a reward why the person that does it is
selling his soul.

All right I said and it dont make no differents does it if the
reward is big or little?

Why no said Joe only the bigger it is the less of a sucker the
person is that goes after it.

Well I said here is Mr Thomas who is vice president of a big
bank and worth a bbl of money and it is just a few days ago
when he lied about his golf score in order so as he would win 9
golf balls instead of a ½ a dozen.

Sure said Joe.

And how about his wife Mrs Thomas I said, who plays for 2
bits a hole and when her ball dont lie good why she picks it up
and pretends to look at it to see if it is hers and then puts it
back in a good lie where she can sock it.

And how about my friend Mrs Doane that made me move

her ball out of a rut to help her beat Miss Rennie out of a party dress.

Well said Joe what of it?

Well I said it seems to me like these people have got a lot of nerve to pan Mr Crane and call him a sucker for doing what he done, it seems to me like $8000 and a swell dame is a pretty fair reward compared with what some of these other people sells their soul for, and I would like to tell them about it.

Well said Joe go ahead and tell them but maybe they will tell you something right back.

What will they tell me?

Well said Joe they might tell you this, that when Mr Thomas asks you how many shots he has had and you say 4 when you know he has had 5, why you are selling your soul for a $1.00 tip. And when you move Mrs Doanes ball out of a rut and give it a good lie what are you selling your soul for? Just a smile.

O keep your mouth shut I said to him.

I am going to said Joe and would advice you to do the same.

WILLIAM SAROYAN

The
Fifty Yard Dash

AFTER a certain letter came to me from New York the year I was twelve, I made up my mind to become the most powerful man in my neighborhood. The letter was from my friend Lionel Strongfort. I had clipped a coupon from *Argosy All-Story Magazine,* signed it, placed it in an envelope, and mailed it to him. He had written back promptly, with an enthusiasm bordering on pure delight, saying I was undoubtedly a man of uncommon intelligence, potentially a giant, and—unlike the average run-of-the-mill people of the world who were, in a manner of speaking, dreamwalkers and daydreamers—a person who would some day be somebody.

His opinion of me was very much like my own. It was pleasant, however, to have the opinion so emphatically corroborated, particularly by a man in New York—and a man with the greatest chest expansion in the world. With the letter came several photographic reproductions of Mr. Strongfort wearing nothing but a little bit of leopard skin. He was a tremendous man and claimed that at one time he had been puny. He was loaded all over with muscle and appeared to be somebody who could lift a 1920 Ford roadster and tip it over.

It was an honor to have him for a friend.

The only trouble was—I didn't have the money. I forget how much the exact figure was at the beginning of our acquaintanceship, but I haven't forgotten that it was an amount completely out of the question. While I was eager to be grateful to Mr. Strongfort for his enthusiasm, I didn't seem to be able to find words with which to explain about not having the money, without immediately appearing to be a dreamwalker and a daydreamer myself. So, while waiting from one day to another, looking everywhere for words that would not blight our friendship and degrade me to commonness, I talked the matter over with my uncle Gyko, who was studying Oriental philosophy at the time. He was amazed at my curious ambition, but quite pleased. He said the secret of greatness, according to Yoga, was the releasing within one's self of those mysterious vital forces which are in all men.

These strength, he said in English which he liked to affect when speaking to me, ease from God. I tell you, Aram, eat ease wonderful.

I told him I couldn't begin to become the powerful man I had decided to become until I sent Mr. Strongfort some money.

Mohney! my uncle said with contempt. I tell you, Aram, mohney is nawthing. You cannot bribe God.

Although my uncle Gyko wasn't exactly a puny man, he was certainly not the man Lionel Strongfort was. In a wrestling match I felt certain Mr. Strongfort would get a headlock or a half-nelson or a toe hold on my uncle and either make him give up or squeeze him to death. And then again, on the other hand, I wondered. My uncle was nowhere near as big as Mr. Strongfort, but neither was Mr. Strongfort as dynamically furious as my uncle. It seemed to me that, at best,

Mr. Strongfort, in a match with my uncle, would have a great deal of unfamiliar trouble—I mean with the mysterious vital forces that were always getting released in my uncle, so that very often a swift glance from him would make a big man quail and turn away, or, if he had been speaking, stop quickly.

Long before I had discovered words with which to explain to Mr. Strongfort about the money, another letter came from him. It was as cordial as the first, and as a matter of fact if anything, a little more cordial. I was delighted and ran about, releasing mysterious vital forces, turning handsprings, scrambling up trees, turning somersaults, trying to tip over 1920 Ford roadsters, challenging all comers to wrestle, and in many other ways alarming my relatives and irritating the neighbors.

Not only was Mr. Strongfort not sore at me, he had reduced the cost of the course. Even so, the money necessary was still more than I could get hold of. I was selling papers every day, but *that* money was for bread and stuff like that. For a while I got up very early every morning and went around town looking for a small satchel full of money. During six days of this adventuring I found a nickel and two pennies. I found also a woman's purse containing several foul smelling cosmetic items, no money, and a slip of paper on which was written in an ignorant hand: Steve Hertwig, 376 Ventura Avenue.

Three days after the arrival of Mr. Strongfort's second letter, his third letter came. From this time on our correspondence became one-sided. In fact, I didn't write at all. Mr. Strongfort's communications were overpowering and not at all easy to answer, without money. There was, in fact, almost nothing to say.

It was wintertime when the first letter came, and it was then that I made up my mind to become the most powerful man in my neighborhood and ultimately, for all I knew, one of the most powerful men in the world. I had ideas of my own as to how to go about getting that way, but I had all the warm friendship and high regard of Mr. Strongfort in New York, and the mystical and furious guardianship of my uncle Gyko, at home.

The letters from Mr. Strongfort continued to arrive every two or three days all winter and on into springtime. I remember, the day apricots were ripe enough to steal, the arrival of a most charming letter from my friend in New York. It was a hymn to newness on earth, the arrival of springtime, the time of youth in the heart, of renewal, fresh strength, fresh determination, and many other things. It was truly a beautiful epistle, probably as fine as any to the Romans or anybody else. It was full of the legend-quality, the world-feeling, and the dignity-of-strength-feeling so characteristic of Biblical days. The last paragraph of the lovely hymn brought up, apologetically, the coarse theme of money. The sum was six or seven times as little as it had been originally, and a new element had come into Mr. Strongfort's program of changing me over from a nobody to a giant of tremendous strength, and extreme attractiveness to women. Mr. Strongfort had decided, he said, to teach me everything in one fell swoop, or one sweep fall, or something of that sort. At any rate, for three dollars, he said, he would send me all his precious secrets in one envelope and the rest would be up to me, and history.

I took the matter up with my uncle Gyko, who by this time had reached the stage of fasting, meditating, walking for hours, and vibrating. We had had discussions two or three times a week all winter and he had told me in his own unique broken-English way all the secrets *he* had been learning from Yoga.

I tell you, Aram, he said, I can do *anything*. Eat ease wonderful.

I believed him, too, even though he had lost a lot of weight, couldn't sleep, and had a strange dynamic blaze in his eyes. He was very scornful of the world that year and was full of pity for the dumb beautiful animals that man was mistreating, killing, eating, domesticating, and teaching to do tricks.

I tell you, Aram, he said, eat ease creaminal to make the horses work. To keal the cows. To teach the dogs to jump, and the monkeys to smoke pipes.

I told him about the letter from Mr. Strongfort.

Mohney! he said. Always he wants mohney. I do not like heem.

My uncle was getting all his dope free from the theosophy-philosophy-astrology-and-miscellaneous shelf at the Public Library. He believed, however, that he was getting it straight from God. Before he took up Yoga he had been one of the boys around town and a good drinker of *rakhi,* but after the light began to come to him he gave up drinking. He said he was drinking liquor finer than *rakhi* or anything else.

What's that? I asked him.

Aram, he said, eat ease weasdom.

Anyhow, he had little use for Mr. Strongfort and regarded the man as a charlatan.

He's all right, I told my uncle.

But my uncle became furious, releasing mysterious vital forces, and said, I wheel break hease head, fooling all you leatle keads.

He ain't fooling, I said. He says he'll give me all his secrets for three dollars.

I tell you, Aram, my uncle Gyko said, he does not know any seacrets. He ease a liar.

I don't know, I said. I'd like to try that stuff out.

Eat ease creaminal, my uncle Gyko said, but I wheel geave you tree dollar.

My uncle Gyko gave me the necessary three dollars and I sent them along to Mr. Strongfort. The envelope came from New York, full of Mr. Strongfort's secrets. They were strangely simple. It was all stuff I had known anyhow but had been too lazy to pay any attention to. The idea was to get up early in the morning and for an hour or so to do various kinds of acrobatic exercises, which were illustrated. Also to drink plenty of water, get plenty of fresh air, eat good wholesome food, and keep it up until you were a giant.

I felt a little let down and sent Mr. Strongfort a short polite note saying so. He ignored the note and I never heard from him again. In the meantime, I had been following the rules and growing more powerful every day. When I say *in the meantime*, I mean for four days I followed the rules. On the fifth day I decided to sleep instead of getting up and filling the house with noise and getting my grandmother sore. She used to wake up in the darkness of early morning and shout that I was an impractical fool and would never be rich. She would go back to sleep for five minutes, wake up, and then shout that I would never buy and sell for a profit. She would sleep a little more, waken, and shout that there were once three sons of a king; one was wise like his father; the other was crazy about girls; and the third had less brains than a bird. Then she would get out of bed, and, shouting steadily, tell me the whole story while I did my exercises.

The story would usually warn me to be sensible and not go around waking her up before daybreak all the time. That would always be the moral, more or less, although the story itself would be about three sons of some king, or three brothers, each of them very wealthy and usually very greedy, or three daughters, or three proverbs, or three roads, or something else like that.

She was wasting her breath, though, because I wasn't enjoying the early-morning acrobatics any more than she was. In fact, I was beginning to feel that it was a lot of nonsense, and that my uncle Gyko had been right about Mr. Strongfort in the first place.

So I gave up Mr. Strongfort's program and returned to my own, which was more or less as follows: to take it easy and grow to be the most powerful man in the neighborhood without any trouble or exercise. Which is what I did.

That spring Longfellow School announced that a track meet was to be held, one school to compete against another; *everybody* to participate.

Here, I believed, was my chance. In my opinion I would be first in every event.

Some how or other, however, continuous meditation on the theme of athletics had the effect of growing into a fury of anticipation that continued all day and all night, so that before the day of the track meet I had run the fifty-yard dash any number of hundreds of times, had jumped the running broad jump, the standing broad jump, and the high jump, and in each event had made my competitors look like weaklings.

This tremendous inner activity, which was strictly Yoga, changed on the day of the track meet into fever.

The time came at last for me and three other athletes, one of them a Greek, to go to our marks, get set, and go; and I did, in a blind rush of speed which I knew had never before occurred in the history of athletics.

It seemed to me that never before had any living man moved so swiftly. Within myself I ran the fifty yards fifty times before I so much as opened my eyes to find out how far back I had left the other runners. I was very much amazed at what I saw.

Three boys were four yards ahead of me and going away.

It was incredible. It was unbelievable, but it was obviously the truth. There ought to be some mistake, but there wasn't. There they were, ahead of me, going away.

Well, it simply meant that I would have to overtake them, with my eyes open, and win the race. This I proceeded to do. They continued, incredibly, however, to go away, in spite of my intention. I became irritated and decided to put them in their places for the impertinence, and began releasing all the mysterious vital forces within myself that I had. Somehow or other, however, not even this seemed to bring me any closer to them and I felt that in some way I was being betrayed. If so, I decided, I would shame my betrayer by winning the race in spite of the betrayal, and once again I threw fresh life and energy into my running. There wasn't a great distance still to go, but I knew I would be able to do it.

Then I knew I wouldn't.

The race was over.

I was last, by ten yards.

Without the slightest hesitation I protested and challenged the runners to another race, same distance, back. They refused to consider the proposal, which proved, I knew, that they were afraid to race me. I told them they knew very well I could beat them.

It was very much the same in all the other events.

When I got home I was in high fever and very angry. I was delirious all night and sick three days. My grandmother took very good care of me and probably was responsible for my not dying. When my uncle Gyko came to visit me he was no longer hollow-cheeked. It seems he had finished his fast, which had been a long one—forty days or so; and nights too, I believe. He had stopped meditating, too, because he had practically exhausted the subject. He was again one of the boys around town, drinking, staying up all hours, and following the women.

I tell you, Aram, he said, we are a great family. We can do *anything*.

RUDYARD KIPLING

The
Maltese Cat

THEY had good reason to be proud, and better reason to be afraid, all twelve of them; for though they had fought their way, game by game, up the teams entered for the polo tournament, they were meeting the Archangels that afternoon in the final match; and the Archangels men were playing with half a dozen ponies apiece. As the game was divided into six quarters of eight minutes each, that meant a fresh pony after every halt. The Skidars' team, even supposing there were no accidents, could only supply one pony for every other change; and two to one is heavy odds. Again as Shiraz, the grey Syrian, pointed out, they were meeting the pink and pick of the polo-ponies of Upper India, ponies that had cost from a thousand rupees each, while they themselves were a cheap lot gathered often from country-carts, by their masters, who belonged to a poor but honest native infantry regiment.

"Money means pace and weight," said Shiraz, rubbing his black-silk nose dolefully along his neat-fitting boot, "and by the maxims of the game as I know it—"

109

"Ah, but we aren't playing the maxims," said The Maltese Cat. "We're playing the game; and we've the great advantage of knowing the game. Just think a stride, Shiraz! We've pulled up from bottom to second place in two weeks against all those fellows on the ground here. That's because we play with our heads as well as our feet."

"It makes me feel undersized and unhappy all the same," said Kittiwynk, a mouse-colored mare with a red brow-band and the cleanest pair of legs that ever an aged pony owned. "They've twice our style, these others."

Kittiwynk looked at the gathering and sighed. The hard, dusty polo-ground was lined with thousands of soldiers, black and white, not counting hundreds and hundreds of carriages and drags and dog-carts, and ladies with brilliant-colored parasols, and officers in uniform and out of it and crowds of natives behind them; and orderlies on camels, who had halted to watch the game, instead of carrying letters up and down the station; and native horse-dealers running about on thineared Biluchi mares, looking for a chance to sell a few first-class polo-ponies. Then there were the ponies of thirty teams that had entered for the Upper India Free-for-All Cup—nearly every pony of worth and dignity, from Mhow to Peshawar, from Allahabad to Multan; prize ponies, Arabs, Syrian, Barb, Country-bred, Deccanee, Waziri, and Kabul ponies of every color and shape and temper that you could imagine. Some of them were in mat-roofed stables, close to the polo-ground, but most were under saddle, while their masters, who had been defeated in the earlier games, trotted in and out and told the world exactly how the game should be played.

It was a glorious sight, and the come and go of the little, quick hooves, and the incessant salutations of ponies that had met before on other polo-grounds or racecourses were enough to drive a four-footed thing wild.

But the Skidars' team were careful not to know their neighbors, though half the ponies on the ground were

anxious to scrape acquaintance with the little fellows that had
come from the North, and, so far, had swept the board.

"Let's see," said a soft gold-colored Arab, who had been
playing very badly the day before, to The Maltese Cat; "didn't
we meet in Abdul Rahman's stable in Bombay, four seasons
ago? I won the Paikpattan Cup next season, you may remember?"

"Not me," said The Maltese Cat, politely. "I was at Malta
then, pulling a vegetable-cart. I don't race. I play the game."

"Oh!" said the Arab, cocking his tail and swaggering off.

"Keep yourselves to yourselves," said The Maltese Cat to
his companions. "We don't want to rub noses with all those
goose-rumped half-breeds of Upper India. When we've won
this Cup they'll give their shoes to know *us*."

"We sha'n't win the Cup," said Shiraz. "How do you feel?"

"Stale as last night's feed when a muskrat has run over it,"
said Polaris, a rather heavy-shouldered grey; and the rest of
the team agreed with him.

"The sooner you forget that the better," said The Maltese
Cat, cheerfully. "They've finished tiffin in the big tent. We
shall be wanted now. If your saddles are not comfy, kick. If
your bits aren't easy, rear, and let the *saises* know whether
your boots are tight."

Each pony had his *sais*, his groom, who lived and ate and
slept with the animal, and had betted a good deal more than
he could afford on the result of the game. There was no chance
of anything going wrong, but to make sure, each *sais* was
shampooing the legs of his pony to the last minute. Behind the
saises sat as many of the Skidars' regiment as had leave to
attend the match—about half the native officers, and a
hundred or two dark, black-bearded men with the regimental
pipers nervously fingering the big, beribboned bagpipes. The
Skidars were what they call a Pioneer regiment, and the
bagpipes made the national music of half their men. The
native officers held bundles of polo-sticks, long cane-handled

mallets, and as the grandstand filled after lunch they arranged themselves by ones and twos at different points round the ground, so that if a stick were broken the player would not have far to ride for a new one. An impatient British Cavalry Band struck up "If you want to know the time, ask a p'leeceman!" and the two umpires in light dust-coats danced out on two little excited ponies. The four players of the Archangels' team followed, and the sight of their beautiful mounts made Shiraz groan again.

"Wait till we know," said The Maltese Cat. "Two of 'em are playing in blinkers, and that means they can't see to get out of the way of their own side, or they *may* shy at the umpires' ponies. They've *all* got white web-reins that are sure to stretch or slip!"

"And," said Kittiwynk, dancing to take the stiffness out of her, "they carry their whips in their hands instead of on their wrists. Hah!"

"True enough. No man can manage his stick and his reins and his whip that way," said The Maltese Cat. "I've fallen over every square yard of the Malta ground, and I ought to know."

He quivered his little, flea-bitten withers just to show how satisfied he felt; but his heart was not so light. Ever since he had drifted into India on a troop-ship, taken, with an old rifle, as part payment for a racing debt, The Maltese Cat had played and preached polo to the Skidars' team on the Skidars' stony polo-ground. Now a polo-pony is like a poet. If he is born with a love for the game, he can be made. The Maltese Cat knew that bamboos grew solely in order that polo-balls might be turned from their roots, that grain was given to ponies to keep them in hard condition, and that ponies were shod to prevent them slipping on a turn. But, besides all these things, he knew every trick and device of the finest game in the world, and for two seasons had been teaching the others all he knew or guessed.

"Remember," he said for the hundredth time, as the riders came up, "you *must* play together, and you *must* play with your heads. Whatever happens, follow the ball. Who goes out first?"

Kittiwynk, Shiraz, Polaris, and a short high little bay fellow with tremendous hocks and no withers worth speaking of (he was called Corks) were being girthed up, and the soldiers in the background stared with all their eyes.

"I want you men to keep quiet," said Lutyens, the captain of the team, "and especially not to blow your pipes."

"Not if we win, Captain Sahib?" asked the piper.

"If we win you can do what you please," said Lutyens, with a smile, as he slipped the loop of his stick over his wrist, and wheeled to canter to his place. The Archangels' ponies were a little bit above themselves on account of the many-colored crowds so close to the ground. Their riders were excellent players, but they were a team of crack players instead of a crack team; and that made all the difference in the world. They honestly meant to play together, but it is very hard for four men, each the best of the team he is picked from, to remember that in polo no brilliancy in hitting or riding makes up for playing alone. Their captain shouted his orders to them by name, and it is a curious thing that if you call his name aloud in public after an Englishman you make him hot and fretty. Lutyens said nothing to his men because it had all been said before. He pulled up Shiraz, for he was playing "back," to guard the goal. Powell on Polaris was half-back, and Macnamara and Hughes on Corks and Kittiwynk were forwards. The tough, bamboo ball was set in the middle of the ground, one hundred and fifty yards from the ends, and Hughes crossed sticks, heads up, with the Captain of the Archangels, who saw fit to play forward; that is a place from which you cannot easily control your team. The little click as the cane-shafts met was heard all over the ground, and then Hughes made some sort of quick wrist-stroke that just dribbled the ball a few yards. Kittiwynk knew that stroke of old, and followed as a cat follows a mouse. While the Captain of the Archangels was wrenching his pony round, Hughes struck with all his strength, and next instant Kittiwynk was away, Corks following close behind her, their little feet pattering like raindrops on glass.

"Pull out to the left," said Kittiwynk between her teeth; "it's coming your way, Corks!"

The back and half-back of the Archangels were tearing down on her just as she was within reach of the ball. Hughes leaned forward with a loose rein, and cut it away to the left almost under Kittiwynk's foot, and it hopped and skipped off to Corks, who saw that, if he was not quick it would run beyond the boundaries. That long bouncing drive gave the Archangels time to wheel and send three men across the ground to head off Corks. Kittiwynk stayed where she was; for she knew the game. Corks was on the ball half a fraction of a second before the others came up, and Macnamara, with a backhanded stroke, sent it back across the ground to Hughes, who saw the way clear to the Archangels' goal, and smacked the ball in before any one quite knew what had happened.

"That's luck," said Corks, as they changed ends. "A goal in three minutes for three hits, and no riding to speak of."

"Don't know," said Polaris. "We've made them angry too soon. Shouldn't wonder if they tried to rush us off our feet next time."

"Keep the ball hanging, then," said Shiraz. "That wears out every pony that is not used to it."

Next time there was no easy galloping across the ground. All the Archangels closed up as one man, but there they stayed, for Corks, Kittiwynk, and Polaris were somewhere on the top of the ball marking time among the rattling sticks, while Shiraz circled about outside, waiting for a chance.

"We can do this all day," said Polaris, ramming his quarters into the side of another pony. "Where do you think you're shoving to?"

"I'll—I'll be driven in an *ekka* if I know," was the gasping reply, "and I'd give a week's feed to get my blinkers off. I can't see anything."

"The dust is rather bad. Whew! That was one for my off-hock. Where's the ball, Corks?"

"Under my tail. At least the man's looking for it there! This is beautiful. They can't use their sticks, and it's driving 'em wild. Give old Blinkers a push and then he'll go over."

"Here, don't touch me! I can't see. I'll—I'll back out, I think," said the pony in blinkers, who knew that if you can't see all round your head, you cannot prop yourself against the shock.

Corks was watching the ball where it lay in the dust, close to his near fore-leg, with Macnamara's shortened stick tap-tapping it from time to time. Kittiwynk was edging her way out of the scrimmage, whisking her stump of a tail with nervous excitement.

"Ho! They've got it," she snorted. "Let me out!" and she galloped like a rifle-bullet just behind a tall lanky pony of the Archangels, whose rider was swinging up his stick for a stroke.

"Not today, thank you," said Hughes, as the blow slid off his raised stick, and Kittiwynk laid her shoulder to the tall pony's quarters, and shoved him aside just as Lutyens on Shiraz sent the ball where it had come from, and the tall pony went skating and slipping away to the left. Kittiwynk, seeing that Polaris had joined Corks in the chase for the ball up the ground, dropped into Polaris' place, and then "time" was called.

The Skidars' ponies wasted no time in kicking or fuming. They knew that each minute's rest meant so much gain, and trotted off to the rails, and their *saises* began to scrape and blanket and rub them at once.

"Whew!" said Corks, stiffening up to get all the tickle of the big vulcanite scraper. "If we were playing pony for pony, we would bend those Archangels double in half an hour. But they'll bring up fresh ones and fresh ones and fresh ones after that—you see."

"Who cares?" said Polaris. "We've drawn first blood. Is my hock swelling?"

"Looks puffy," said Corks. "You must have had rather a wipe. Don't let it stiffen. You'll be wanted again in half an hour."

"What's the game like?" said The Maltese Cat.

"Ground's like your shoe, except where they put too much water on it, said Kittiwynk. "Then it's slippery. Don't play in the centre. There's a bog there. I don't know how their next four are going to behave, but we kept the ball hanging, and made 'em lather for nothing. Who goes out? Two Arabs and a couple of country-breds! That's bad. What a comfort it is to wash your mouth out!"

Kitty was talking with a neck of a lather-covered soda-water bottle between her teeth, and trying to look over withers at the same time. This gave her a very coquettish air.

"What's bad?" said Grey Dawn, giving to the girth and admiring his well-set shoulders.

"You Arabs can't gallop fast enough to keep yourselves warm—that's what Kitty means," said Polaris, limping to show that his hock needed attention. "Are you playing back, Grey Dawn?"

"Looks like it," said Grey Dawn, as Lutyens swung himself up. Powell mounted The Rabbit, a plain bay country-bred much like Corks, but with mulish ears. Macnamara took Faiz-Ullah, a handy, short-backed little red Arab with a long tail, and Hughes mounted Benami, an old and sullen brown beast, who stood over in front more than a polo-pony should.

"Benami looks like business," said Shiraz. "How's your temper, Ben?" The old campaigner hobbled off without answering, and The Maltese Cat looked at the new Archangel ponies prancing about on the ground. They were four beautiful blacks, and they saddled big enough and strong enough to the Skidar's team and gallop away with the meal inside them.

"Blinkers again," said The Maltese Cat. "Good enough!"

"They're chargers—cavalry chargers!" said Kittiwynk, indignantly. *"They'll* never see thirteen-three again."

"They've all been fairly measured, and they've all got their certificates," said The Maltese Cat, "or they wouldn't be here. We must take things as they come along, and keep your eyes on the ball."

The game began, but this time the Skidars were penned to their own end of the ground, and the watching ponies did not approve of that.

"Faiz-Ullah is shirking—as usual," said Polaris, with a scornful grunt.

"Faiz-Ullah is eating whip," said Corks. They could hear the leather-thonged polo-quirt lacing the little fellow's well-rounded barrel. Then The Rabbit's shrill neigh came across the ground.

"I can't do all the work," he cried, desperately.

"Play the game—don't talk." The Maltese Cat whickered; and all the ponies wriggled with excitement, and the soldiers and the grooms gripped the railings and shouted. A black pony with blinkers had singled out old Benami, and was interfering with him in every possible way. They could see Benami shaking his head up and down and flapping his under lip.

"There'll be a fall in a minute," said Polaris. "Benami is getting stuffy."

The game flickered up and down between goal-post and goal-post, and the black ponies were getting more confident as they felt they had the legs of the others. The ball was hit out of a little scrimmage, and Benami and The Rabbit followed it, Faiz-Ullah only too glad to be quiet for an instant.

The blinkered black pony came up like a hawk, with two of

his own side behind him, and Benami's eye glittered as he raced. The question was which pony should make way for the other, for each rider was perfectly willing to risk a fall in a good cause. The black, who had been driven nearly crazy by his blinkers, trusted to his weight and his temper; but Benami knew how to apply his weight and how to keep his temper. They met, and there was a cloud of dust. The black was lying on his side, all the breath knocked out of his body. The Rabbit was a hundred yards up the ground with the ball, and Benami was sitting down. He had slid nearly ten yards on his tail, but he had had his revenge and sat cracking his nostrils till the black pony rose.

"That's what you get for interfering. Do you want any more?" said Benami, and he plunged into the game. Nothing was done that quarter, because Faiz-Ullah would not gallop, though Macnamara beat him whenever he could spare a second. The fall of the black pony had impressed his companions tremendously, and so the Archangels could not profit by Faiz-Ullah's bad behaviour.

But as The Mastese Cat said when "time" was called, and the four came back blowing and dripping, Faiz-Ullah ought to have been kicked all round Umballa. If he did not behave better next time The Maltese Cat promised to pull out his Arab tail by the roots and—eat it.

There was no time to talk, for the third four were ordered out.

The third quarter of a game is generally the hottest, for each side thinks that the others must be pumped; and most of the winning play in a game is made about that time.

Lutyens took over The Maltese Cat with a pat and a hug, for Lutyens valued him more than anything else in the world; Powell had Shikast, a little grey rat with no pedigree and no manners outside polo; Macnamara mounted Bamboo, the largest of the team; and Hughes Who's Who, alias The Animal. He was supposed to have Australian blood in his

veins, but he looked like a clothes-horse and you could whack
his legs with an iron crow-bar without hurting him.

They went out to meet the very flower of the Archangels'
team; and when Who's Who saw their elegantly booted legs
and their beautiful satin skins, he grinned a grin through his
light, well-worn bridle.

"My word!" said Who's Who. "We must give 'em a little
football. These gentlemen need a rubbing down."

"No biting," said The Maltese Cat, warningly; for once or
twice in his career Who's Who had been known to forget
himself in that way.

"Who said anything about biting? I'm not playing tiddly-
winks. I'm playing the game."

The Archangels came down like a wolf on the fold, for they
were tired of football, and they wanted polo. They got it more
and more. Just after the game began, Lutyens hit a ball that
was coming towards him rapidly, and it rolled in the air, as a
ball sometimes will, with the whirl of a frightened partridge.
Shikast heard but could not see it for the minute though he
looked everywhere and up into the air as The Maltese Cat had
taught him. When he saw it ahead and overhead he went
forward with Powell, as fast as he could put foot to ground. It
was then that Powell, a quiet and level-headed man as a rule,
became inspired, and played a stroke that sometimes comes
off successfully after long practice. He took his stick in both
hands, and, standing up in his stirrups, swiped at the ball in
the air, Munipore fashion. There was one second of paralyzed
astonishment, and then all four sides of the ground went up in
a yell of applause and delight as the ball flew true (you could
see the amazed Archangels ducking in their saddles to dodge
the line of flight, and looking at it with open mouths), and the
regimental pipes of the Skidars squealed from the railings as
long as the pipers had breath.

Shikast heard the stroke; but he heard the head of the stick
fly off at the same time. Nine hundred and ninety-nine ponies

out of a thousand would have gone tearing on after the ball
with a useless player pulling at their heads; but Powell knew
him, and he knew Powell; and the instant he felt Powell's right
leg shift a trifle on the saddle-flap, he headed to the boundary,
where a native officer was frantically waving a new stick.
Before the shouts had ended, Powell was armed again.

Once before in his life The Maltese Cat had heard that very
same stroke played off his own back, and had profited by the
confusion it wrought. This time he acted on experience, and
leaving Bamboo to guard the goal in case of accidents, came
through the others like a flash, head and tail low—Lutyens
standing up to ease him—swept on and on before the other
side knew what was the matter, and nearly pitched on his head
between the Archangels's goal-post as Lutyens kicked the ball
in after a straight scurry of a hundred and fifty yards. If there
was one thing more than another upon which The Maltese Cat
prided himself, it was on this quick, streaking kind of run half
across the ground. He did not believe in taking balls round the
field unless you were clearly overmatched. After this they gave
the Archangels five-minutes of football; and an expensive fast
pony hates football because it rumples his temper.

Who's Who showed himself even better than Polaris in this
game. He did not permit any wriggling away, but bored
joyfully into the scrimmage as if he had his nose in a feed-box
and was looking for something nice. Little Shikast jumped on
the ball the minute it got clear, and every time an Archangel
pony followed it, he found Shikast standing over it, asking
what was the matter.

"If we can live through this quarter," said The Maltese Cat,
"I sha'n't care. Don't take it out of yourselves. Let them do the
lathering."

So the ponies, as their riders explained afterwards, "shut-
up." The Archangels kept them tied fast in front of their goal,
but it cost the Archangels' ponies all that was left of their
tempers; and ponies began to kick, and men began to repeat

compliments, and they chopped at the legs of Who's Who, and he set his teeth and stayed where he was, and the dust stood up like a tree over the scrimmage until that hot quarter ended.

They found the ponies very excited and confident when they went to their *saises*; and The Maltese Cat had to warn them that the worst of the game was coming.

"Now *we* are all going in for the second time," said he, "and *they* are trotting out fresh ponies. You think you can gallop, but you'll find you can't; and then you'll be sorry."

"But two goals to nothing is a halter-long lead," said Kittiwynk, prancing.

"How long does it take to get a goal?" The Maltese Cat answered. "For pity's sake, don't run away with a notion that the game is half-won just because we happen to be in luck *now!* They'll ride you into the grandstand, if they can; you must not give 'em a chance. Follow the ball."

"Football, as usual?" said Polaris. "My hock's half as big as a nose-bag."

"Don't let them have a look at the ball, if you can help it. Now leave me alone. I must get all the rest I can before the last quarter."

He hung down his head and let all his muscles go slack, Shikast, Bamboo, and Who's Who copying his example.

"Better not watch the game," he said. "We aren't playing, and we shall only take it out of ourselves if we grow anxious. Look at the ground and pretend it's fly-time."

They did their best, but it was hard advice to follow. The hooves were drumming and the sticks were rattling all up and down the ground, and yells of applause from the English troops told that the Archangels were pressing the Skidars hard. The native soldiers behind the ponies groaned and grunted, and said things in undertones, and presently they heard a long-drawn shout and a clatter of hurrahs.

"One to the Archangels," said Shikast, without raising his head. "Time's nearly up. Oh, my sire—and dam!"

"Faiz-Ullah," said The Maltese Cat, "if you don't play to the last nail in your shoes this time, I'll kick you on the ground before all the other ponies."

"I'll do my best when the time comes," said the little Arab sturdily.

The *saises* looked at each other gravely as they rubbed their ponies' legs. This was the time when long purses began to tell, and everybody knew it. Kittiwynk and the others came back, the sweat dripping over their hooves and their tails telling sad stories.

"They're better than we are," said Shiraz. "I knew how it would be."

"Shut your big head," said The Maltese Cat; "we've one goal to the good yet."

"Yes; but it's two Arabs and two country-breds to play now," said Corks. "Faiz-Ullah, remember!" He spoke in a biting voice.

As Lutyens mounted Grey Dawn he looked at his men, and they did not look pretty. They were covered with dust and sweat in streaks. Their yellow boots were almost black, their wrists were red and lumpy, and their eyes seemed two inches deep in their heads; but the expression in the eyes was satisfactory.

"Did you take anything at tiffin?" said Lutyens; and the team shook their heads. They were too dry to talk.

"All right. The Archangels did. They are worse pumped than we are."

"They've got the better ponies," said Powell. "I sha'n't be sorry when this business is over."

That fifth quarter was a painful one in every way. Faiz-Ullah played like a little red demon, and The Rabbit seemed to be everywhere at once, and Benami rode straight at anything and everything that came in his way; while the umpires on their ponies wheeled like gulls outside the shifting game. But the Archangels had the better mounts—they had kept their racers till late in the game—and never allowed the Skidars to play football. They hit the ball up and down the width of the ground till Benami and the rest were outpaced. Then they went forward, and time and again Lutyens and Grey Dawn were just, and only just, able to send the ball away with a long, spitting backhander. Grey Dawn forgot that he was an Arab, and turned from grey to blue as he galloped. Indeed, he forgot too well, for he did not keep his eyes on the ground as an Arab should, but stuck out his nose and scuttled for the dear honor of the game. They had watered the ground once or twice between the quarters, and a careless waterman had emptied the last of his skinful all in one place near the Skidars' goal. It was close to the end of the play, and for the tenth time Grey Dawn was bolting after the ball, when his near hind-foot slipped on the greasy mud, and he rolled over and over, pitching Lutyens just clear of the goal-post; and the triumphant Archangels made their goal. Then "time" was called—two goals all; but Lutyens had to be helped up, and Grey Dawn rose with his near hindleg strained somewhere.

"What's the damage?" said Powell, his arm around Lutyens.

"Collar-bone, *of course*," said Lutyens, between his teeth. It was the third time he had broken it in two years, and it hurt him.

Powell and the others whistled.

"Game's up," said Hughes.

"Hold on. We've five good minutes yet, and it isn't my right hand. We'll stick it out."

"I say," said the Captain of the Archangels, trotting up, "are you hurt, Lutyens? We'll wait if you care to put in a substitute. I wish—I mean—the fact is, you fellows deserve this game if any team does. Wish we could give you a man, or some of our ponies—or something."

"You're awfully good, but we'll play it to a finish, I think."

The captain of the Archangels stared for a little. "That's not half bad," he said, and went back to his own side, while Lutyens borrowed a scarf from one of his native officers and made a sling of it. Then an Archangel galloped up with a big bath-sponge, and advised Lutyens to put it under his armpit to ease his shoulder and between them they tied up his left arm scientifically; and one of the native officers leaped forward with four long glasses that fizzed and bubbled.

The team looked at Lutyens piteously, and he nodded. It was the last quarter, and nothing would matter after that. They drank out the dark golden drink, and wiped their moustaches, and things looked more hopeful.

The Maltese Cat had put his nose into the front of Lutyens' shirt and was trying to say how sorry he was.

"He knows," said Lutyens, proudly. "The beggar knows. I've played him without a bridle before now—for fun."

"It's no fun now," said Powell. "But we haven't a decent substitute."

"No," said Lutyens. "It's the last quarter, and we've got to make our goal and win. I'll trust The Cat."

"If you fall this time, you'll suffer a little," said Macnamara.

"I'll trust The Cat," said Lutyens.

"You hear that?" said The Maltese Cat, proudly, to the others. "It's worth while playing polo for ten years to have that said of you. Now then, my sons, come along. We'll kick up a little bit, just to show the Archangels this team haven't suffered."

And, sure enough, as they went on to the ground, The Maltese Cat, after satisfying himself that Lutyens was home in the saddle, kicked out three or four times, and Lutyens laughed. The reins were caught up anyhow in the tips of his strapped left hand, and he never pretended to rely on them. He knew The Cat would answer to the least pressure of the leg, and by way of showing off—for his shoulder hurt him very much—he bent the little fellow in a close figure-of-eight in and out between the goal-posts. There was a roar from the native officers and men, who dearly loved a piece of *dagabashi* (horse-trick work), as they called it, and the pipes very quietly and scornfully droned out the first bars of a common bazaar tune called "Freshly Fresh and Newly New," just as a warning to the other regiments that the Skidars were fit. All the natives laughed.

"And now," said The Maltese Cat, as they took their place, "remember that this is the last quarter, and follow the ball!"

"Don't need to be told," said Who's Who.

"Let me go on. All those people on all four sides will begin to crowd in—just as they did at Malta. You'll hear people calling out, and moving forward and being pushed back; and that is going to make the Archangel ponies very unhappy. But if a ball is struck to the boundary, you go after it, and let the people get out of your way. I went over the pole of a four-in-hand once, and picked a game out of the dust by it. Back me up when I run, and follow the ball."

There was a sort of an all-round sound of sympathy and wonder as the last quarter opened, and then there began exactly what The Maltese Cat had foreseen. People crowded in close to the boundaries, and the Archangels' ponies kept looking sideways at the narrowing space. If you know how a man feels to be cramped at tennis—not because he wants to run out of the court, but because he likes to know that he can at a pinch—you will guess how ponies must feel when they are playing in a box of human beings.

"I'll bend some of those men if I can get away," said Who's Who, as he rocketed behind the ball; and Bamboo nodded without speaking. They were playing the last ounce in them, and The Maltese Cat had left the goal undefended to join them. Lutyens gave him every order that he could to bring him back, but his was the first time in his career that the little wise grey had ever played polo on his own responsibility, and he was going to make the most of it.

"What are you doing here?" said Hughes, as The Cat crossed in front of him and rode off an Archangel.

"The Cat's in charge—mind the goal!" shouted Lutyens, and bowing forward hit the ball full, and followed on, forcing the Archangels towards their own goal.

"No football," said The Maltese Cat. "Keep the ball by the boundaries and cramp 'em. Play open order, and drive 'em to the boundaries."

Across and across the ground in big diagonals flew the ball, and whenever it came to a flying rush and a stroke close to the boundaries the Archangel ponies moved stiffly. They did not care to go headlong at a wall of men and carriages, though if the ground had been open they could have turned on a sixpence.

"Wriggle her up the sides," said The Cat. "Keep her close to the crowd. They hate the carriages. Shikast, keep her up this side."

Shikast and Powell lay left and right behind the uneasy scuffle of an open scrimmage, and every time the ball was hit away Shikast galloped on it at such an angle that Powell was forced to hit it towards the boundary; and when the crowd had been driven away from that side, Lutyens would send the ball over to the other, and Shikast would slide desperately after it till his friends came down to help. It was billiards, and no football, this time—billiards in a corner pocket; and the cues were not well chalked.

"If they get us out in the middle of the ground they'll walk away from us. Dribble her along the sides," cried The Maltese Cat.

So they dribbled all along the boundary, where a pony could not come on their right-hand side; and the Archangels were furious and the umpires had to neglect the game to shout at the people to get back, and several blundering mounted policemen tried to restore order, all close to the scrimmage, and the nerves of the Archangels' ponies stretched and broke like cobwebs.

Five or six times an Archangel hit the ball up into the middle of the ground, and each time the watchful Shikast gave Powell his chance to send it back, and after each return, when the dust had settled, men could see that the Skidars had gained a few yards.

Every now and again there were shouts of "Side! Off side!" from the spectators; but the teams were too busy to care, and the umpires had all they could do to keep their maddened ponies clear of the scuffle.

At last Lutyens missed a short easy stroke, and the Skidars had to fly back helter-skelter to protect their own goal, Shikast leading. Powell stopped the ball with a backhander when it was not fifty yards from the goal-posts, and Shikast spun round with a wrench that nearly hoisted Powell out of his saddle.

"Now's our last chance," said The Cat, wheeling like a cockchafer on a pin. "We've got to ride it out. Come along."

Lutyens felt the little chap take a deep breath, and, as it were, crouch under his rider. The ball was hopping towards the right-hand boundary, an Archangel riding for it with both spurs and a whip; but neither spur nor whip would make his pony stretch himself as he neared the crowd. The Maltese Cat glided under his very nose, picking up his hind legs sharp, for there was not a foot to spare between his quarters and the other pony's bit. It was as neat an exhibition as fancy figure-skating. Lutyens hit with all the strength he had left, but the stick slipped a little in his hand, and the fall flew off to the left instead of keeping close to the boundary. Who's Who was far across the ground, thinking hard as he galloped. He repeated stride for stride The Cat's maneuvres with another Archangel pony, nipping the ball away from under his bridle, and clearing his opponent by half a fraction of an inch, for Who's Who was clumsy behind. Then he drove away towards the right as The Maltese Cat came up from the left; and Bamboo held a middle course exactly between them. The three were making a sort of Government-broad-arrow-shaped attack; and there was only the Archangels' back to guard the goal; but immediately behind them were three Archangels racing all they knew, and mixed up with them was Powell sending Shikast along on what he felt was their last hope. It takes a very good man to stand up to the rush of seven crazy ponies in the last quarters of a Cup game, when men are riding with their necks for sale, and the ponies are delirious. The Archangels' back missed his stroke and pulled aside just in time to let the rush go by. Bamboo and Who's Who shortened stride to give The Cat room, and Lutyens got the goal with a clean, smooth, smacking stroke that was heard all over the field. But there was no stopping the ponies. They poured through the goal-posts in one mixed mob, winners and losers together, for the pace had been terrific. The Maltese Cat knew by experience what would happen, and, to save Lutyens, turned to the right with one last effort, that strained a back-sinew beyond hope of repair. As he did so he heard the right-hand goal-post crack as a pony cannoned into it—crack, splinter and fall like a mast. It had been sawed three parts through in cases of accidents, but it upset the pony nevertheless, and he blundered into another, who blundered into the left-hand post, and then there was confusion and dust and wood. Bamboo was lying on the ground seeing stars; an Archangel pony rolled beside him, breathless and angry; Shikast had sat down dog-fashion to avoid falling over the others, and was sliding along on his little bobtail in a cloud of dust; and Powell was sitting on the ground hammering with his stick and trying to cheer. All the others were shouting at the top of what was left of their voices, and the men who had been spilt were shouting too. As soon as the people saw no one was hurt, ten thousand natives and

English shouted and clapped and yelled, and before any one could stop them the pipers of the Skidars broke on to the ground, with all the native officers and men behind them, and marched up and down, playing a wild Northern tune called "Zakhme Bagán," and through the insolent blaring of the pipes and the high-pitched native yells you could hear the Archangels' band hammering, "For they are all jolly good fellows," and then reproachfully to the losing team, "Ooh, Kafoozalum! Kafoozalum! Kafoozalum!"

Besides all these things and many more, there was a Commander-in-chief, and an Inspector-General of Cavalry, and the principal veterinary officer of all India standing on the top of a regimental coach, yelling like school-boys; and brigadiers and colonels and commissioners, and hundreds of pretty ladies joined the chorus. But The Maltese Cat stood with his head down, wondering how many legs were left to him; and Lutyens watched the men and ponies pick themselves out of the wreck of the two goal-posts, and he patted The Maltese Cat very tenderly.

"I say," said the Captain of the Archangels, spitting a pebble out of his mouth, "will you take three thousand for that pony—as he stands?"

"No thank you. I've an idea he's saved my life," said Lutyens, getting off and lying down at full length. Both teams were on the ground too, waving their boots in the air, and coughing and drawing deep breaths, as the *saises* ran up to take away the ponies, and an officious water-carrier sprinkled the players with dirty water till they sat up.

"My aunt!" said Powell, rubbing his back, and looking at the stumps of the goal-posts. "That was a game!"

They played it over again, every stroke of it, that night at the big dinner, when the Free-for-All Cup was filled and passed down the table, and emptied and filled again, and everybody made most eloquent speeches. About two in the morning, when there might have been some singing, a wise little, plain little, grey little head looked in through the open door.

"Hurrah! Bring him in," said the Archangels; and his *sais,* who was very happy indeed, patted The Maltese Cat on the flank, and he limped in to the blaze of light and the glittering uniforms looking for Lutyens. He was used to messes, and men's bedrooms, and places where ponies are not usually encouraged, and in his youth had jumped on and off a mess-table for a bet. So he behaved himself very politely, and ate bread dipped in salt, and was petted all round the table, moving gingerly; and they drank his health, because he had done more to win the Cup than any man or horse on the ground.

That was glory and honor enough for the rest of his days, and The Maltese Cat did not complain much when the veterinary surgeon said that he would be no good for polo any more. When Lutyens married, his wife did not allow him to play, so he was forced to be an umpire; and his pony on these occasions was flea-bitten grey with a neat polo-tail, lame all round, but desperately quick on his feet, and, as everybody knew, Past Pluperfect Prestissimo Player of the Game.

IRVIN S. COBB

The Plural of
Moose Is Mise

At the outset, when our expedition was still in the preparatory stages, we collectively knew a few sketchy details regarding the general architectural plan and outward aspect of the moose. One of us had once upon a time, years and years before, shot at or into—this point being debatable —a moose up in Maine. Another professed that in his youth he had seriously annoyed a moose with buckshot somewhere in Quebec. The rest of us had met the moose only in zoos with iron bars between us and him or in dining halls, where his head, projecting in a stuffed and mounted condition from the wall, gave one the feeling of dining with somebody out of the Old Testament. Speaking with regard to his family history, we understood he was closely allied to the European elk—the Unabridged told us that—and we gathered that, viewed at a distance, he rather suggested a large black mule with a pronounced Roman nose and a rustic hatrack sprouted out between his ears. Also, through our reading upon the subject, we knew that next to the buffalo he was the largest vegetarian in North America, and, next to a man who believes in the forecast of a campaign manager on the eve of an election, the stupidest native mammal that we have. By hearsay we had been made aware that he possessed a magnificent sense of smell and a perfectly wonderful sense of hearing, but was woefully shy on the faculty of thought, the result being that while by the aid of his nose and his ear he might all day elude you, if then perchance you did succeed in getting within gunning range of him he was prone to remain right where he was, peering blandly at you and accommodatingly shifting his position so as to bring his shape broadside on, thereby offering a better target until you, mastering the tremors of eagerness, succeeded in implanting a leaden slug in one of his vital areas.

But, offhand, we couldn't decide what the plural of him was. Still if the plural of goose were geese and the plural of mouse were mice it seemed reasonable to assume that the plural of moose should be mise. Besides, we figured that when we had returned and met friends and told them about our trip it would sound more impressive, in fact more plural, to say that we had slain mise rather than that we had slaughtered moose. In the common acceptance of the term as now used, moose might mean one moose or a herd of them, but mise would mean at least a bag of two of these mighty creatures and from two on up to any imaginable number.

One mentally framed the conversation:

"Well, I hear you've been up in Canada moose hunting." This is the other fellow speaking. "Kill any moose?"

"Kill any moose? Huh, we did better than that—we killed mise."

So by agreement we arranged that mise it should be. This being settled we went ahead with plans for outfitting ourselves against our foray into the game country. We equipped ourselves with high-powered rifles, with patent bedding rolls, with fanciful conceits in high boots and blanket overcoats. We bought everything that the clerk in the shop, who probably had never ventured north of the Bronx in all the days of his sheltered life, thought we should buy, including wicked-looking sheath knives and hand axes to be carried in the belt, tomahawk fashion, and pocket compasses. Personally, I have never been able to figure out the exact value of a compass to a man adrift in a strange country. What is the use of knowing where north is if you don't know where *you* are? Nevertheless, I was prevailed upon to purchase a compass, along with upward of a great gross of other articles large and small which the clerk believed would be needful to one starting upon such an expedition as we contemplated.

On my account he did a deal of thinking. Not since the fall of 1917, when we were making the world safe for the sporting-goods dealers of America, could he have spent so busy and so happy an afternoon as the afternoon when I dropped in on him.

By past experience I should have known better than to permit myself to be swept off my feet by this tradesman's flood of suggestions and recommendations. Already I had an ample supply of khaki shirts that were endeared to me by associations of duck-hunting forays in North Carolina and chill evenings in an Adirondack camp and a memorable journey to Wyoming, where the sage hen abides. I treasured a pair of comfortable hunting boots that had gone twice to European battlefields and down into the Grand Canyon and up again and across the California desert, without ever breeding a blister or chafing a shin. Among my most valued possessions I counted an ancient shooting coat, wearing which I had missed quail in Kentucky, snipe on Long Island, grouse in Connecticut, doves in Georgia, and woodcock in New York State. Finally, had I but taken time for sober second consideration, I should have recalled that the guides I have from time to time known considered themselves properly accoutred for the chase when they put on the oldest suit of store clothes they owned and stuck an extra pair of wool socks in their pockets. But to the city-bred sportsman half the joy of going on a camping trip consists in getting ready for it. So eminent an authority as Emerson Hough is much given to warning the amateur sportsman against burdening himself with vain adornments, and yet I am reliably informed that the said Hough has a larger individual collection of pretty devices in canvas and leather than any person in this republic.

That clerk had a seductive way about him; he had a positive gift. Otherwise I suppose he would have been handling some line which practically sells itself, such as oil stocks or mining shares. Under the influence of his blandishments I invested in a sweater of a pattern which he assured me was being favored by the really prominent moose hunters in the current season, and a pair of corduroy hunting pants which, when walked in, gave off a pleasant swishing sound like a softshoe dancer starting to do a sand jig. I was particularly drawn to these latter garments as being the most vocal pants I had ever seen. As I said before, I bought ever and ever so many other things; I am merely mentioning some of the main items.

We assembled the most impassive group of guides in the whole Dominion—men who, filled with the spirit of the majestic wilds, had never been known publicly to laugh at the expense of a tender-footed stranger. They did not laugh at Harry Leon Wilson's conception of the proper equipment for a man starting upon such an excursion as this one. Wilson on being wired an invitation to go on a hunt for moose promptly telegraphed back that to the best of his recollection he had not lost any moose, but that if any of his friends had been so unfortunate or so careless as to mislay one he gladly would join in the quest for the missing. He brought along an electric flashlight, in case the search should be prolonged after nightfall, a trout rod and a camera. The guides did not laugh at

Colonel Tillinghast Houston's unique notion of buying an
expensive rifle and a hundred rounds of ammunition and then
spending his days in camp sitting in his tent reading a history
of the Maritime Provinces in two large volumes. They did not
laugh at Colonel Bozeman Bulger's overseas puttees or at
Damon Runyon's bowie knife, or at Major McGeehan's eight-
pound cartridge belt—it weighed more than that when loaded;
I am speaking of it, *net*—or at Frank Stevens' sleeping-cap or
at Bill MacBeth's going-away haircut—the handiwork of a
barber who plainly was a person looking with abhorrence upon
the thought of leaving any hair upon the human neck when it
is so easy to shave all exposed surfaces smooth and clean from
a point drawn across the back of the head at the level of the
tops of the ears on down as far as the rear collar button. He
must have been a lover of the nude in necks, that barber.

The guides did not laugh even at my vociferous corduroys
which, at every step I took, went *"Hist, hist,"* as though
entreating their wearer to be more quiet so they might the
better be heard.

By a series of relay journeys we moved up across the line
into Quebec, thence back again below the boundary and
across the State of Maine, thence out of Maine into New
Brunswick and to the thriving city of St. John, with its justly
celebrated reversible falls which, by reason of the eccentrici-
ties of the tide, tumble upstream part of the time and
downstream part of the time, thence by steamer across that
temperamental body of water known as the Bay of Fundy, and
so on into the interior of Nova Scotia. If anywhere on this
continent there is a lovelier spot than the southern part of
Nova Scotia in mid-fall I earnestly desire that, come next
October, someone shall take me by the hand and lead me to it
and let me rave. It used to be the land of Evangeline and the
Acadians; now it is the land of the apple. You ran out of the

finnan haddie belt in and around Digby into the wonderful valley of the apples. On every hand are apples—on this side of the right-of-way, orchards stretching down to the blue waters of one of the most beautiful rivers in America; on that side, orchards climbing up the flanks of the rolling hills to where the combing of thick timber comes down and meets them; and everywhere, at roadside, on the verges of thickets, in pastures and old fields, are seedlings growing singly, in pairs and in clumps. They told us that the valley scenically considered is at its best in the spring after the bloom bursts out upon the trees and the whole countryside turns to one vast pink and white bridal bouquet, but hardly can one picture it revealing itself as a more delectable vision than when the first frosts have fallen and every bough of every tree is studded with red and green and yellow globes and the scent of the ripened fruit rises like an incense of spices and wine.

The transition from the pastoral to the wilderness is abrupt. You leave Annapolis Royal in a motor car—that is, you do if you follow in our footsteps—and almost immediately you strike into the big game country. Not that the big game does not lap over into the settlements and even into the larger towns on occasion, for it does. It is recorded that on a certain day a full-grown moose—and a full-grown moose is almost the largest full-grown thing you ever saw—strolled through one of the principal streets of St. John and sought to enter—this being in the old sinful times—a leading saloon. A prominent lawyer of the same city told me that some four weeks before our arrival a woman client of his, living some two miles from the corporate limits, called him on the telephone at his office to ask his professional advice as to how legally she might go about getting rid of a bull moose which insisted on frequenting her orchard and frightening her children when they went to gather pippins. She felt, she said, that a lawyer was the proper person to seek in the emergency that had arisen, seeing that the closed season for moose was still on and it would be unlawful to take a shot at the intruder, so what she particularly desired to know was whether she couldn't have him impounded for trespass or something of that nature.

But such things as these do not happen every day. Probably a man could spend months on end in St. John without seeing the first of the above-mentioned animals rambling down the sidewalk in the manner of a young moose-about-town and trying to drop into the place where the saloon used to be, only to back out again, with chagrin writ large upon his features, upon discovering that the establishment in question had been transformed into a hat store.

To meet the moose where frequently he is and not merely where occasionally he is, one must go beyond the outlying orchards and on into the vasty expanse of the real moose country—hundreds of hundreds of miles of virgin waste, trackless except for game trails and portages across the ridges between waterways. It is a country of tamaracks and hemlocks, of maples and beech and birch, of berries and flowering shrubs, of bogs and barrens and swampy swales, of great granite boulders left behind by the glaciers when the world was young and thawing, of countless lakes and brawling white rapids and deep blue pools where, in the spawning season, the speckled trout are so thick that the small trout have to travel on the backs of the larger ones to avoid being crushed in the jam. I did not see this last myself; my authority for the statement is my friend the veracious lawyer of St. John. But I saw all the rest of it—the woods wearing the flaunting warpaint colors of the wonderful Canadian Indian summer—crimson of huckleberry, tawny of tamarack, yellow of birch, scarlet of maple; the ruffed grouse strutting, unafraid as barnyard fowl and, thanks be to a three-year period of protection, almost as numerous as sparrows in a city street; the signs of hoofed and padded creatures crossing and crisscrossing wherever the earth was soft enough to register the foot tracks of wild things.

And if you want to know how interior New Brunswick looked after Nova Scotia, you are respectfully requested to reread the foregoing paragraph, merely leaving out some of the lakes and most of the boulders.

On a flawless morning, in a motorboat we crossed a certain lake, and I wish I knew the language that might serve to describe the glory of the colors that ringed that lake around and were reflected, to the last flame-tipped leaf and the last smooth white column of birchen trunk, in its still waters, but I don't. I'll go further and say I can't believe Noah Webster had the words to form the picture, and he had more words than anybody up until the time William J. Bryan went actively into politics. As for myself, I can only say that these colors fairly crackled. There were hues and combinations of hues, shadings and contrasts such as no artist ever has painted and no artist will care to paint, either, for fear of being called a nature faker.

The scene shifts to our main camp. We have met our guides and have marveled at their ability to trot over steep up-and-down-hill portages carrying, each one of them, upon his back a load which no humane man would load on a mule, and have marveled still more when these men, having deposited their mountainous burdens at the farther end of the carry, go hurrying back across the ridge presently to reappear bearing upon their shoulders upturned canoes, their heads hidden inside the inverted interiors and yet by some magic gift peculiar to their craft, managing somehow to dodge the overhanging boughs of trees and without losing speed or changing gait to skip along from one slick round-topped boulder top to another.

Now we are in the deep woods, fifty miles from a railroad and thirty miles from a farmhouse. We sleep at night in canvas lean-tos, with log fires at our feet; we wash our faces and hands in the lake and make high resolves—which we never carry out—to take dips in that same frosty water; we breakfast

at sun-up and sup at dusk in a log shanty set behind the cluster
of tents, and between breakfast and supper we seek, under
guidance, for fresh meat and dining-room trophies.

We have come too late for the calling season, it seems. In
the calling season Mr. Moose desires female society, and by all
accounts desires it mightily. So the guide takes a mean advantage of his social cravings. Generally afoot, but sometimes in
a canoe, he escorts the gunner to a likely feeding ground or a
drinking place, and through a scroll of birch bark rolled up in a
megaphone shape, he delivers a creditable imitation of the call
of the flirtatious cow moose. There are guides who can sound
the love note through their cupped hands, but most of the
fraternity favor the birchen cornucopia. The sound—part
lonely bleat, part plaintive bellow—travels across the silent
reaches for an incredible distance. Once when the wind was
right there is a record of a moose call having been heard six
miles away from where it was uttered, but in this case the
instrumentalist was Louis Harlowe, a half-breed Micmac
Indian, the champion moose caller of Nova Scotia and perhaps
of the world.

In the bog where he is lying, or on the edge of the barren
where he is feeding, the bull hears the pleading entreaty and
thereby is most grossly deceived. Forgetting the caution which
guides his course at other times, he hurries to where the
deceiver awaits him, in his haste smashing down saplings,
clattering his great horns against the tree boles, splashing
through the brooks. And then when he bursts forth into the
open, snorting and puffing and grunting, the hunter beholds
before him a target which in that setting and with that
background must loom up like a grain elevator. Yet at a
distance of twenty yards or thirty, he has been known to miss
the mark clean and to keep on missing it, the while the vast
creature stands there, its dull brain filled with wonder that the
expected cow should not be where he had had every vocal
assurance that she would be, and seemingly only mildly

disturbed by the crashing voice of the repeater and by the unseen, mysterious things which pass whistling over his back or under his belly as the gun quivers in the uncertain grasp of the overanxious or mayhap the buckague-stricken sportsman.

Once though he has made up his sluggish mind that all is not well for him in that immediate vicinity, he vanishes into deep cover as silently as smoke and as suddenly as a wink.

The mating time comes in mid-September and lasts about a month, more or less; and since the open season does not begin until October the first, it behooves the hunter who wishes to bag his moose with the least amount of physical exertion to be in camp during the first two weeks of October, for after that the bull moose is reverting to bachelorhood again. He may answer the call, but the chances are that he will not.

A little later on, after the snows have come, one may trail him with comparative ease. Besides, he is browsing more liberally then and consequently is moving pretty constantly. But between the time when the leaves begin to fall and the time when the snow begins to fly he is much given to staying in the densest coverts he can find and doing the bulk of his grazing by night.

So he must be still-hunted, as the saying goes, and it was still-hunting that we are called upon to do. The guide takes his birch-bark horn along each morning when he starts out, carrying it under one arm and an axe under the other, and upon his back a pouch containing the ingredients for the midday lunch and the inevitable fire-blackened teapot which he calls always by the affectionate name of "kittle." He never speaks of stopping for lunch. When the sun stands overhead and your foreshortened shadow has snuggled up close beneath your feet like a friendly black puppy, he suggests the advisability of "biling a kittle," by which he means building a fire and making tea. So the pack between his shoulders is necessary but the moose call is largely ornamental; it is habit for him to tote it and tote it he does; but mainly he depends upon his eyes and his ears and his uncanny knowledge of the ways of the thing we aim to destroy.

Yes, they call it still-hunting and still-hunting it truly is so far as Louis Harlowe, the half-breed, or Sam Glode, the full-blood Micmac, or Charley Charlton, the head guide, is concerned, as he goes worming his way through the under-growth in his soft-soled moccasins, instinctively avoiding the rotted twig, the loose bit of stone and the swishy bough. But the pair of us, following in his footsteps, in our hard-bot-tomed, hobnailed boots, our creaky leather gear and our noisy waterproofed nether garments, cannot, by the widest latitude in descriptive terminology, be called still-hunters. Carrying small avalanches with us, we slide down rocky slopes which the guide on ahead of us negotiated in pussy-footed style; and we blunder into undergrowth; and we trip over logs and we flounder into bogs and out of them again with loud, churning sounds. Going into second on a hillside we pant like switch engines. I was two weeks behind with my panting when I came out of Canada and in odd times now I still pant briskly, trying to catch up.

Reaching level ground we reverse gears and halt to blow. Toward mid-afternoon, on the homebound hike, our weary legs creak audibly at the joints and our tired feet blunder and fumble among the dried leaves. We create all the racket which, without recourse to bass drums or slide trombones, it is humanly possible for a brace of overdressed, city-softened sojourners to create in deep woods. And still our guide—that person so utterly lacking in a sense of humor—speaks of our endeavor as still-hunting. If an ethical Nova Scotian guide—and all professional guides everywhere, so far as I have observed, are most ethical—were hired to chaperon Sousa's band on a still-hunt through the wilderness and on the way Mr. Sousa should think up a new march full of oom-pahs and everything, and the band should practice it while cruising from bog to barren, the guide, returning to the settlements after the outing, would undoubtedly refer to it as a still-hunt.

In our own case, I trust that our eagerness in some measure compensated for our awkwardness. At least, we worked hard —worked until muscles that we never before knew we had achingly forced themselves upon our attention. Yes, if for the first day or two our exertion brought us no reward in the shape of antlered frontlets or great black pelts drying on the rocks at the canoe landing or savory moose steaks in the frying pan; if it seemed that after all we would have to content ourselves with taking home a stuffed guide's head or so; if twilight found us reuniting at the supper table each with tales of endless miles of tramping to our credit but no game, nevertheless and notwithstanding, the labor we spent was not without its plenteous compensations.

To begin with, there was ever the hope that beyond the next thicket or across the next swale old Mr. Sixty-Inch Spread would be browsing about waiting for us to come stealing upon him with all the stealthy approach of a runaway moving van and blow him over. There was the joy of watching our guide trailing, he reading the woods as a scholar reads a book and seeing there plain as print what we never would have seen— the impress of a great splayed hoof in the yellowed moss, the freshly gnawed twigs of the moose wood, the scarred bark high up on a maple to show that here a bull had whetted his horns, the scuffed earth where a bear had been digging for grubs, the wallow a buck deer had made at a crossing. And when he told us that the moose had passed this way, trotting, less than an hour before, but that the deer's bed was at least two nights old, while the bear's scratching dated back for days, we knew that he knew. Real efficiency in any line carries its own credentials and needs no bolstering affidavits. There may be better eyes in some human head than the pair Louis Harlowe owns or than that equally keen pair belonging to Harry Allen, the dean of

New Brunswick guides, but I have yet to see their owner, and I am quite sure that for woodcraft there are no better equipped men anywhere than the two I have named.

We couldn't decide which was the finer—the supper at night with a great log fire chasing back the dense shadows, and the baked beans and the talk and the crisp bacon and the innocent lies passing back and forth, or the midday lunch out in the tangy, painted forest, miles and miles away from anywhere at all, with the chickadees and the snowbirds and the robins flittering about, waiting their chance to gather the crumbs they knew we would leave behind for them and with the moose birds informally dropping in on us before ever the kettle had begun to sing.

Naturalists know the moose bird, I believe, as the Canada jay and over the line in the States they call him the venison hawk, but by any name he is a handsome, saucy chap, as smart as Satan and as impudent as they make 'em. The first thin wisp of your fire, rising above the undergrowth, is his signal. For some of the denizens of the wilderness it may be just twelve o'clock, but to him it's feeding time. Here he comes in his swooping flight, a graceful, slate-blue figure with his snowy bib and tucker like a trencherman prepared. And there, following close behind him, are other members of his tribe. There always is one in the flock more daring than the rest. If you sit quietly, this fellow will flit closer and closer, his head cocked on one side, uttering half-doubtful, half-confident cheeps until he is snatching up provender right under your feet or even out of your hand. His preference is for meat—raw meat for choice, but his taste is catholic; he'll eat anything. Small morsels he swallows on the spot; larger tidbits he takes in his bill and flies away with to hide in a nearby tree crotch. His friends watch him, and by the time he has returned for another helping they have stolen his cache, so that chiefly what he gets out of the burden of his thriftful industry is the exercise. I do not know whether this should teach us that it is better to strive to lay something against a rainy day and take a chance on the honesty of the neighbors or to seize our pleasure when and where we find it and forget the morrow. Aesop might be able to figure it out, but, being no Aesop, I must continue to register uncertainty.

Campfire suppers and high noon barbecues and glorious sunrises and shooting the rapids in the rivers and paddling across the blue lakes, scaring up the black duck and the loons from before us, and all the rest of it, was fine enough in its way, but it was not killing the bull moose. So we hunted and we hunted. We dragged our reluctant feet through moose bogs —beaver meadows these are in the Adirondacks—and we ranged the high ground and the low. Cow moose we encountered frequently and calves aplenty. But the adult male was what we sought.

We had several close calls, or perhaps I should say he did. One of our outfit—nameless here because I have no desire to heap shame upon an otherwise well-meaning and always dependable companion—had been cruising through thick timber all day without seeing anything to fire at. Emerging into an open glade over a ridge above Little Red Lake, he was moved to try his new and virgin automatic at a target. So he loosed off at one of the big black crows of the North that was perched, like a disconsolate undertaker, with bunched shoulders and drooping head, on a dead tamarack fifty yards away. He did not hit Brother Corbie but he tore the top out of the tamarack snag. And then when he and the guide had rounded the shoulder of the little hill and descended to a swamp below they read in certain telltale signs a story which came near to moving the marksman to tears.

Moving up the slope from the other side the guide had been calling, a bull moose—and a whaling big one, to judge by his hoof marks—had been stirred to inquire into the circumstances. He had quitted the swamp and had ambled up the hill to within a hundred yards of the crest when—as the guide deduced it—the sound of the shot just above caused him to halt and swing about and depart from that neighborhood at his very best gait. But for that unlucky rifle report he probably would have walked right into the enemy. My friend does not now feel toward crows as he formerly felt. He thinks they should be abolished.

An experience of mine was likewise fraught with the germs of a tragic disappointment. In a densely thicketed district, my guide, with a view to getting a view of the surrounding terrain above the tops of the saplings, scaled the steep side of a boulder that was as big as an icehouse and then beckoned to me to follow.

But as a scaler I am not a conspicuous success. By main strength and awkwardness I managed to clamber up. Just as I reached the top and put my rifle down so that I might fan breath into myself with both hands, my boot soles slipped off the uncertain surface and I slid off my perch into space. Wildly I threw out both arms in a general direction. My clutching fingers closed on a limb of a maple which overshadowed the rock and I swung out into the air twelve feet or so above the inhospitable earth, utterly unable to reach with my convulsively groping feet the nearermost juts of granite. For an agonized moment it seemed probable that the only thing that might break my fall would be myself. But I kept my presence of mind. I flatter myself that in emergencies I am a quick thinker. As I dangled there an expedient came to me. I let go gradually.

And then as I plumped with a dull sickening thud into the herbage below and lay there weaponless, windless and jarred I saw, vanishing into the scrub not a hundred feet away, the black shape of a big and startled moose. I caught one fleeting glimpse of an enormous head, of a profile which might have belonged to one of the major prophets, of a set of horns outspreading even as the fronded palm outspreads itself, of a switching tail and a slab-sided rump, and then the shielding bushes closed and the apparition was gone, and gone for keeps. For my part there was nothing to do but to sit there for a spell and cherish regrets. Under the circumstances, trailing a frightened bull moose would have been about as satisfactory as trailing a comet, and probably not a bit more successful as to results.

For the majority of the members of our troupe the duration of the hunt had a time limit. On the afternoon of the last day in camp two of the party strolled into the immediate presence of a fair-sized bull and, firing together, one of them put a slug of lead in a twitching ear which he turned toward them. It must have been his deaf ear, else he would have been aware of their approach long before. But one moose was singular and the achievement of the plural number was our ambition. So four of us crossed back into New Brunswick, where, according to all native New Brunswickers, the moose grow larger than they do in the sister province; Nova Scotians taking the opposing side and being willing to argue it at all times.

With unabated determination the gallant quartet of us hunted and hunted. Three big deer died to make holiday for us but the moose displayed a coyness and diffidence which might be accounted for only on the ground that they heard we were coming. Indeed they could not very well help hearing it.

Each morning under the influences of the frost the flaming frost colors showed a dimming hue. Day before yesterday they had been like burning brands, yesterday there were dulled embers, today smoldering coals; and tomorrow they would be as dead ashes. Each night the sun went down in a nimbus of cold gray clouds. There was a taste and a smell as of snow in the air. The last tardy robin packed up and went south; the swarms of juncos grew thicker; wedge-shaped flights of coot and black duck passed overhead, their bills all pointing toward the Gulf of Mexico. Then on the last day there fell a rain which turned to sleet and the sleet to snow—four inches of it —and in the snow on that last day the reward which comes— sometimes—to the persevering was ours.

To know the climactic sensation which filled the triumphant amateur you must first of all care for the outdoors and for big-game shooting, and in the second place you must have known the feeling of hope deferred, and in the third place you must have reached the eleventh hour, so to speak, of your stay in these parts with the anticipation you had been nurturing for all these weeks since the trip was first proposed still unrealized in your soul.

You and your camp mate and your guide were on the last lap of the journey back to camp; the sun was slipping down the western wall of the horizon; the shadows were deepening under the spruces; you rounded the shoulder of a ridge and stood for a moment at your guide's back looking out across a fire-burned barren. He stiffened like a pointer on a warm scent and pointed straight ahead. Your eye followed where his finger aimed, and two hundred yards away you saw a dark blot against a background of faded tamarack—a bull standing head-on. You shot together, you and your companion. Apparently, the animal swung himself about and started moving at the seemingly languid lope of the moose, which really is a faster gait than you would suppose until you measure the length of his stride. You kept on firing, both of you, as rapidly almost as you could pull the triggers of your automatics. Twice he shook himself and humped his hindquarters as though stung, but he did not check his speed. You emptied your magazine—five shots. Your mate's fifth shell jammed in the chamber, putting him out of the running for the moment. In desperate haste you fumbled one more shell into your rifle, and just as the fugitive topped a little rise before disappearing for good into the shrouding second growth you got your sight full on the mark and sent a farewell bullet whistling on its way. The black hulk vanished magically.

"That'll do," said your guide, grinning broadly. "You got 'im. But load up again before we go down there. He's down and down for keeps, I think, judgin' by the way he flopped, but he might get up again."

But he didn't get up again. You came on him where he lay, still feebly twitching, with two flesh wounds in his flanks and a third hole right through him behind the shoulders—a thousand pounds of meat, a head worth saving and mounting and bragging about in the years to come, a pelt as big as a double blanket and at last the accomplished plural of moose was mise.

So then you did what man generally does when language fails to express what he feels. You harked back sundry thousands of years and you did as your remote ancestor, the cave dweller, did when he slew the sabre-toothed whatyoumaycallhim. About the carcass of your kill you executed a war dance; at least you did if you chambered the emotions which filled the present writer to the choking point.

And then the next day, back in the settlements, when you reunited with the two remaining members of the outfit who had been in camp eight miles away from the camp where you stayed, and when you learned that now there was a total tally of three deceased beasties, the war dance was repeated, only this time it was a four-handed movement instead of a solo number.

JAMES THURBER

You Could
Look It Up

IT all begun when we dropped down to C'lumbus, Ohio, from Pittsburgh to play a exhibition game on our way out to St. Louis. It was gettin' on into September, and though we'd been leadin' the league by six, seven games most of the season, we was now in first place by a margin you could 'a' got it into the eye of a thimble, bein' only a half a game ahead of St. Louis. Our slump had given the boys the leapin' jumps, and they was like a bunch a old ladies at a lawn fete with a thunderstorm comin' up, runnin' around snarlin' at each other, eatin' bad and sleepin' worse, and battin' for a team average of maybe .186. Half the time nobody'd speak to nobody else, without it was to bawl 'em out.

Squawks Magrew was managin' the boys at the time, and he was darn near crazy. They called him "Squawks" 'cause when things was goin' bad he lost his voice, or perty near lost it, and squealed at you like a little girl you stepped on her doll or

153

somethin'. He yelled at everybody and wouldn't listen to nobody, without maybe it was me. I'd been trainin' the boys for ten year, and he'd take more lip from me than from anybody else. He knowed I was smarter'n him, anyways, like you're goin' to hear.

This was thirty, thirty-one year ago; you could look it up, 'cause it was the same year C'lumbus decided to call itself the Arch City, on account of a lot of iron arches with electric-light bulbs into 'em which stretched acrost High Street. Thomas Albert Edison sent 'em a telegram, and they was speeches and maybe even President Taft opened the celebration by pushin' a button. It was a great week for the Buckeye capital, which was why they got us out there for this exhibition game.

Well, we just lose a double-header to Pittsburgh, 11 to 5 and 7 to 3, so we snarled all the way to C'lumbus, where we put up at the Chittaden Hotel, still snarlin'. Everybody was tetchy, and when Billy Klinger took a sock at Whitey Cott at breakfast, Whitey throwed marmalade all over his face.

"Blind each other, whatta I care?" says Magrew. "You can't see nothin' anyways."

C'lumbus win the exhibition game, 3 to 2, whilst Magrew set in the dugout, mutterin' and cursin' like a fourteen-year-old Scotty. He bad-mouthed everybody on the ball club and he bad-mouthed everybody offa the ball club, includin' the Wright brothers, who, he claimed, had yet to build a airship big enough for any of our boys to hit it with a ball bat.

"I wisht I was dead," he says to me. "I wisht I was in heaven with the angels."

I told him to pull hisself together, 'cause he was drivin' the boys crazy, the way he was goin' on, sulkin' and bad-mouthin' and whinin'. I was older'n he was and smarter'n he was, and he knowed it. I was ten times smarter'n he was about this Pearl du Monville, first time I ever laid eyes on the little guy, which was one of the saddest days of my life.

Now, most people name of Pearl is girls; but this Pearl du

Monville was a man, if you could call a fella a man who was only thirty-four, thirty-five inches high. Pearl du Monville was a midget. He was part French and part Hungarian, and maybe even part Bulgarian or somethin'. I can see him now, a sneer on his little pushed-in pan, swingin' a bamboo cane and smokin' a big cigar. He had a gray suit with a big black check into it, and he had a gray felt hat with one of them rainbow-colored hatbands onto it, like the young fellas wore in them days. He talked like he was talkin' into a tin can, but he didn't have no foreign accent. He might a been fifteen or he might a been a hundred, you couldn't tell. Pearl du Monville.

After the game with C'lumbus, Magrew headed straight for the Chittaden bar—the train for St. Louis wasn't goin' for three, four hours—and there he set, drinkin' rye and talkin' to this bartender.

"How I pity me, brother," Magrew was tellin' this bartender. "How I pity me." That was alwuz his favorite tune. So he was settin' there, tellin' this bartender how heartbreakin' it was to be manager of a bunch a blindfolded circus clowns, when up pops this Pearl du Monville outa nowheres.

It give Magrew the leapin' jumps. He thought at first maybe the D.T.'s had come back on him; he claimed he'd had 'em once, and little guys had popped up all around him, wearin' red, white and blue hats.

"Go on, now!" Magrew yells. "Get away from me!"

But the midget clumb up on a chair acrost the table from Magrew and says, "I seen that game today, Junior, and you ain't got no ball club. What you got there, Junior," he says, "is a side show."

"Whatta ya mean, 'Junior'?" says Magrew, touchin' the little guy to satisfy hisself he was real.

"Don't pay him no attention, mister," says the bartender. "Pearl calls everybody 'Junior' 'cause it alwuz turns out he's a year older'n anybody else."

"Yeh?" says Magrew. "How old is he?"

"How old are you, Junior?" says the midget.

"Who, me? I'm fifty-three," says Magrew.

"Well, I'm fifty-four," says the midget.

Magrew grins and asts him what he'll have, and that was the beginnin' of their beautiful friendship, if you don't care what you say.

Pearl du Monville stood up on his chair and waved his cane around and pretended like he was ballyhooin' for a circus. "Right this way, folks!" he yells. "Come on in and see the greatest collection of freaks in the world! See the armless pitchers, see the eyeless batters, see the infielders with five thumbs!" and on and on like that, feedin' Magrew gall and handin' him a laugh at the same time, you might say.

You could hear him and Pearl du Monville hootin' and hollerin' and singin' way up to the fourth floor of the Chittaden, where the boys was packin' up. When it come time to go to the station, you can imagine how disgusted we was when we crowded into the doorway of that bar and seen them two singin' and goin' on.

"Well, well, well," says Magrew, lookin' up and spottin' us. "Look who's here. . . . Clowns, this is Pearl du Monville, a monseer of the old, old school. . . . Don't shake hands with 'em, Pearl, 'cause their fingers is made of chalk and would bust right off in your paws," he says, and he starts guffawin' and Pearl starts titterin' and we stand there givin' 'em the iron eye, it bein' the lowest ebb a ball-club manager'd got hisself down to since the national pastime was started.

Then the midget begun givin' us the ballyhoo. "Come on in!" he says, wavin' his cane. "See the legless base runners, see the outfielders with the butter fingers, see the southpaw with the arm of a little chee-ild!"

Then him and Magrew begun to hoop and holler and nudge each other till you'd of thought this little guy was the funniest guy than even Charlie Chaplin. The fellas filed outa the bar without a word and went on up to the Union Depot, leavin' me to handle Magrew and his new-found crony.

Well, I got 'em outa there finely. I had to take the little guy along, 'cause Magrew had a holt onto him like a vise and I couldn't pry him loose.

"He's comin' along as masket," says Magrew, holdin' the midget in the crouch of his arm like a football. And come along he did, hollerin' and protestin' and beatin' at Magrew with his little fists.

"Cut it out, will ya, Junior?" the little guy kept whinin'. "Come on, leave a man loose, will ya, Junior?"

But Junior kept a holt onto him and begun yellin', "See the guys with the glass arm, see the guys with the cast-iron brains, see the fielders with the feet on their wrists!"

So it goes, right through the whole Union Depot, with people starin' and catcallin', and he don't put the midget down till he gets him through the gates.

"How'm I goin' to go along without no toothbrush?" the midget asts. "What'm I goin' to do without no other suit?" he says.

"Doc here," says Magrew, meanin' me—"doc here will look after you like you was his own son, won't you, doc?"

I give him the iron eye, and he finely got on the train and prob'ly went to sleep with his clothes on.

This left me alone with the midget. "Lookit," I says to him. "Why don't you go on home now? Come mornin', Magrew'll forget all about you. He'll prob'ly think you was somethin' he seen in a nightmare maybe. And he ain't goin' to laugh so easy in the mornin', neither," I says. "So why don't you go on home?"

"Nix," he says to me. "Skiddoo," he says, "twenty-three for you," and he tosses his cane up into the vestibule of the coach and clam'ers on up after it like a cat. So that's the way Pearl du Monville come to go to St. Louis with the ball club.

I seen 'em first at breakfast the next day, settin' opposite each other; the midget playin' "Turkey in the Straw" on a harmonium and Magrew starin' at his eggs and bacon like they was a uncooked bird with its feathers still on.

"Remember where you found this?" I says, jerkin' my thumb at the midget. "Or maybe you think they come with breakfast on these trains," I says, bein' a good hand at turnin' a sharp remark in them days.

The midget puts down the harmonium and turns on me. "Sneeze," he says; "your brains is dusty." Then he snaps a couple drops of water at me from a tumbler. "Drown," he says, tryin' to make his voice deep.

Now, both them cracks is Civil War cracks, but you'd of thought they was brand new and the funniest than any any crack Magrew'd ever heard in his whole life. He started hoopin' and hollerin', and the midget started hoopin' and hollerin', so I walked on away and set down with Bugs Courtney and Hank Metters, payin' no attention to this weak-minded Damon and Phidias acrost the aisle.

Well, sir, the first game with St. Louis was rained out, and there we was facin' a double-header next day. Like maybe I told you, we lose the last three double-headers we play, makin' maybe twenty-five errors in the six games, which is all right for the intimates of a school for the blind, but is disgraceful for the world's champions. It was too wet to go to the zoo, and Magrew wouldn't let us go to the movies, 'cause they flickered so bad in them days. So we just set around, stewin' and frettin'.

One of the newspaper boys come over to take a pitture of Billy Klinger and Whitey Cott shakin' hands—this reporter'd heard about the fight—and whilst they was standin' there, toe to toe, shakin' hands, Billy give a back lunge and a jerk, and throwed Whitey over his shoulder into a corner of the room, like a sack a salt. Whitney come back at him with a chair, and Bethlehem broke loose in that there room. The camera was tromped to pieces like a berry basket. When we finally got 'em pulled apart, I heard a laugh, and there was Magrew and the midget standin' in the door and givin' us the iron eye.

"Wrasslers," says Magrew, cold-like, "that's what I got for a ball club, Mr. Du Monville, wrasslers—and not very good wrasslers at that, you ast me."

"A man can't be good at everythin'," says Pearl, "but he oughta be good at somethin'."

This sets Magrew guffawin' again, and away they go, the midget taggin' along by his side like a hound dog and handin' him a fast line of so-called comic cracks.

When we went out to face that battlin' St. Louis club in a double-header the next afternoon, the boys was jumpy as tin toys with keys in their back. We lose the first game, 7 to 2, and are trailin', 4 to 0, when the second game ain't but ten minutes old. Magrew set there like a stone statue, speakin' to nobody. Then, in their half a the fourth, somebody singled to center and knocked in two more runs for St. Louis.

That made Magrew squawk. "I wisht one thing," he says, "I wisht I was manager of a old ladies' sewin' circus 'stead of a ball club."

"You are, Junior, you are," says a familyer and disagreeable voice.

It was that Pearl du Monville again, poppin' up outa nowheres, swingin' his bamboo cane and smokin' a cigar that's three sizes too big for his face. By this time we'd finely got the other side out, and Hank Metters slithered a bat acrost the ground, and the midget had to jump to keep both his ankles from bein' broke.

I thought Magrew'd bust a blood vessel. "You hurt Pearl and I'll break your neck!" he yelled.

Hank muttered somethin' and went on up to the plate and struck out.

We managed to get a couple runs acrost in our half a the sixth, but they come back with three more in their half a the seventh, and this was too much for Magrew.

"Come on, Pearl," he says. "We're gettin' outa here."

"Where you think you're goin'?" I ast him.

"To the lawyer's again," he says cryptly.

"I didn't know you'd been to the lawyer's once, yet," I says.

"Which that goes to show how much you don't know," he says.

With that, they was gone, and I didn't see 'em the rest of the day, nor know what they was up to, which was a God's blessin'. We lose the nightcap, 9 to 3, and that puts us into second place plenty, and as low in our mind as a ball club can get.

The next day was a horible day, like anybody that lived through it can tell you. Practice was just over and the St. Louis club was takin' the field, when I hears this strange sound from the stands. It sounds like the nervous whickerin' a horse gives when he smells somethin' funny on the wind. It was the fans ketchin' sight of Pearl du Monville, like you have prob'ly guessed. The midget had popped up onto the field all dressed up in a minacher club uniform, sox, cap, little letters sewed onto his chest, and all. He was swingin' a kid's bat and the only thing kept him from lookin' like a real ballplayer seen through the wrong end of a microscope was this cigar he was smokin'.

Bugs Courtney reached over and jerked it outa his mouth and throwed it away. "You're wearin' that suit on the playin' field," he says to him, severe as a judge. "You go insultin' it and I'll take you out to the zoo and feed you to the bears."

Pearl just blowed some smoke at him which he still has in his mouth.

Whilst Whitey was foulin' off four or five prior to strikin' out, I went on over to Magrew. "If I was as comic as you," I says, "I'd laugh myself to death," I says. "Is that any way to treat the uniform, makin' a mockery out of it?"

"It might surprise you to know I ain't makin' no mockery

outa the uniform," says Magrew. "Pearl du Monville here has been made a bone-of-fida member of this so-called ball club. I fixed it up with the front office by long-distance phone."

"Yeh?" I says. "I can just hear Mr. Dillworth or Bart Jenkins agreein' to hire a midget for the ball club. I can just hear 'em." Mr. Dillworth was the owner of the club and Bart Jenkins was the secretary, and they never stood for no monkey business. "May I be so bold as to inquire," I says, "just what you told 'em?"

"I told 'em," he says, "I wanted to sign up a guy they ain't no pitcher in the league can strike him out."

"Uh-huh," I says, "and did you tell 'em what size of a man he is?"

"Never mind about that," he says. "I got papers on me, made out legal and proper, constitutin' one Pearl du Monville a bone-of-fida member of this former ball club. Maybe that'll shame them big babies into gettin' in there and swingin', knowin' I can replace any one of 'em with a midget, if I have a mind to. A St. Louis lawyer I seen twice tells me it's all legal and proper."

"A St. Louis lawyer would," I says, "seein' nothin' could make him happier than havin' you makin' a mockery outa this one-time baseball outfit," I says.

Well, sir, it'll all be there in the papers of thirty, thirty-one year ago, and you could look it up. The game went along without no scorin' for seven innings, and since they ain't nothin' much to watch but guys poppin' up or strikin' out, the fans pay most of their attention to the goin's-on of Pearl du Monville. He's out there in front a the dugout, turnin' hand-springs, balancin' his bat on his chin, walkin' a imaginary line, and so on. The fans clapped and laughed at him, and he ate it up.

So it went up to the last a the eighth, nothin' to nothin', not more'n seven, eight hits all told, and no errors on neither side. Our pitcher gets the first two men out easy in the eighth. Then up come a fella name of Porter or Billings, or some such name, and he lammed one up against the tobacco sign for three bases. The next guy up slapped the first ball out into left for a base hit, and in come the fella from third for the only run of the ball game so far. The crowd yelled, the look a death come onto Magrew's face again, and even the midget quit his tom-foolin'. Their next man fouled out back a third, and we come up for our last bats like a bunch a schoolgirls steppin' into a pool of cold water. I was lower in my mind than I'd been since the day in nineteen-four when Chesbro throwed the wild pitch in the ninth inning with a man on third and lost the pennant for the Highlanders. I knowed something just as bad was goin' to happen, which shows I'm a clairvoyun, or was then.

When Gordy Mills hit out to second, I just closed my eyes. I opened 'em up again to see Dutch Muller standin' on second, dustin' off his pants, him havin' got his first hit in maybe twenty times to the plate. Next up was Harry Loesing, battin' for our pitcher, and he got a base on balls, walkin' on a fourth one you could a combed your hair with.

Then up come Whitey Cott, our lead-off man. He crotches down in what was prob'ly the most fearsome stanch in organized ball, but all he can do is pop out to short. That brung up Billy Klinger, with two down and a man on first and second. Billy took a cut at one you could a knocked a plug hat offa this here Carnera with it, but then he gets sense enough to wait 'em out, and finely he walks, too, fillin' the bases.

Yes, sir, there you are; the tyin' run on third and the winnin' run on second, first a the ninth, two men down, and Hank Metters comin' to the bat. Hank was built like a Pope-Hartford and he couldn't run no faster'n President Taft, but he had five home runs to his credit for the season, and that wasn't bad in them days. Hank was still hittin' better'n anybody else on the ball club, and it was mighty heartenin', seein' him stridin' up towards the plate. But he never got there.

"Wait a minute!" yells Magrew, jumpin' to his feet. "I'm sendin' in a pinch hitter!" he yells.

You could a heard a bomb drop. When a ball-club manager says he's sendin' in a pinch hitter for the best batter on the club, you know and I know and everybody knows he's lost his holt.

"They're goin' to be sendin' the funny wagon for you, if you don't watch out," I says, grabbin' a holt of his arm.

But he pulled away and run out towards the plate, yellin', "Du Monville battin' for Metters!"

All the fellas begun squawlin' at once, except Hank, and he just stood there starin' at Magrew like he'd gone crazy and was claimin' to be Ty Cobb's grandma or somethin'. Their pitcher stood out there with his hands on his hips and a disagreeable look on his face, and the plate umpire told Magrew to go on and get a batter up. Magrew told him again Du Monville was battin' for Metters, and the St. Louis manager finely got the idea. It brung him outa his dugout, howlin' and bawlin' like he'd lost a female dog and her seven pups.

Magrew pushed the midget towards the plate and he says to him, he says, "Just stand up there and hold that bat on your shoulder. They ain't a man in the world can throw three strikes in there 'fore he throws four balls!" he says.

"I get it, Junior!" says the midget. "He'll walk me and force in the tyin' run!" And he starts on up to the plate as cocky as if he was Willie Keeler.

I don't need to tell you Bethlehem broke loose on that there ball field. The fans got onto their hind legs, yellin' and whistlin', and everybody on the field begun wavin' their arms and hollerin' and shovin'. The plate umpire stalked over to Magrew like a traffic cop, waggin' his jaw and pointin' his finger, and the St. Louis manager kept yellin' like his house was on fire. When Pearl got up to the plate and stood there, the pitcher slammed his glove down onto the ground and started stompin' on it, and they ain't nobody can blame him. He's just walked two normal-sized human bein's, and now here's a guy up to the plate they ain't more'n twenty inches between his knees and his shoulders.

The plate umpire called in the field umpire, and they talked a while, like a couple doctors seein' the bucolic plague or somethin' for the first time. Then the plate umpire come over to Magrew with his arms folded acrost his chest, and he told him to go on and get a batter up, or he'd forfeit the game to St. Louis. He pulled out his watch, but somebody batted it outa his hand in the scufflin', and I thought there'd be a free-for-all, with everybody yellin' and shovin' except Pearl du Monville, who stood up at the plate with his little bat on his shoulder, not movin' a muscle.

Then Magrew played his ace. I seen him pull some papers outa his pocket and show 'em to the plate umpire. The umpire begun lookin' at 'em like they was bills for somethin' he not only never bought it, he never even heard of it. The other umpire studied 'em like they was a death warren, and all this time the St. Louis manager and the fans and the players is yellin' and hollerin'.

Well, sir, they fought about him bein' a midget, and they fought about him usin' a kid's bat, and they fought about where'd he been all season. They was eight or nine rule books brung out and everybody was thumbin' through em, tryin' to find out what it says about midgets, but it don't say nothin' about midgets, 'cause this was somethin' never'd come up in the history of the game before, and nobody'd ever dreamed about it, even when they has nightmares. Maybe you can't send no midgets in to bat nowadays, 'cause the old game's changed a lot, mostly for the worst, but you could then, it turned out.

The plate umpire finely decided the contrack papers was all legal and proper, like Magrew said, so he waved the St. Louis players back to their places and he pointed his finger at their manager and told him to quit hollerin' and get on back in the dugout. The manager says the game is percedin' under protest, and the umpire bawls, "Play ball!" over'n' above the yellin' and booin', him havin' a voice like a hog-caller.

The St. Louis pitcher picked up his glove and beat at it with his fist six or eight times, and then got set on the mound and studied the situation. The fans realized he was really goin' to pitch to the midget, and they went crazy, hoopin' and hollerin' louder'n ever, and throwin' pop bottles and hats and cushions down onto the field. It took five, ten minutes to get the fans quieted down again, whilst our fellas that was on base set down on the bags and waited. And Pearl du Monville kept standin' up there with the bat on his shoulder, like he'd been told to.

So the pitcher starts studyin' the setup again, and you got to admit it was the strangest setup in a ball game since the players cut off their beards and begun wearin' gloves. I wisht I could call the pitcher's name—it wasn't old Barney Pelty nor Nig Jack Powell nor Harry Howell. He was a big right-hander, but I can't call his name. You could look it up. Even in a crotchin' position, the ketcher towers over the midget like the Washington Monument.

The plate umpire tries standin' on his tiptoes, then he tries crotchin' down, and he finely gets hisself into a stanch nobody'd ever seen on a ball field before, kinda squattin' down on his hanches.

Well, the pitcher is sore as a old buggy horse in fly time. He slams in the first pitch, hard and wild, and maybe two foot higher'n the midget's head.

"Ball one!" hollers the umpire over 'n' above the racket, 'cause everybody is yellin' worsten ever.

The ketcher goes on out towards the mound and talks to the pitcher and hands him the ball. This time the big right-hander tried a under-shoot, and it comes in a little closer, maybe no higher'n a foot, foot and a half above Pearl's head. It would a been a strike with a human bein' in there, but the umpire's got to call it, and he does.

"Ball two!" he bellers.

The ketcher walks on out to the mound again, and the whole infield comes over and gives advice to the pitcher about what they'd do in a case like this, with two balls and no strikes on a batter that oughta be in a bottle of alcohol 'stead of up there at the plate in a big-league game between the teams that is fightin' for first place.

For the third pitch, the pitcher stands there flatfooted and tosses up the ball like he's playin' ketch with a little girl.

Pearl stands there motionless as a hitchin' post, and the ball comes in big and slow and high—high for Pearl, that is, it bein' about on a level with his eyes, or a little higher'n a grown man's knees.

They ain't nothin' else for the umpire to do, so he calls, "Ball three!"

Everybody is onto their feet, hoopin' and hollerin', as the pitcher sets to throw ball four. The St. Louis manager is makin' signs and faces like he was a contorturer, and the infield is givin' the pitcher some more advice about what to do this time. Our boys who was on base stick right onto the bag, runnin' no risk of bein' nipped for the last out.

Well, the pitcher decides to give him a toss again, seein' he come closer with that than with a fast ball. They ain't nobody ever seen a slower ball throwed. It come in big as a balloon and slower'n any ball ever throwed before in the major leagues. It come right in over the plate in front of Pearl's chest, lookin' prob'ly big as a full moon to Pearl. They ain't never been a minute like the minute that followed since the United States was founded by the Pilgrim grandfathers.

Pearl du Monville took a cut at that ball, and he hit it! Magrew give a groan like a poleaxed steer as the ball rolls out in front a the plate into fair territory.

"Fair ball!" yells the umpire, and the midget starts runnin' for first, still carryin' that little bat, and makin' maybe ninety foot an hour. Bethlehem breaks loose on that ball field and in them stands. They ain't never been nothin' like it since creation was begun.

The ball's rollin' slow, on down towards third, goin' maybe eight, ten foot. The infield comes in fast and our boys break from their bases like hares in a brush fire. Everybody is standin' up, yellin' and hollerin', and Magrew is tearin' his hair outa his head, and the midget is scamperin' for first with all the speed of one of them little dashhounds carryin' a satchel in his mouth.

The ketcher gets to the ball first, but he boots it on out past the pitcher's box, the pitcher fallin' on his face tryin' to stop it, the shortstop sprawlin' after it full length and zaggin' it on over towards the second baseman, whilst Muller is scorin' with the tyin' run and Loesing is roundin' third with the winnin' run. Ty Cobb could a made a three-bagger outa that bunt, with everybody fallin' over theirself tryin' to pick the ball up. But Pearl is still maybe fifteen, twenty feet from the bag, toddlin' like a baby and yeepin' like a trapped rabbit, when the second baseman finely gets a holt of that ball and slams it over to first. The first baseman ketches it and stomps on the bag, the base umpire waves Pearl out, and there goes your old ball game, the craziest ball game ever played in the history of the organized world.

Their players start runnin' in, and then I see Magrew. He starts after Pearl, runnin' faster'n any man ever run before. Pearl sees him comin' and runs behind the base umpire's legs and gets a holt onto 'em. Magrew comes up, pantin' and roarin', and him and the midget plays ring-around-a-rosy with the umpire, who keeps shovin' at Magrew with one hand and tryin' to slap the midget loose from his legs with the other.

Finally Magrew ketches the midget, who is still yeepin' like a stuck sheep. He gets holt of that little guy by both his ankles and starts whirlin' him round and round his head like Magrew was a hammer thrower and Pearl was the hammer. Nobody can stop him without gettin' their head knocked off, so everybody just stands there and yells. Then Magrew lets the midget fly. He flies on out towards second, high and fast, like a human home run, headed for the soap sign in center field.

Their shortstop tries to get to him, but he can't make it, and I knowed the little fella was goin' to bust to pieces like a dollar watch on a asphalt street when he hit the ground. But it so happens their center fielder is just crossin' second, and he starts runnin' back, tryin' to get under the midget, who had took to spiralin' like a football 'stead of turnin' head over foot, which give him more speed and more distance.

I know you never seen a midget ketched, and you prob'ly never even seen one throwed. To ketch a midget that's been throwed by a heavy-muscled man and is flyin' through the air, you got to run under him and pull your hands and arms back and down when you ketch him, to break the compact of his body, or you'll bust him in two like a matchstick. I seen Bill Lange and Willie Keeler and Tris Speaker make some wonderful ketches in my day, but I never seen nothin' like that center fielder. He goes back and back and still further back and he pulls that midget down outa the air like he was liftin' a sleepin' baby from a cradle. They wasn't a bruise onto him, only his face was the color of cat's meat and he ain't got no air in his chest. In his excitement, the base umpire, who was runnin' back with the center fielder when he ketched Pearl, yells, "Out!" and that give hysterics to the Bethlehem which was ragin' like Niagry on that ball field.

Everybody was hoopin' and hollerin' and yellin' and runnin', with the fans swarmin' onto the field, and the cops tryin' to keep order, and some guys laughin' and some of the women fans cryin', and six or eight of us holdin' onto Magrew to keep him from gettin' at that midget and finishin' him off. Some of the fans picks up the St. Louis pitcher and the center fielder, and starts carryin' 'em around on their shoulders, and they was the craziest goin's-on knowed to the history of organized ball on this side of the 'Lantic Ocean.

I seen Pearl du Monville strugglin' in the arms of a lady fan with a ample bosom, who was laughin' and cryin' at the same time, and him beatin' at her with his little fists and bawlin' and yellin'. He clawed his way loose finely and disappeared in the forest of legs which made that ball field look like it was Coney Island on a hot summer's day.

That was the last I ever seen of Pearl du Monville. I never seen hide nor hair of him from that day to this, and neither did nobody else. He just vanished into the thin of the air, as the fella says. He was ketched for the final out of the ball game and that was the end of him, just like it was the end of the ball game, you might say, and also the end of our losin' streak, like I'm goin' to tell you.

That night we piled onto a train for Chicago, but we wasn't snarlin' and snappin' any more. No, sir, the ice was finely broke and a new spirit come into that ball club. The old zip come back with the disappearance of Pearl du Monville out back a second base. We got to laughin' and talkin' and kiddin' together, and 'fore long Magrew was laughin' with us. He got a human look onto his pan again, and he quit whinin' and complainin' and wishtin' he was in heaven with the angels.

Well, sir, we wiped up that Chicago series, winnin' all four games, and makin' seventeen hits in one of 'em. Funny thing was, St. Louis was so shook up by that last game with us, they never did hit their stride again. Their center fielder took to misjudgin' everything that come his way, and the rest a the fellas followed suit, the way a club'll do when one guy blows up.

'Fore we left Chicago, I and some of the fellas went out and bought a pair of them little baby shoes, which we had 'em golded over and give 'em to Magrew for a souvenir, and he took it all in good spirit. Whitey Cott and Billy Klinger made up and was fast friends again, and we hit our home lot like a ton of dynamite and they was nothin' could stop us from then on.

I don't recollect things as clear as I did thirty, forty year ago. I can't read no fine print no more, and the only person I got to check with on the golden days of the national pastime, as the fella says, is my friend, old Milt Kline, over in Springfield, and his mind ain't as strong as it once was.

He gets Rube Waddell mixed up with Rube Marquard, for one thing, and anybody does that oughta be put away where he won't bother nobody. So I can't tell you the exact margin we win the pennant by. Maybe it was two and a half games, or maybe it was three and a half. But it'll all be there in the newspapers and record books of thirty, thirty-one year ago and, like I was sayin', you could look it up.

WILLIAM HAZLETT UPSON

A
Quiet Wedding

ON THURSDAY AFTERNOON, in the front office of the Coliseum at Prairie City, Iowa, Bill Bozeman, three-hundred pound black-bearded professional wrestler, was conferring with his manager, a buxom and highly efficient young woman by the name of Miss Bella Jones, who a few years previously had abandoned her career as a circus bareback rider to devote her peculiar talents to the commercial side of the professional wrestling game. Bill and Bella were discussing their approaching marriage.

"What I want," Bill said, "is just a simple, quiet wedding."

"What you're going to have," Bella said, "is an elaborate, noisy brawl—with plenty of vulgar excitement, and as big a mob as we can drag in. It's a wonderful chance to put over a lot of swell publicity."

"Maybe so," Bill said. "And I don't mind publicity about my wrestling. But when we're getting married, I figure it is our own personal business. So what we want is just a nice quiet—"

"Listen," said Bella. "Before you took me on as your manager you were just a ham. Now you're the best box-office attraction in the Middle West. And what did it? Publicity!"

"Not entirely," Bill said. "Don't forget that I'm a pretty good wrestler."

"I know it. But it isn't straight wrestling that brings in the cash customers. You've built yourself up as a swell drawing-card by following my advice and giving the fans a good show —wearing those whiskers and billing yourself as the Bearded Behemoth, roaring and snarling and tearing around the ring like a drunken gorilla, and pulling off stunts like that fight out in the street last week and so on."

"Well," Bill said, "I still got my beard. I can still roar when I'm in the ring. And if you want, I could stage another street fight."

"No," Bella said. "That's old stuff now. We got to give them something new. And this wedding is just the chance we need. So I've figured out a setup that will just naturally drive the fans crazy."

"And just what are you planning to do?" asked Bill, suspiciously.

"I'm announcing that I can't make up my mind whether to marry you or Clarence Alford. So it's going to be decided by the wrestling match next Saturday night. Whichever one of you wins gets me as a prize."

"What! You mean you'd actually consider marrying that low-down, chicken-livered ex-acrobat, Clarence Alford?"

"Certainly not," snorted Bella. "I'm working out the scenario for the bout so Clarence will almost get you, but you'll flatten him in the end."

"We don't need any scenario for that," said Bill, indignantly. "I can flatten that rat any time I feel like it."

"All right," said Bella. "So after you've won the bout, we'll have the wedding right there in the ring. I'm going to have a full brass band—"

"I won't stand for it," said Bill.

"You've got to," said Bella. "It is all decided. And here's the advance publicity." She flashed a copy of the *Prairie City Evening Times*. With glowing indignation Bill read the following item:

"GRUNT AND GROAN BOYS EMULATE KNIGHTS OF OLD—JOUST FOR HAND OF FAIR LADY

"Just as the plumed knights of yore were wont to engage in deadly combat for the hand of some fair lady, so two mighty gladiators of today, Clarence Alford, the Akron (Ohio) Adonis, and Bill Bozeman, the Bearded Behemoth, will clash in a bitterly contested wrestling bout on Saturday evening at the local Coliseum to decide which is to win the hand in marriage of Miss Bella Jones, beautiful and attractive local business girl.

"When interviewed this afternoon, Miss Jones expressed her warm regard for the Akron Adonis, who is renowned from coast to coast for his beautifully developed body, for his clean sportsmanship, and for his gentlemanly tactics in the ring. On the other hand, Miss Jones admitted that she is deeply fascinated by the sheer brute power, and the animal cruelty of the hideously hairy Bearded Behemoth. Unable to choose between the curiously contrasting charms of these two ardent suitors, she says she has decided to stake her entire future on the outcome of the wrestling match to be held next Saturday night.

"The exact motives underlying Miss Jones's strange decision are the subject of considerable discussion by local psychologists. It is possible that she may be honestly and sincerely bewildered when she attempts to evaluate the relative charms of her two manly lovers, and that she has hit upon this wrestling match as the only possible means of solving dilemma which tears her now this way, now that. On the other hand there are many who charge that she is actuated by overweening pride and selfish vanity—by a neurotic craving for the thrill that will come when she witnesses this epic battle, and realizes that these mighty men are fighting for her, and her alone.

"In any event, the general delectability and oomph possessed by the prize are sure to inspire a battle of unprecedented and blood-curdling ferocity. The customers are certain to get their money's worth."

As Bill finished reading, Bella smiled proudly. "What do you think of it?" she asked.

"It's a bunch of tripe," said Bill. "I don't see how these sporting writers can produce such stuff."

"They can't," said Bella. "They haven't the ability. I wrote the whole thing myself."

"I still say it's tripe," said Bill. "And I bet Sammy Ringo will agree with me." Sammy Ringo was the owner of the Coliseum and producer of the wrestling bouts.

"I explained the whole thing to Sammy yesterday," said Bella. "He thought it was swell. He told me to go ahead. And he's the boss around here, so what he says goes. You know that."

"Just the same, I don't like it, and I won't stand for it. Have you told Clarence yet?"

"Yes."

"What did he say?"

"Oh, he had a lot of childish objections. He said in the first place he didn't like me, and in the second place he had a wife already, so he couldn't pretend he wanted to marry me."

"And what did you say to that?"

"I told him I wouldn't marry him for a million dollars because I like him even less than he doesn't like me—and he doesn't have to worry about his wife, because he hasn't lived with her for years, and she is way back east in Newark, New

Jersey, or some such place, where she won't even hear about this business. And, finally, I told him it was all according to orders from Sammy Ringo himself, so Clarence had to agree —just the way you're going to agree."

"I'll never agree," said Bill. "What I want is just a nice quiet—"

"I'm sorry," interrupted Bella, "but I got no time to argue. I got to go and work up some more publicity."

The next day—Friday—the local paper carried another article playing up the coming wrestling bout and wedding. There was also a letter to the editor, as follows:

"To the Editor of the *Times*. Sir:—For some time past the more thoughtful members of the community have viewed with alarm the increasing wave of indecency and loose-living which seems to be sweeping across this country. Those of us who wish to preserve the sanctity of the American home and the purity of American womanhood have stood aghast at the inroads being made by the forces of communism, nazism, atheism, companionship marriage, free love, Trojan horses, easy divorce, birth control, selfishness, greed, irreverence, the liquor traffic, gambling, and the so-called freedom of the younger generation. But the climax of all these iniquitous movements is reached in the shocking performance announced in today's paper. I refer to the so-called wrestling match which is planned for Saturday night at the Coliseum, where, according to your paper, some shameless hussy—I will not dignify her by the name of woman—is brazenly offering her body as a prize to the victor of a brutal and degrading physical combat. In the name of common decency I call upon you, Mr. Editor, to exclude from your columns all further publicity and advertising for this affair, and, in the name of the law, I call upon the police of Prairie City to stop this degenerate spectacle. (Signed) Outraged Womanhood."

Bill showed the letter to Bella.

"This shows," he said, "what we're getting into by exploiting ourselves this way. I don't like it. I won't stand for people calling you a—what was it, now?" He looked over the letter again. "Oh, here it is—a shameless hussy."

"It's all good publicity, Bill. If we can sell the public the idea that this is an immoral exhibition, we're sure to pack the house. That's why I wrote the letter."

"You mean you wrote it?"

"Sure—and the sporting editor was kind enough to see that it got published. Hot stuff, isn't it?"

"Bella, I'm ashamed of you."

"I'm not," said Bella. "But now I have a lot of other things to do. Good-bye." And Bella was gone.

On Saturday afternoon, the papers came out with more publicity, more objections, and an item stating that a member of the State Athletic Commission had decided to attend the bout in person. The Commissioner was quoted as saying that he stood—first, last and all the time—for good, clean sport. And there had been so much publicity and controversy about the coming bout, that he felt it his duty to make sure that everything was on the level and in accordance with the high moral standards heretofore always associated with the manly art of wrestling throughout the state.

Bill was considerably worried at the prospect of having the Athletic Commissioner at the bout. But Bella, merely laughed:

"All you have to do is follow my advice, and everything will be all right."

"I'm not so sure," said Bill.

"You're not losing your faith in me, are you?" asked Bella. "Don't you love me any more?"

"Bella," said Bill, "you are the most wonderful woman in the world. You know I'm just crazy about you. Without you to handle things for me, I never would have amounted to anything. But this time I wish you would listen to me. It would be so much nicer to have just a simple quiet—"

"Bill," said Bella, "you're just too sweet for words, and I

love you very much, and I just know you're going to carry this thing through the way I want you to."

"Well," said Bill, doubtfully. "If you insist—"

"Atta boy!" said Bella. She kissed him affectionately on his cheek just above the point where his beard began. "And now," she went on, briskly, "we've got to go down and see Clarence, and make the final arrangements."

Taking Bill by the hand, she led him down to the small Coliseum gymnasium, where Clarence Alford had just finished his afternoon workout. The term "Akron Adonis" fitted him fairly well. His face was rather weak and uninspiring, but his physical development was pretty much all right—broad shoulders, rippling muscles, and an undeniably graceful carriage. Bella motioned to Clarence. The three of them sat down on a bench, and Bella explained the details of the coming match.

"For the first ten or fifteen minutes," she said, "you guys can slam each other around in the usual way. But this is a very special occasion, so we ought to give the fans something new in the way of a finish. Here is the scenario: Clarence pulls a few flying tackles, maybe a couple of those phony flying handsprings, and Bill begins to act groggy. Then Clarence knocks Bill through the ropes, and Bill falls down in front of the first row of fans, and rolls in under the edge of the platform. Clarence stands looking down at the place where Bill disappeared and waiting for him to come back."

"There's nothing new about that," Clarence objected.

"Wait till you hear the rest," Bella said. "Instead of coming up where he went down, Bill creeps along under the platform and comes up into the ring on the far side. Clarence doesn't see him, because he has his back turned, and he's looking for him at the place where he disappeared. So Bill takes Clarence by surprise, slams him on the canvas, and wins the match. If you ask me, it's a good trick. The fans ought to eat it up."

"Yes, I guess it ought to work out all right," Bill admitted.

"But you want to be very careful, Bill," said Clarence, "when you hit me from behind. If you aren't careful you might hurt me."

"Don't you worry," Bill said. "I'll lay you down as gentle as if you were a crate of eggs."

"All right, then," Bella said. "It's settled. Now I have to go see about my wedding dress."

That was the last they saw of her until the evening performance.

When the doors were opened, there were already long lines of people waiting in the street. Sammy had boosted the prices, and the fans did a lot of grumbling, but they turned out just the same.

The last preliminary bout was over at half-past nine. The announcer then stepped up into the ring and explained that the grand entrance of the wedding party was about to take place. Afterward, the final bout would go on, and then the beautiful Miss Bella Jones would marry the winner.

As the announcer finished speaking, an orchestra arrived from the basement by means of the small stairway under the ring. The musicians climbed through the ropes, settled themselves on camp chairs, and started in on the well-known strains of *Oh Promise Me*. The words were sung by the announcer—amplified to a terrific roar by the public address system.

The fans, on the whole, did not like it. The lads in the cheap seats started a rhythmic stamping which almost drowned out the music. And the song ended in such a chorus of hoots and hisses that the announcer decided to skip *I Love You Truly*.

The orchestra swung into the opening bars of the *Lohengrin Wedding March*. A deep hush fell over the audience, accompanied by a great craning of necks as the wedding procession entered a rear door and moved down the aisle.

In front were two little flower girls—daughters of one of the preliminary wrestlers. They carried baskets of roses which they scattered before them as they advanced. There was some undignified scrambling around by nearby members of the audience who could not refrain from grabbing these roses as souvenirs. After the flower girls were six bridesmaids hired by a leading department store to model its latest gowns.

And then came Bella herself, a truly majestic figure in white satin, with a long veil. She leaned gracefully on the arm of Mr. Sammy Ringo, the promoter, who was beautifully dressed in full evening attire—including a white tie, white stiff shirt with large diamond studs, white satin vest, a coat with tails. Behind Bella were two little pages, sons of another wrestler, who carried her train.

The entire bridal party clambered into the ring, joined by the minister and the two bridegrooms, who came up from the basement. The timid-looking minister wore a dingy frock coat. The two bridegrooms were attired in wrestling trunks and bathrobes. Each was accompanied by a combination best man and second, clad in white pants and white sweater, and carrying a towel.

The crowd burst into loud and enthusiastic applause. The announcer introduced the minister, the blushing bride, and the unhappy-looking bridegrooms. Then the orchestra disappeared into the basement. And the entire bridal party, with the exception of the two bridegrooms, climbed down into a section of the ringside seats which had been blocked off by white ribbon. Here also sat the Athletic Commissioner of the State.

The referee held his inevitable conference with the wrestlers. They removed their bathrobes, the big bell rang, and the great battle for the beautiful lady began.

Bill employed all his usual tricks for exciting the interest of the crowd. He expanded his vast hairy chest and beat upon it with his fists. He rumpled his hair and beard. He bared his teeth and growled and roared. And he went charging about the ring in his usual mad-bull fashion. Clarence employed the same Toreador tactics which he had used in the past—gracefully side-stepping Bill's wild rushes, wiggling out of tight places, and occasionally closing in and taking a good pull at the heavy black beard of his opponent. From time to time the two men would grapple with each other and fall heavily. Bill would get an apparently effective hold and almost push Clarence's shoulders to the mat. And then, with a mighty heave, Clarence would wiggle loose and escape. It was a good show, and it had the fans roaring with delight.

Finally Clarence caught Bill off his guard and bounded off the ropes with a beautiful flying tackle that sent Bill sprawling. As Bill staggered to his feet, Clarence floored him with another tackle. Then Clarence pulled his most spectacular stunt—the flying handspring—striking Bill square in the chest with his feet, and knocking him backward into the ropes. As Bill dropped heavily over the edge and rolled in under the platform, the crowd leaped to its feet in a frenzy of excitement. Clarence waited, tense and expectant, just inside the ropes.

Slowly the referee began to count. According to the rules, if Bill failed to get back into the ring in twenty seconds he would lose the match. When the referee had reached the count of ten, he began to slow down. By the time he got to fifteen he was proceeding at about half the normal speed. And at sixteen he stopped entirely and began to look around in a puzzled sort of way.

The State Athletic Commissioner was on his feet. "You keep on counting," he shouted. "I'm here to see that this is a fair match!"

Reluctantly the referee took up his slow count.

Bella slid out of her seat, got down on her knees and peered under the platform. In the semi-darkness she was able to make out the vast form of Bill, partly hidden by the complicated network of criss-cross timbers which supported the platform. He had reached a point directly under the center of the ring.

"Hey, there," Bella shouted. "You better hurry."

"I am," Bill answered. "But I'm caught. I seem to be wedged in between two of these timbers."

Bella went scuttling in under the platform—bridal veil and all. She crawled around, put her shoulder behind Bill and pushed.

Bill heaved and struggled until the entire platform swayed and shook. Then one of the timbers came loose with a crash, and Bill was on his way once more, with Bella right after him.

But it was too late. By the time he emerged at the side of the ring, the referee had reached the count of twenty, and the State Athletic Commissioner was shouting, "All right, what are you waiting for? Hold up the hand of the winner!"

The referee walked over and lifted Clarence's hand high in the air. The crowd was cheering and clapping and stamping. The little minister—thinking, no doubt, of the generous fee of twenty-five dollars which Bella had promised him—climbed eagerly into the ring. He opened his prayer book.

Down on the main floor beside the ring Bella spoke rapidly into Bill's ear. "I can't back out of this very well myself," she said. "So there's only one thing to do."

"What's that?" asked Bill.

"You've got to kidnap me by violence. Come on—pick me up and carry me out of here! And don't mind if I put up a fight. I got to stage a bit of a show for the benefit of the fans."

After a few seconds hesitation, Bill went into action. With one sweep of his mighty arm he swung the far-from-unsubstantial form of his fiancée across his shoulders in a fireman's carry. But before he could start for the door he was diverted by a sudden commotion.

A large determined-looking woman came marching down the aisle. She reached the ring, climbed through the ropes, and walked over in front of Clarence.

"So this is what you are doing, you dirty little weasel!" she said in a shrill and angry voice. "Getting ready to commit bigamy!"

"I can explain the whole thing," Clarence whined.

"I know all about it already," said the woman. "Apparently I was just in time. You can forget all about this new wedding, and from now on you're going to turn over all your spare cash to me, or I'll have you put in jail for non-support and desertion."

"Who are you?" asked the minister.

The lady pointed her finger at the cringing Clarence, and answered in a voice that came over the public address system like the roar of a Texas tornado: "I am this man's lawful wife!"

"Say," grunted Bella from her uncomfortable position across Bill's shoulders. "That's swell! It shows how far the publicity went; all the way to Newark, New Jersey. Now nobody can expect me to marry Clarence. So you can let me down, and you and I will get married according to the original plan."

"Bella," said Bill, "you got real brains. But I got the muscle."

"Put me down," yelled Bella.

"Shut up," said Bill. "I got you where I want you. And from now on I'm going to boss this affair."

He went up the aisle like a charging elephant. He carried the kicking and screaming Bella through the lobby, down to the dressing-rooms where he picked up his clothes, and out to the street where he hailed a passing taxi.

As they drove off, Bill braced himself for a terrific bawling out. But Bella merely gazed at him with love and admiration. "What a man!" she said. An hour later they were married by a minister in an outlying village. It was a simple, quiet wedding.

ARTHUR C. CLARKE

Big
Game Hunt

ALTHOUGH BY general consent Harry Purvis stands unrivalled among the "White Hart" *clientele* as a purveyor of remarkable stories (some of which, we suspect, may be slightly exaggerated) it must not be thought that his position has never been challenged. There have even been occasions when he has gone into temporary eclipse. Since it is always entertaining to watch the discomfiture of an expert, I must confess that I take a certain glee in recalling how Professor Hinckelberg disposed of Harry on his own home ground.

Many visiting Americans pass through the "White Hart" in the course of the year. Like the residents, they are usually scientists or literary men, and some distinguished names have been recorded in the visitors' book that Drew keeps behind the bar. Sometimes the newcomers arrive under their own power, diffidently introducing themselves as soon as they have the opportunity. (There was the time when a shy Nobel Prize winner sat unrecognized in a corner for an hour before he plucked up enough courage to say who he was.) Others arrive with letters of introduction, and not a few are escorted in by regular customers and then thrown to the wolves.

Professor Hinckelberg glided up one night in a vast fish-tailed Cadillac he'd borrowed from the fleet in Grosvenor Square. Heaven only knows how he had managed to insinuate it through the side streets that lead to the "White Hart," but amazingly enough all the fenders seemed intact. He was a large lean man, with that Henry-Ford-Wilbur-Wright kind of face that usually goes with the slow, taciturn speech of the sun-tanned pioneer. It didn't in Professor Hinckelberg's case. He could talk like an L.P. record on a 78 turntable. In about ten seconds we'd discovered that he was a zoologist on leave of absence from a North Virginia college, that he was attached to the Office of Naval Research on some project to do with plankton, that he was tickled pink with London and even liked English beer, that he'd heard about us through a letter in *Science* but couldn't believe we were true, that Stevenson was O.K. but if the Democrats wanted to get back they'd better import Winston, that he'd like to know what the heck was wrong with all our telephone call boxes and could he retrieve the small fortune in coppers of which they had mulcted him, that there seemed to be a lot of empty glasses around and how about filling them up, boys?

On the whole the Professor's shock-tactics were well received, but when he made a momentary pause for breath I thought to myself, "Harry'd better look out. This guy can talk rings round him." I glanced at Purvis, who was only a few feet away from me, and saw that his lips were pursed into a slight frown. I sat back luxuriously and awaited results.

As it was a fairly busy evening, it was quite some time before Professor Hinckelberg had been introduced to everybody. Harry, usually so forward at meeting celebrities, seemed to be keeping out of the way. But eventually he was cornered by Arthur Vincent, who acts as informal club secretary and makes sure that everyone signs the visitors' book.

"I'm sure you and Harry will have a lot to talk about," said Arthur, in a burst of innocent enthusiasm. "You're both scientists, aren't you? And Harry's had some most extraordinary things happen to him. Tell the Professor about the time you found that U 235 in your letter-box. . . ."

"I don't think," said Harry, a trifle too hastily, "that Professor—ah—Hinckelberg wants to listen to my little adventure. I'm sure he must have a lot to tell *us.*"

I've puzzled my head about that reply a good deal since then. It wasn't in character. Usually, with an opening like this, Purvis was up and away. Perhaps he was sizing up the enemy, waiting for the Professor to make the first mistake, and then swooping in to the kill. If that was the explanation, he'd misjudged his man. He never had a chance, for Professor Hinckelberg made a jet-assisted take-off and was immediately in full flight.

"Odd you should mention that," he said. "I've just been dealing with a most remarkable case. It's one of these things that can't be written up as a proper scientific paper, and this seems a good time to get it off my chest. I can't often do that, because of this darned security—but so far no one's gotten round to classifying Dr. Grinnell's experiments, so I'll talk about them while I can."

Grinnell, it seemed, was one of the many scientists trying to interpret the behavior of the nervous system in terms of electrical circuits. He had started, as Grey Walter, Shannon and others had done, by making models that could reproduce the simpler actions of living creatures. His greatest success in this direction had been a mechanical cat that could chase mice and could land on its feet when dropped from a height. Very quickly, however, he had branched off in another direction owing to his discovery of what he called "neural induction." This was, to simplify it greatly, nothing less than a method of actually *controlling* the behavior of animals.

It had been known for many years that all the processes that take place in the mind are accompanied by the production of minute electric currents, and for a long time it has been possible to record these complex fluctuations—though their exact interpretation is still unknown. Grinnell had not attempted the intricate task of analysis; what he had done was a good deal simpler, though its achievement was still complicated enough. He had attached his recording device to various animals, and thus been able to build up a small library, if one could call it that, of electrical impulses associated with their behavior. One pattern of voltage might correspond to a movement to the right, another with travelling in a circle, another with complete stillness, and so on. That was an interesting enough achievement, but Grinnell had not stopped there. By "playing back" the impulses he had recorded, he could compel his subjects to repeat their previous actions— whether they wanted to or not.

That such a thing might be possible in theory almost any neurologist would admit, but few would have believed that it could be done in practice owing to the enormous complexity of the nervous system. And it was true that Grinnell's first experiments were carried out on very low forms of life, with relatively simple responses.

"I saw only one of his experiments," said Hinckelberg. "There was a large slug crawling on a horizontal piece of glass, and half a dozen tiny wires led from it to a control panel which Grinnell was operating. There were two dials—that was all—and by suitable adjustments he could make the slug move in any direction. To a layman, it would have seemed a trivial experiment, but I realized that it might have tremendous implications. I remember telling Grinnell that I hoped his device could never be applied to human beings. I'd been reading Orwell's '1984' and I could just imagine what Big Brother would do with a gadget like this.

"Then, being a busy man, I forgot all about the matter for a year. By the end of that time, it seems, Grinnell had improved his apparatus considerably and had worked up to more complicated organisms, though for technical reasons he had restricted himself to invertebrates. He had now built up a substantial store of 'orders' which he could then play back to his subjects. You might think it surprising that such diverse creatures as worms, snails, insects, crustaceans and so on would be able to respond to the same electrical commands, but apparently that was the case.

"If it had not been for Dr. Jackson, Grinnell would probably have stayed working away in the lab for the rest of his life, moving steadily up the animal kingdom. Jackson was a very remarkable man—I'm sure you must have seen some of his films. In many circles he was regarded as a publicity-hunter rather than a real scientist, and academic circles were suspicious of him because he had far too many interests. He'd led expeditions into the Gobi Desert, up the Amazon, and had even made one raid on the Antarctic. From each of these trips he had returned with a best-selling book and a few miles of Kodachrome. And despite reports to the contrary, I believe he *had* obtained some valuable scientific results, even if they were slightly incidental.

"I don't know how Jackson got to hear of Grinnell's work, or how he talked the other man into co-operating. He could be very persuasive, and probably dangled vast appropriations before Grinnell's eyes—for he was the sort of man who could get the ear of the trustees. Whatever happened, from that moment Grinnell became mysteriously secretive. All we knew was that he was building a much larger version of his apparatus, incorporating all the latest refinements. When challenged, he would squirm nervously and say 'We're going big game hunting.'

"The preparations took another year, and I expect that Jackson—who was always a hustler—must have been mighty impatient by the end of that time. But at last everything was ready. Grinnell and all his mysterious boxes vanished in the general direction of Africa.

"*That* was Jackson's work. I suppose he didn't want any premature publicity, which was understandable enough when you consider the somewhat fantastic nature of the expedition. According to the hints with which he had—as we later discovered —carefully mislead us all, he hoped to get some really remarkable pictures of animals in their wild state, using Grinnell's apparatus. I found this rather hard to swallow, unless Grinnell had somehow succeeded in linking his device to a radio transmitter. It didn't seem likely that he'd be able to attach his wires and electrodes to a charging elephant. . . .

"They'd thought of that, of course, and the answer seems obvious now. Sea water is a good conductor. They weren't going to Africa at all, but were heading out into the Atlantic. But they hadn't lied to us. They were after big game, all right. The biggest game there is. . . .

"We'd never have known what happened if their radio operator hadn't been chattering to an amateur friend over in the States. From his commentary it's possible to guess the sequence of events. Jackson's ship—it was only a small yacht, bought up cheaply and converted for the expedition—was lying-to not far from the Equator off the west coast of Africa, and over the deepest part of the Atlantic. Grinnell was angling: his electrodes had been lowered into the abyss, while Jackson waited impatiently with his camera.

"They waited a week before they had a catch. By that time, tempers must have been rather frayed. Then, one afternoon on a perfectly calm day, Grinnell's meters started to jump. Something was caught in the sphere of influence of the electrodes.

"Slowly, they drew up the cable. Until now, the rest of the crew must have thought them mad, but everyone must have shared their excitement as the catch rose up through all those thousands of feet of darkness until it broke surface. Who can blame the radio operator if, despite Jackson's orders, he felt an urgent need to talk things over with a friend back on the safety of dry land?

"I won't attempt to describe what they saw, because a master has done it before me. Soon after the report came in, I turned up my copy of 'Moby Dick' and re-read the passage; I can still quote it from memory and don't suppose I'll ever forget it. This is how it goes, more or less:

" 'A vast pulpy mass, furlongs in length, of a glancing cream-color, lay floating on the water, innumerable long arms radiating from its centre, curling and twisting like a nest of anacondas, as if blindly to catch at any hapless object within reach.'

"Yes: Grinnell and Jackson had been after the largest and most mysterious of all living creatures—the giant squid. Largest? Almost certainly: *Bathyteuthis* may grow up to a hundred feet long. He's not as heavy as the sperm whales who dine upon him, but he's a match for them in length.

"So here they were, with this monstrous beast that no human being had ever before seen under such ideal conditions. It seems that Grinnell was calmly putting it through its paces while Jackson ecstatically shot off yards of film. There was no danger, though it was twice the size of their boat. To Grinnell, it was just another mollusc that he could control like a puppet by means of his knobs and dials. When he had finished, he would let it return to its normal depths and it could swim away again, though it would probably have a bit of a hangover.

"What one wouldn't give to get hold of that film! Altogether apart from its scientific interest, it would be worth a fortune in Hollywood. You must admit that Jackson knew what he was doing: he'd seen the limitations of Grinnell's apparatus and put it to its most effective use. What happened next was not his fault."

Professor Hinckelberg sighed and took a deep draught of beer, as if to gather strength for the finale of his tale.

"No, if anyone is to blame it's Grinnell. Or, I should say, it *was* Grinnell, poor chap. Perhaps he was so excited that he overlooked a precaution he would undoubtedly have taken in the lab. How otherwise can you account for the fact that he didn't have a spare fuse handy when the one in the power supply blew out?

"And you can't really blame *Bathyteuthis,* either. Wouldn't *you* have been a little annoyed to be pushed about like this? And when the orders suddenly ceased and you were your own master again, you'd take steps to see it remained that way. I sometimes wonder, though, if Jackson stayed filming to the very end. . . ."

P. G. WODEHOUSE

The Clicking
of Cuthbert

THE YOUNG MAN came into the smoking room of the clubhouse, and flung his bag with a clatter on the floor. He sank moodily into an armchair and pressed the bell.

"Waiter!"

"Sir?"

The young man pointed at the bag with every evidence of distaste.

"You may have these clubs," he said. "Take them away. If you don't want them yourself, give them to one of the caddies."

Across the room the Oldest Member gazed at him with a grave sadness through the smoke of his pipe. His eye was deep and dreamy—the eye of a man who, as the poet says, has seen Golf steadily and seen it whole.

"You are giving up golf?" he said.

He was not altogether unprepared for such an attitude on the young man's part, for from his eyrie on the terrace above the ninth green he had observed him start out on the afternoon's round and had seen him lose a couple of balls in the lake at the second hole after taking seven strokes at the first.

"Yes!" cried the young man fiercely. "For ever, dammit! Footling game! Blanked infernal fatheaded silly ass of a game! Nothing but a waste of time."

The Sage winced.

"Don't say that, my boy."

"But I do say it. What earthly good is golf? Life is stern and life is earnest. We live in a practical age. All round us we see foreign competition making itself unpleasant. And we spend our time playing golf! What do we get out of it? Is golf any *use?* That's what I'm asking you. Can you name me a single case where devotion to this pestilential pastime has done a man any practical good?"

The Sage smiled gently.

"I could name a thousand."

"One will do."

"I will select," said the Sage, "from the innumerable memories that rush to my mind, the story of Cuthbert Banks."

"Never heard of him."

"Be of good cheer," said the Oldest Member. "You are going to hear of him now."

It was in the picturesque little settlement of Wood Hills (said the Oldest Member) that the incidents occurred which I am about to relate. Even if you have never been in Wood Hills, that suburban paradise is probably familiar to you by name. Situated at a convenient distance from the city, it combines in a notable manner the advantages of town life with the pleasant surroundings and healthful air of the country. Its inhabitants live in commodious houses, standing in their own grounds, and enjoy so many luxuries—such as gravel soil, main drainage, electric light, telephone, baths (h. and c.), and company's own water, that you might be pardoned for imagining life to be so ideal for them that no possible improvement could be added to their lot. Mrs. Willoughby Smethurst was under no such delusion. What Wood Hills needed to make it perfect, she realized, was Culture. Material comforts are all very well, but, if the *summum bonum* is to be achieved, the Soul also demands a look in, and it was Mrs. Smethurst's unfaltering resolve that never while she had her strength should the Soul be handed the loser's end. It was her intention to make Wood Hills a center of all that was most cultivated and refined, and, golly! how she had succeeded. Under her presidency the Wood Hills Literary and Debating Society had tripled its membership.

But there is always a fly in the ointment, a caterpillar in the salad. The local golf club, an institution to which Mrs. Smethurst strongly objected, had also tripled its membership; and the division of the community into two rival camps, the Golfers and the Cultured, had become more marked than ever. This division, always acute, had attained now to the dimensions of a Schism. The rival sects treated one another with a cold hostility.

Unfortunate episodes came to widen the breach. Mrs. Smethurst's house adjoined the links, standing to the right of the fourth tee; and, as the Literary Society was in the habit of entertaining visiting lecturers, many a golfer had foozled his drive owing to sudden loud outbursts of applause coinciding with his down swing. And not long before this story opens a sliced ball, whizzing in at the open window, had come within an ace of incapacitating Raymond Parsloe Devine, the rising young novelist (who rose at that moment a clear foot and a half) from any further exercise of his art. Two inches, indeed, to the right, and Raymond must inevitably have handed in his dinner pail.

To make matters worse, a ring at the front doorbell followed almost immediately, and the maid ushered in a young man of pleasing appearance in a sweater and baggy knickerbockers who apologetically but firmly insisted on playing his ball where it lay, and what with the shock of the lecturer's narrow escape and the spectacle of the intruder standing on the table and working away with a niblick, the afternoon's session had to be classed as a complete frost. Mr. Devine's determination, from which no argument could swerve him, to deliver the rest of his lecture in the coal cellar gave the meeting a jolt from which it never recovered.

I have dwelt upon this incident, because it was the means of introducing Cuthbert Banks to Mrs. Smethurst's niece, Adeline. As Cuthbert, for it was he who had so nearly reduced the muster roll of rising novelists by one, hopped down from the table after his stroke, he was suddenly aware that a beautiful girl was looking at him intently. As a matter of fact, everyone in the room was looking at him intently, none more so than Raymond Parsloe Devine, but none of the others were beautiful girls. Long as the members of Wood Hills Literary Society were on brain, they were short on looks, and, to Cuthbert's excited eye, Adeline Smethurst stood out like a jewel in a pile of coke.

He had never seen her before, for she had only arrived at her aunt's house on the previous day, but he was perfectly certain that life, even when lived in the midst of gravel soil, main drainage, and company's own water, was going to be a pretty poor affair if he did not see her again. Yes, Cuthbert was in love; and it is interesting to record, as showing the effect of the tender emotion on a man's game, that twenty minutes after he had met Adeline he did the short eleventh in one, and as near as a toucher got a three on the four-hundred-yard twelfth.

I will skip lightly over the intermediate stages of Cuthbert's courtship and come to the moment when—at the annual ball in aid of the local Cottage Hospital, the only occasion during the year on which the lion, so to speak, lay down with the lamb, and the Golfers and the Cultured met on terms of easy comradeship, their differences temporarily laid aside—he proposed to Adeline and was badly stymied.

That fair, soulful girl could not see him with a spyglass.

"Mr. Banks," she said, "I will speak frankly."

"Charge right ahead," assented Cuthbert.

"Deeply sensible as I am of—"

"I know. Of the honor and the compliment and all that. But, passing lightly over all that guff, what seems to be the trouble? I love you to distraction—"

"Love is not everything."

"You're wrong," said Cuthbert earnestly. "You're right off it. Love—" And he was about to dilate on the theme when she interrupted him.

"I am a girl of ambition."

"And very nice, too," said Cuthbert.

"I am a girl of ambition," repeated Adeline, "and I realize that the fulfillment of my ambitions must come through my husband. I am very ordinary myself—"

"What!" cried Cuthbert. "You ordinary? Why, you are a pearl among women, the queen of your sex. You can't have been looking in a glass lately. You stand alone. Simply alone. You make the rest look like battered repaints."

"Well," said Adeline, softening a trifle, "I believe I am fairly good-looking—"

"Anybody who was content to call you fairly good-looking would describe the Taj Mahal as a pretty nifty tomb."

"But that is not the point. What I mean is, if I marry a nonentity I shall be a nonentity myself for ever. And I would sooner die than be a nonentity."

"And, if I follow your reasoning, you think that that lets *me* out?"

"Well, really, Mr. Banks, *have* you done anything, or are you likely ever to do anything worth while?"

Cuthbert hesitated.

"It's true," he said, "I didn't finish in the first ten in the

Open, and I was knocked out in the semifinal of the Amateur, but I won the French Open last year."

"The—what?"

"The French Open Championship. Golf, you know."

"Golf! You waste all your time playing golf. I admire a man who is more spiritual, more intellectual."

A pang of jealousy rent Cuthbert's bosom.

"Like What's-his name Devine?" he said sullenly.

"Mr. Devine," replied Adeline, blushing faintly, "is going to be a great man. Already he has achieved much. The critics say that he is more Russian than any other young American writer."

"And is that good?"

"Of course it's good."

"I should have thought the wheeze would be to be more American than any other young American writer."

"Nonsense! Who wants an American writer to be American? You've got to be Russian or Spanish or something to be a real success. The mantle of the great Russians has descended on Mr. Devine."

"From what I've heard of Russians, I should hate to have that happen to *me*."

"There is no danger of that," said Adeline scornfully.

"Oh! Well, let me tell you that there is a lot more in me than you think."

"That might easily be so."

"You think I'm not spiritual and intellectual," said Cuthbert, deeply moved. "Very well. Tomorrow I join the Literary Society."

Even as he spoke the words his leg was itching to kick himself for being such a chump, but the sudden expression of pleasure on Adeline's face soothed him; and he went home that night with the feeling that he had taken on something rather attractive. It was only in the cold, gray light of the morning that he realized what he had let himself in for.

I do not know if you have had any experience of suburban literary societies, but the one that flourished under the eye of Mrs. Willoughby Smethurst at Wood Hills was rather more so than the average. With my feeble powers of narrative, I cannot hope to make clear to you all that Cuthbert Banks endured in the next few weeks. And, even if I could, I doubt if I should do so. It is all very well to excite pity and terror, as Aristotle recommends, but there are limits. In the ancient Greek tragedies it was an ironclad rule that all the real rough stuff should take place off stage, and I shall follow this admirable principle. It will suffice if I say merely that J. Cuthbert Banks had a thin time. After attending eleven debates and fourteen lectures on *vers libre* Poetry, the Seventeenth-Century Essayists, the Neo-Scandinavian Movement in Portuguese Literature, and other subjects of a similar nature, he grew so enfeebled that, on the rare occasions when he had time for a visit to the links, he had to take a full iron for his mashie shots.

It was not simply the oppressive nature of the debates and lectures that sapped his vitality. What really got right in amongst him was the torture of seeing Adeline's adoration of Raymond Parsloe Devine. The man seemed to have made the deepest possible impression upon her plastic emotions. When he spoke, she leaned forward with parted lips and looked at him. When he was not speaking—which was seldom—she leaned back and looked at him. And when he happened to take the next seat to her, she leaned sideways and looked at him. One glance at Mr. Devine would have been more than enough for Cuthbert; but Adeline found him a spectacle that never palled. She could not have gazed at him with a more rapturous intensity if she had been a small child and he a saucer of ice cream. All this Cuthbert had to witness while still endeavoring to retain the possession of his faculties sufficiently to enable him to duck and back away if somebody suddenly asked him what he thought of the somber realism of Vladimir Brusiloff. It is little wonder that he tossed in bed, picking at the coverlet, through sleepless nights, and had to have all his waistcoats taken in three inches to keep them from sagging.

This Vladimir Brusiloff to whom I have referred was the famous Russian novelist, and, owing to the fact of his being in the country on a lecturing tour at the moment, there had been something of a boom in his works. The Wood Hills Literary Society had been studying them for weeks, and never since his first entrance into intellectual circles had Cuthbert Banks come nearer to throwing in the towel. Vladimir specialized in gray studies of hopeless misery, where nothing happened till page three hundred and eighty, when the moujik decided to commit suicide. It was tough going for a man whose deepest reading hitherto had been Vardon on the push shot, and there can be no greater proof of the magic of love than the fact that Cuthbert stuck it without a cry. But the strain was terrible and I am inclined to think that he must have cracked, had it not been for the daily reports in the papers of the internecine strife which was proceeding so briskly in Russia. Cuthbert was an optimist at heart, and it seemed to him that, at the rate at which the inhabitants of that interesting country were murdering one another, the supply of Russian novelists must eventually give out.

One morning, as he tottered down the road for the short walk which was now almost the only exercise to which he was equal, Cuthbert met Adeline. A spasm of anguish flitted through all his nerve centers as he saw that she was accompanied by Raymond Parsloe Devine.

"Good morning, Mr. Banks," said Adeline.

"Good morning," said Cuthbert hollowly.

"Such good news about Vladimir Brusiloff."

"Dead?" said Cuthbert, with a touch of hope.

"Dead? Of course not. Why should he be? No, Aunt Emily met his manager after his lecture at Queen's Hall yesterday, and he has promised that Mr. Brusiloff shall come to her next Wednesday reception."

"Oh, ah!" said Cuthbert dully.

"I don't know how she managed it. I think she must have told him that Mr. Devine would be there to meet him."

"But you said he was coming," argued Cuthbert.

"I shall be very glad," said Raymond Devine, "of the opportunity of meeting Brusiloff."

"I'm sure," said Adeline, "he will be very glad of the opportunity of meeting you."

"Possibly," said Mr. Devine. "Possibly. Competent critics have said that my work closely resembles that of the great Russian Masters."

"Your psychology is so deep."

"Yes, yes."

"And your atmosphere."

"Quite."

Cuthbert in a perfect agony of spirit prepared to withdraw from this love feast. The sun was shining brightly, but the world was black to him. Birds sang in the treetops, but he did not hear them. He might have been a moujik for all the pleasure he found in life.

"You will be there, Mr. Banks?" said Adeline, as he turned away.

"Oh, sure," said Cuthbert.

When Cuthbert had entered the drawing room on the following Wednesday and had taken his usual place in a distant corner where, while able to feast his gaze on Adeline, he had a sporting chance of being overlooked or mistaken for a piece of furniture, he perceived the great Russian thinker seated in the midst of a circle of admiring females. Raymond Parsloe Devine had not yet arrived.

His first glance at the novelist surprised Cuthbert. Doubtless with the best motives, Vladimir Brusiloff had permitted his face to become almost entirely concealed behind a dense zareba of hair, but his eyes were visible through the undergrowth, and it seemed to Cuthbert that there was an expression in them not unlike that of a cat in a strange backyard surrounded by small boys. The man looked forlorn and hopeless, and Cuthbert wondered whether he had had bad news from home.

This was not the case. The latest news which Vladimir Brusiloff had had from Russia had been particularly cheering. Three of his principal creditors had perished in the last massacre of the *bourgeoisie,* and a man whom he had owed for years for a samovar and a pair of overshoes had fled the country, and had not been heard of since. It was not bad news from home that was depressing Vladimir. What was wrong with him was the fact that this was the eighty-second suburban literary reception he had been compelled to attend since he had landed in the country on his lecturing tour, and he was sick to death of it. When his agent had first suggested the trip, he had signed on the dotted line without an instant's hesitation. Worked out in rubles, the fees offered had seemed just about right. But now, as he peered through the brushwood at the faces round him, and realized that eight out of ten of those present had manuscripts of some sort concealed on their persons, and were only waiting for an opportunity to whip them out and start reading, he wished that he had stayed at his quiet home in Nijni-Novgorod, where the worst thing that could happen to a fellow was a brace of bombs coming in through the window and mixing themselves up with his breakfast egg.

At this point in his meditations he was aware that his hostess was looming up before him with a pale young man in horn-rimmed spectacles at her side. There was in Mrs. Smethurst's demeanor something of the unction of the master of ceremonies at the big fight who introduces the earnest gentleman who wishes to challenge the winner.

"Oh, Mr. Brusiloff," said Mrs. Smethurst, "I do so want you to meet Mr. Raymond Parsloe Devine, whose work I expect you know. He is one of our younger novelists."

The distinguished visitor peered in a wary and defensive manner through the shrubbery, but did not speak. Inwardly he was thinking how exactly like Mr. Devine was to the eighty-one other younger novelists to whom he had been introduced at various hamlets throughout the country. Raymond Parsloe Devine bowed courteously, while Cuthbert, wedged into his corner, glowered at him.

"The critics," said Mr. Devine, "have been kind enough to say that my poor efforts contain a good deal of the Russian spirit. I owe much to the great Russians. I have been greatly influenced by Sovietski."

Down in the forest something stirred. It was Vladimir Brusiloff's mouth opening, as he prepared to speak. He was not a man who prattled readily, especially in a foreign tongue. He gave the impression that each word was excavated from his interior by some up-to-date process of mining. He glared bleakly at Mr. Devine, and allowed three words to drop out of him.

"Sovietski no good!"

He paused for a moment, set the machinery working again, and delivered five more at the pithead.

"I spit me of Sovietski!"

There was a painful sensation. The lot of a popular idol is in many ways an enviable one, but it has the drawback of uncertainty. Here today and gone tomorrow. Until this moment Raymond Parsloe Devine's stock had stood at something considerably over par in Wood Hills intellectual circles, but now there was a rapid slump. Hitherto he had been greatly admired for being influenced by Sovietski, but it appeared now that this was not a good thing to be. It was evidently a rotten thing to be. The law could not touch you for being influenced by Sovietski, but there is an ethical as well as a legal code, and this it was obvious that Raymond Parsloe Devine had transgressed. Women drew away from him slightly, holding their skirts. Men looked at him censoriously. Adeline Smethurst started violently, and dropped a teacup. And Cuthbert Banks, doing this popular imitation of a sardine in his corner, felt for the first time that life held something of sunshine.

Raymond Parsloe Devine was plainly shaken, but he made an adroit attempt to recover his lost prestige.

"When I say I have been influenced by Sovietski, I mean, of course, that I was once under his spell. A young writer commits many follies. I have long since passed through that phase. The false glamor of Sovietski has ceased to dazzle me. I now belong wholeheartedly to the school of Nastikoff."

There was a reaction. People nodded at one another sympathetically. After all, we cannot expect old heads on young shoulders, and a lapse at the outset of one's career should not be held against one who has eventually seen the light.

"Nastikoff no good," said Vladimir Brusiloff coldly. He paused, listening to the machinery.

"Nastikoff worse than Sovietski."

He paused again.

"I spit me of Nastikoff!" he said.

This time there was no doubt about it. The bottom had dropped out of the market, and Raymond Parsloe Devine Preferred were down in the cellar with no takers. It was clear to the entire assembled company that they had been all wrong about Raymond Parsloe Devine. They had allowed him to play on their innocence and sell them a pup. They had taken him at his own valuation, and had been cheated into admiring him as a man who amounted to something, and all the while he had belonged to the school of Nastikoff. You never can tell. Mrs. Smethurst's guests were well-bred, and there was consequently no violent demonstration, but you could see by their faces what they felt. Those nearest Raymond Parsloe jostled to get further away. Mrs. Smethurst eyed him stonily through a raised lorgnette. One or two low hisses were heard, and over at the other end of the room somebody opened the window in a marked manner.

Raymond Parsloe Devine hesitated for a moment, then, realizing his situation, turned and slunk to the door. There was an audible sigh of relief as it closed behind him.

Vladimir Brusiloff proceeded to sum up.

"No novelists any good except me. Sovietski—yah! Nastikoff—bah! I spit me of zem all. No novelists anywhere any good except me. P. G. Wodehouse and Tolstoi not bad. Not good, but not bad. No novelists any good except me."

And, having uttered this dictum, he removed a slab of cake from a nearby plate, steered it through the jungle, and began to champ.

It is too much to say that there was a dead silence. There could never be that in any room in which Vladimir Brusiloff was eating cake. But certainly what you might call the general chitchat was pretty well down and out. Nobody liked to be the first to speak. The members of the Wood Hills Literary Society looked at one another timidly. Cuthbert, for his part, gazed at Adeline; and Adeline gazed into space. It was plain that the girl was deeply stirred. Her eyes were opened wide, a faint flush crimsoned her cheeks, and her breath was coming quickly.

Adeline's mind was in a whirl. She felt as if she had been walking gaily along a pleasant path and had stopped suddenly on the very brink of a precipice. It would be idle to deny that Raymond Parsloe Devine had attracted her extraordinarily. She had taken him at his own valuation as an extremely hot potato, and her hero worship had gradually been turning into love. And now her hero had been shown to have feet of clay. It was hard, I consider, on Raymond Parsloe Devine, but that is how it goes in this world. You get a following as a celebrity, and then you run up against another bigger celebrity and your admirers desert you. One could moralize on this at considerable length, but better not, perhaps. Enough to say that the glamor of Raymond Devine ceased abruptly in that moment for Adeline, and her most coherent thought at this juncture was the resolve, as soon as she got up to her room, to burn the three signed photographs he had sent her and to give the autographed presentation set of his books to the grocer's boy.

Mrs. Smethurst, meanwhile, having rallied somewhat, was endeavoring to set the feast of reason and flow of soul going again.

"And how do you like America, Mr. Brusiloff?" she asked.

The celebrity paused in the act of lowering another segment of cake.

"Dam good," he replied cordially.

"I suppose you have traveled all over the country by this time?"

"You said it," agreed the Thinker.

"Have you met many of our great public men?"

"Yais— Yais— Quite a few of the nibs—the President, I meet him. But—" Beneath the matting a discontented expression came into his face, and his voice took on a peevish note. "But I not meet your *real* great men—your Volterragin, your Veener Sirahzen—I not meet them. That's what gives me the pipovitch. Have *you* ever met Volterragin and Veener Sirahzen?"

A strained, anguished look came into Mrs. Smethurst's face and was reflected in the faces of the other members of the circle. The eminent Russian had sprung two entirely new ones on them, and they felt that their ignorance was about to be exposed. What would Vladimir Brusiloff think of the Wood Hills Literary Society? The reputation of the Wood Hills Literary Society was at stake, trembling in the balance, and coming up for the third time. In dumb agony Mrs. Smethurst rolled her eyes about the room searching for someone capable of coming to the rescue. She drew blank.

And then, from a distant corner, there sounded a deprecating cough, and those nearest Cuthbert Banks saw that he had stopped twisting his right foot around his left ankle and his left foot round his right ankle and was sitting up with a light of almost human intelligence in his eyes.

"Er—" said Cuthbert, blushing as every eye in the room seemed to fix itself on him, "I think he means Walter Hagen and Gene Sarazen."

"Walter Hagen and Gene Sarazen?" repeated Mrs. Smethurst blankly. "I never heard of—"

"Yais! Yais! Most! Very!" shouted Vladimir Brusiloff enthusiastically. "Volterragin and Veener Sirahzen. You know them, yes, what, no, perhaps?"

"I've played with Walter Hagen often, and I was partnered with Gene Sarazen in last year's Open."

The great Russian uttered a cry that shook the chandelier.

"You play in ze Open? Why," he demanded reproachfully of Mrs. Smethurst, "was I not been introduced to this young man who play in opens?"

"Well, really," faltered Mrs. Smethurst. "Well, the fact is, Mr. Brusiloff—"

She broke off. She was unequal to the task of explaining, without hurting anyone's feelings, that she had always regarded Cuthbert as a piece of cheese and a blot on the landscape.

"Introduct me!" thundered the Celebrity.

"Why, certainly, certainly, of course. This is Mr.—" She looked appealingly at Cuthbert.

"Banks," prompted Cuthbert.

"Banks!" cried Vladimir Brusiloff. "Not Cootaboot Banks?"

"Is your name Cootaboot?" asked Mrs. Smethurst faintly.

"Well, it's Cuthbert."

"Yais! Yais! Cootaboot!" There was a rush and swirl, as the effervescent Muscovite burst his way through the throng and rushed to where Cuthbert sat. He stood for a moment eying him excitedly, then, stooping swiftly, kissed him on both cheeks before Cuthbert could get his guard up. "My dear young man, I saw you win ze French Open. Great! Great! Grand! Superb! Hot stuff, and you can say I said so! Will you permit one who is but eighteen at Nijni-Novgorod to salute you once more?"

And he kissed Cuthbert again. Then, brushing aside one or two intellectuals who were in the way, he dragged up a chair and sat down.

"You are a great man!" he said.

"Oh, no," said Cuthbert modestly.

"Yais! Great. Most! Very! The way you lay your approach putts dead from anywhere!"

"Oh, I don't know."

Mr. Brusiloff drew his chair closer.

"Let me tell you one vairy funny story about putting. It was one day I play at Nijni-Novgorod with the pro against Lenin and Trotsky, and Trotsky had a two-inch putt for the hole. But, just as he addresses the ball, someone in the crowd he tries to assassinate Lenin with a rewolwer—you know that is our great national sport, trying to assassinate Lenin with rewolwers—and the bang puts Trotsky off his stroke and he goes five yards past the hole, and then Lenin, who is rather shaken, you understand, he misses again himself, and we win the hole and match and I clean up three hundred and ninety-six thousand rubles, or five dollars in your money. Some gameovitch! And now let me tell you one other vairy funny story—"

Desultory conversation had begun in murmurs over the rest of the room, as the Wood Hills intellectuals politely endeavored to conceal the fact that they realized that they were about as much out of it at this reunion of twin souls as cats at a dog show. From time to time they started as Vladimir Brusiloff's laugh boomed out. Perhaps it was a consolation to them to know that he was enjoying himself.

As for Adeline, how shall I describe her emotions? She was stunned. Before her very eyes the stone which the builders had rejected had become the main thing, the hundred-to-one shot had walked away with the race. A rush of tender admiration for Cuthbert Banks flooded her heart. She saw that she had been all wrong. Cuthbert, whom she had always treated with a patronizing superiority, was really a man to be looked up to and worshiped. A deep, dreamy sigh shook Adeline's fragile form.

Half an hour later Vladimir and Cuthbert Banks rose.

"Goot-a-bye, Mrs. Smet-thirst," said the Celebrity. "Zank you for a most charming visit. My friend Cootaboot and me we go now to shoot a few holes. You will lend me clobs, friend Cootaboot?"

"Any you want."

"The niblicksky is what I use most. Goot-a-bye, Mrs. Smet-thirst."

They were moving to the door, when Cuthbert felt a light touch on his arm. Adeline was looking up at him tenderly.

"May I come, too, and walk round with you?"

Cuthbert's bosom heaved.

"Oh," he said, with a tremor in his voice, "that you would walk round with me for life!"

Her eyes met his.

"Perhaps," she whispered softly, "it could be arranged."

"And so," (concluded the Oldest Member) "you see that golf can be of the greatest practical assistance to a man in Life's struggle. Raymond Parsloe Devine, who was no player, had to move out of the neighborhood immediately, and is now, I believe, writing scenarios out in California for the Flicker Film Company. Adeline is married to Cuthbert, and it was only his earnest pleading which prevented her from having their eldest son christened Francis Ouimet Ribbed-Faced

Mashie Banks, for she is now as keen a devotee of the great game as her husband. Those who know them say that theirs is a union so devoted, so—"

The Sage broke off abruptly, for the young man had rushed to the door and out into the passage. Through the open door he could hear him crying passionately to the waiter to bring back his clubs.

REX LARDNER

Trials
of the King

Dear Jeff,

Well, I guess you must be dying to hear how the team looked in our first game against Long Beach. Frankly, we looked *rotten,* though the Junior flash did OK. Coach Hetzel, who I'm sure could give Florence Nightingale tips on how to run a basketball team, started Cantwell instead of me at forward. Wouldn't you know that for this game, being the home opener, the five starters were introduced, one by one. So there I am stewing on the bench while Cantwell is taking the bows and making a big show of being peppy and encouraging everybody by patting them on the pants while the Northside fans are going out of their heads screaming.

Cantwell, who is a 6'0'' Senior (emphasis on the 0) and greatly beloved by Hetzel, blew three jumpers and two chippies and dropped three passes in the first quarter, so

217

finally Hetzel put me in. Immediately we began to click. We were 9 points behind when I went in and at half-time we were only 6 behind. Guess who stuck in the basket from the right corner just as the buzzer sounded. Swish. You should have heard them screaming.

I also got four rebounds that half and would have snagged four more if our own man Deke Saunders, who is 6'5" and is burdened with 225 pounds and not too much intelligence, didn't box me out most of the time, all the while stepping on my feet. He is like a Sherman tank, though not as well coordinated as a Sherman tank. Once in the fourth quarter I faked a layup and threw him a beautiful pass over my shoulder and while I passed it I'm thinking, My God, I passed to Saunders! Sure enough, it went right through his hands and out of bounds. Another time I went about 90 feet in the air for a defensive rebound and while I'm bringing it down he snatches it from me and we're fighting for it. So the stupid ref calls a jump ball. Then nobody gets credit for the rebound because the Long Beach guy outjumped Saunders by 15 feet and knocked it to their big guy Olsen and he stuck it in for a quick basket.

Cantwell played the third quarter and we dropped back by 15. In the last quarter Hetzel tilted up the bench and anybody who fell off he stuck in the game. With Hetzel's prize screwballs in I never got the ball. After Long Beach sunk one, one of these green subs would bring the ball downcourt and if he didn't get called for palming or traveling he would sky-rocket a shot from 50 feet out. No passing, no maneuvering, and no basket. They'd get the rebound and a fast two points because nobody plays defense but me. Half the time three of them wouldn't go back but would hang under the Long Beach basket waiting for a long pass so they could pop in a quick two. You can expect Seniors like Burkhart and Rancom never to pass the ball, but the second-string Juniors ought to throw the ball to somebody who can *shoot,* if you know what I mean. We finally lost 74–58.

Hetzel could have won the game if he had used his players right, but he has a genius for sticking the wrong guy in at the wrong time. This is how the team looks: Doug Haley, a 6'2" Senior, is the only ballplayer on the team (besides me) and he played only half the game. The only other Junior who can shoot (besides me) is Norman Parker. He is not a bad rebounder but as for defense, forget it. He is 6'3". He got 16 points and was high scorer. I wound up with six and got two fouls called on me. One of them was a clean stuff on one of their midget guards but was called a hack by the stupid referee. The other was, I admit, a legitimate charge. But what an act their guy pulled when I ran into him! He ran back about 15 feet, fell down and almost turned a backward somersault. What melodrama, clutching his shoulder. It is some move, I will have to pick it up.

But I did stick an elbow into their big guy one time under our boards and it wasn't called, so that makes the refs and I even. It didn't seem to slow him down any, however.

The Old Man, Muth and Terry are fine, along with the cat and goldfish. He has lost interest in them. There is a big red one in there they call Big Larry—after guess-who. He looks *mean.* The Old Man did not see the Long Beach game but he is going to try to see the one against Molinas. I will let you know how we come out.

Regards,
Larry

P.S. On the program they have Rancom down at 5'10" and me at 6'1". They took an inch away from me and gave it to Rancom. With a leap I can touch the rim.

Dec. 12

Jeff baby,

Not to keep you in suspenders, we murdered Molinas 68–53 because Hetzel finally stuck the right line-up in, with your "little" brother in his proper place in the corner. I was 5 for 9 from the floor and 2 for 5 from the foul line for a big 12 points or double figures, as they say. One of my admirers in the stands asked me afterwards why I didn't shoot more and I told him, How can I shoot more when nobody passes me the ball? Actually, I got it about as often as I was open but you have to keep your fans happy.

To keep the score down Hetzel put in the screwball contingent in the last quarter. They went out of their minds trying to score, dashing about, getting the ball stolen and taking steps, committing a whole season's violations in 8 minutes. Every time we got the ball one of them would head fake and shoot from midcourt, happy to even hit the backboard. So Molinas kept crawling up on us, but time ran out on them before they got dangerous. Norman hit for 21 and Doug Haley got 18. Arnie Burkhart, who is the last of the great chuckers, got 14 and he only took 50 shots to do it. The reason I was only 40% from the foul line is because I am concentrating so much on defense, covering for Norman and Burkhart, I can't get relaxed and loose for a foul shot.

When the game was over, what do you think Hetzel yakked about in the locker room for 20 minutes after our impressive win? Not my great defensive play or Norman's field-goal percentage but how lousy our foul shooting was. He says many a game has been won or lost through bad foul shooting and such golden words as that, and we have to practice diligently. Haley, who is kind of funny, whispered to me many more have been lost through rotten substitutions, and I almost broke up.

I forgot to tell you the other day the Press picked Northside to finish sixth in the League! Personally, I think we will take all the marbles and I am saving the clipping to shove in the editor's face when we do it.

I have been asked to a party after the Bay Shore game by a kind of cute blond named Madge Kimbrough, though she talks too much like they all do. She is a cheerleader.

The Old Man said I played pretty good against Molinas. That is the understatement of the year. He gave me a buck to get a hero sandwich. He told Terry about my feats in the game before I came home and when I opened the door she bowed down and said, Hail to the King. So now they are calling me the King around here.

I hope you are making out OK with the townies at Ann Arbor. Muth said to tell you she mailed the calculus text you claim you need out there. Terry sends a big X. I will let you know how I do against Bay Shore.

Regally,

L.

Dec. 15

Dear Big Bro.,

To the consternation of the cretin who makes predictions in the Press—the same clot who picked us for sixth—we creamed Bay Shore 74–68. This despite every coaching mistake a coach can dream up, including not starting the Junior Flash. He had Cantwell in there for me for half the first quarter, playing his usual sterling game, throwing passes to the surprised Bay Shore players, blowing layups and not getting any rebounds except when the ball bounced right into his hands. Talk about deceptive ball-handling. You could set your watch by the way he fakes.

But finally the King went in and rammed home a quick two

buckets—one a 3-point play—and the complection of the game changed, as they say.

Haley and I play good together, mainly because he is the only guy who can handle my deceptive passes and he is one of the few players we have who will pass off to the open man. Burkhart and Rancom never pass to anybody but just keep dribbling around until they can get off a shot or somebody steals the ball from them, and Norman is just psychologically unable to pass. Three guys could be crawling up his back, blocking every kind of shot he could make, and from the look in his eye you know he is desperate and *wants* to pass but he *simply cannot let go of the ball* unless it is to shoot. It is worse than dope. If our opponents ever learn how to stop him from rolling to the right and going up, we are going to have to devise a brand-new scoring play.

Other nutty things Hetzel did was put in the subs in the second quarter, where they quickly blew our 10-point lead, and in the third quarter shifting to a man-for-man defense instead of our usual 2–3 or 1–3–1 zone. In a zone or box-and-one I can cover for Norman and Burkhart while handling my own man, but in man-for-man their guy always beats Norman to the basket and it is often a 3-point play, because either Norman cracks him to make him blow the shot or I have to. So it turns out I am picking up fouls for Norman. Besides that, Norman gets tired when he runs a lot. So he staggered out in the fourth quarter, his tongue hanging out and his hands flapping, and if Haley hadn't kind of taken over we would have been licked. But he was everywhere, picking off passes, scoring on drives, chucking me some good passes for chippies and drawing fouls. And man, he can *sink* them. Between us, we poured in about 15 points (him 11). With two minutes to go the bench came in but even those wild men couldn't blow a 12-point lead.

I wound up with 16 points, my season high, and 13 *official* rebounds, though I am sure it was nearer 20. Haley had 25 points, 11 on foul shots, and Norman a big fat 8.

The family is still breathing and Terry is kind of tall for a 10-year-old. Maybe I will make a center out of her.

Cordially,
The Scholarship Kid

P.S. You remember that party I mentioned? I am through with Madge. It turned out she was *using* me to make the captain of the swimming team jealous. He does a 53.5 freestyle hundred. Big deal. One thing, he will never touch the rim. Well, love 'em and leave 'em, I always say.

Dec. 18

Jeffrey,

I am in kind of a sweat because of some stupid homework thing, so will just include some notes I made evaluating the skills of the team while in study hall this p.m. We walloped Farmington in a 6-quarter scrimmage. But with Hetzel empty-ing the stands almost to give everybody varsity experience, it was a phiasco as far as basketball went. I was in for a quarter and a half and had a cold hand. I figured if Rancom and Burkhart could fling them up from outside all the time, I could too. So every time I got the ball I shot. But the light was reflecting kind of funny off the backboard and nobody would set a pick for me so I was about 4 for 16 or maybe 20. I had a cold hand. Anyway, here is how the team looks with a 3–1 record:

Norman Parker, center—good shot from near the basket, good rebounder, great on tapins. Not crazy about playing defense.

Doug Haley, left forward—Good ball-handler, good shot

from inside and out, good driver, good defense, good passer when he's in the mood. Can dunk.

The King, right forward—Good ball-handler (when he gets it), fair shot from outside, fair driver, superb rebounder, superb on defense, great technical knowledge of the game. Passes are his weakness because they are so well disguised he fools even his own teammates, ha ha. This boy is going places.

Burkhart, backcourt—Should make opponents' All-Opponent team as the player they would most like to play against. Panics, blows layups, good outside shot from constant practice, constitutionally unable to relinquish the ball when he has it except to put it up. No defense. Gives away more points than he gets except when the moon is full.

Manners (Capt.), backcourt—Hasn't played much because of a bad knee thanks to Deke Saunders who flattened him on a rebound in preseason practice. Passes mainly to Seniors.

Cantwell, forward—A candidate for All-Opponent team. Can't pass, can't catch, can't shoot, can't dribble but full of ginger and always patting the other players on the pants. Rebounds OK. Do you know he has played almost as many minutes as I have?

Saunders, center—Rebounds well against his own teammates. Useful if we ever got a game with Attila the Hun. Can dunk in warmup to give crowd a thrill.

Rancom, backcourt—Makes Cantwell look like Oscar Robertson.

What inspired me to make up the list was that in cafeteria Wed. p.m. (beans and franks, you recall), Burkhart came up to me and said he figured out he was the third most valuable player on the team. He had a list. He said Haley was first, Norman second, him third and me fourth. So I blew my stack and told him calmly, Yeah, Haley is first because he's a good ballplayer, Norman is second because he can score for us, but I was definitely third. Burkhart said, Yeah but I'm outscoring you by six points a game. Yeah I said, but that's *all* you can do. You sleep on defense, you won't set a pick and you can't rebound. Look at the shooting percentages, I told him. I'm at least number three, I said, and you're back with the also-rans. Man, I was sore. Stick it in your ear, I told him. I don't know why I even bother talking to him. He is a *complete ass.*

I forgot to say that in the scrimmage one of their forwards lost his contact lens so naturally everything had to stop. Haley was sitting next to me on the bench at the time and while everybody is down on their hands and knees looking for it he says I got an idea. Let's ask Hetzel if the team can do wind sprints up and down the court. He is the kind of guy that would do it, too, but just then Manners found it.

The Old Man has a new clock joke. You remember when you ask him, What time is it? he says, What's time to a horse? Well, last night Muth was in the living room and he was in the kitchen. So she says, What time is it out there? And he calls back, It's 8:35 out here, what time is it in there? And he nearly busts a gut laughing at his own joke. That is grownups for you.

There is a girl named Sue Ann that really has a case on me, I kid you not. She has some hairdo, like one of those Bunckingham Palace guards. She is sending me notes all the time in English class and it is hard to concentrate on Shakespeare. We had a question on a test a couple of days ago, Was Hamlet really mad? So I wrote down, Wouldn't *you* be mad if somebody was trying to gyp you out of your kingdom? I really feel for the guy, you know? I identify with him. I got a B on the test, mainly because Miss Mitchell is crazy about basketball players.

Did you know Peter the Great was 6′9′′? We learned that in Soc class the other day. What a center he would make, eh?

All the best,

L.

P.S. Who would call fouls on him?

Dec. 19

Jeff old sibling,

You did not do me much good when the transcript of your grades came, all A's and B's. That is not bad, considering you can hardly ever have time to go to class. I guess the Pretzel Bell makes a great study hall, eh? Anyway, Muth made some odius comparison between those marks and my C's and D's. Forgetting completely that I never get anything but Outstanding in gym class, except the time I poked that guy on my volleyball team for his lousy serving in the intramural tournament.

Here is my All-Star, All-Historical basketball team if you are interested:

Peter the Great, 6'9", center
Abe Lincoln, 6'4" rf
Andrew Jackson, 6'3", lf
Stonewall Jackson (no relation), 6'2", backcourt
Napoleon Bonaparte, 5'4", backcourt (playmaker)
Referees: Oliver Wendell Holmes and King Solomon

I asked the OM who would be a good backcourt man after I selected the first four players and he said Napoleon—because he would be so good at *freezing*. And he nearly fell down laughing at his own joke. So that is how Napoleon made it. Personally, I think he was out of shape and would be stuffed every time he shot. But maybe Hetzel would get him in shape by doing a lot of wind sprints. The thing is, would Napoleon pass to Peter? They never got along too great.

Cordially,
6'2" brother

P.S. It will be nice having you home for Xmas. You can tell me about the college bunnies and later we can play one-on-

one or maybe you can dig up a college buddy and play Haley and I two-on-two. We can also get up some touch games. You will also be able to see me in three games in the tournament we host over the holidays.

Jan. 12

Dear Jeff,

Well, I guess right now you are telling your Ann Arbor buddies about the scholarship kid at Northside High. Averaging 16 points per game for the tournament is not bad, eh? And I should have had a tap-in the stupid scorer gave to Norman in the Port Jefferson game, but who's counting? So now anyway you know I wasn't snowing you when I talked about Norman's sparkling defensive play and Burkhart's love affair with the backboard.

After we won the tournament the Press rated us No. 2 in the county behind Jericho, and they could do little else, considering our 5–1 record, along with copping the tournament.

Yesterday I had a miserable practice because I am fighting off some kind of cold germ and the night before I was up late —till 11 anyway—on some kind of science project for science. At about 8 I mentioned to the OM I was feeling bushed and might need some help on the thing, since it was due the next day.

He blew his stack. How come this is the first time you mentioned it? he hollers, throwing down his paper. There are screams from Terry, who claims she can't hear. She is watching some family show on TV while the OM is snapping questions at me and I'm trying to straighten him out. TV should tune in on *us* some time. How am I supposed to know when it should be in, I asked him calmly.

Because your teacher should tell you, he screams. She only told us at the last minute, I said. Anyway, let's be calm about this, I told them. Muth was in it by this time. So then I told them a few things that maybe they didn't know about—that the King is leading the No. 2 team in the county in both offensive and defensive rebounds though only a Junior, is a close fourth in scoring, would lead in assists if the stupid scorer knew how to score assists and other things. (To say nothing of leading the team in fouls, ha ha.)

They were not greatly impressed. Anyhow, I told them, I'm dying from fighting off cold germs and I'm going to hit the sack. I told Muth to wake me at 4 a.m. and I would get after the science project. She and the OM exchanged glances and talked around me, and finally with some grumbling he decided he would do it. His final words burned in my ears while I chugged down some hot lemonade that Muth made and piled into the sack.

So he was up for a while grumbling and clipping stuff out of magazines and made a kind of evolutionary family tree— lizards, monkeys, birds and so on—and I got up 15 minutes early and glued it together in the morning. It would have taken me all night to do it, let alone think up the idea, but he is always reading anyway, so it was no big sweat for him to dig up the pictures. Did you know that birds are descended from snakes? The way I am feeling I may not start against Hartsdale.

Hoping you are the same,
Larry

Jan. 16

Dear Jeff,

We murdered Hartsdale so bad I played only about half a quarter like the rest of the first team. The score was 76–54, our season high. The only notable thing about the game was that Hetzel put the screwballs in early to keep the score down and they went crazy putting baskets in from all over the floor and some of them are so puffed up and proud of themselves I feel like socking them.

In practice today Hetzel was experimenting with a new offense because he figures that some of the teams we play a second time have got to hit on a way to stop Norman by double-teaming him or timing his roll so he can't get off a clean shot. So the thing is now for Haley to take a jag step toward the middle, then cut under the basket. Norman is supposed to fake right and then go left and pass to Haley who will have a layup. If he is covered I am supposed to be in his spot, only in more, taking advantage of their defense sagging in, and take a short jumper. Naturally Haley and I are wild about the change because it will give us more chance to score, while Norman and Burkhart are kind of disgruntled. Burkhart has been told not to chuck so much, but I don't think he listens too hard. Norman took a poke at Manners, a real mild guy, in the locker room he was so ticked off about the change, and Hetzel chewed him out good, 19 point average or no 19 point average.

I got back the science project the OM helped me with and got a big fat C on it. This is not too bad since you practicly have to turn in a working model of a cyclotron to get a B from Miss Putnam and the story is she has not given an A on anything since 1921. It is rumored that she once flunked George Washington Carver.

In study hall Haley told me it is a great gag in *his* science class—Mrs. Fuller's—that when some of them are assigned a science project they turn in an *egg*. I mean, an egg is really a *cell*, you know? The yolk is the nucleus and all. And you can't get much more scientific than that.

I was figuring next year if I could turn in an egg every time Mrs. Fuller demanded a science project I could keep picking up solid C's and not waste a lot of time. Because we have lots of eggs and it is no trouble at all to take one out of the fridge and schlepp it over to school. Besides which she could make herself a nice omelette with my eggs and Norman's eggs (I will let him in on the secret) every three weeks or so. But I suppose if we were studying something like earthquakes, which is also science, she would not be too crazy to get eggs. May I would turn in a busted egg. Well, it is something to think about, anyway.

I wish you would be around to see us against Long Beach, because they are the only team that licked us this season and we are out for blood, especially with our new scoring punch, if you know what I mean.

Cordially,
The Big L

Jan. 20

Dear Jeff,

You will be shocked and amazed to learn we nipped Long Beach only by 53–51 and I had a bad game mainly because of the stupid refs. In the first place, Hetzel completely forgot about the new offense and we went back to the same old tired plays of everybody feeding Norman and letting him slap it up or Burkhart chucking from midcourt. Nobody passed to me and I kept playing defense for at least three members of our team, so naturally I did not do much scoring. But the main problem was the stupid refs. I picked up four fouls in the first half—one of which was legitimate—and was benched in the third quarter. In the fourth quarter I had to play cautious because they were calling them so tight on me.

Get this: One time I took down a rebound with my elbows out—strictly in self-defense because I was getting murdered under the basket by Olsen—and *that* was a foul. Long Beach got the ball outside. Then one time I picked off a defensive rebound and was dribbling downcourt for an easy layup when one of their guys—Unger, a backcourt man—ran down after me, slammed into my back so I nearly went into the wall, and it was called a foul on *me*. Unbelievable! You should have heard the howls of anguish that roared up from the stands. The ref completely *choked*.

Another time I stuffed Olsen *clean*. It was a fantastic play because he is 6'5". I hit the ball so hard when he tried to shoot he wound up sitting on the floor. Hetzel is all red in the face hollering Clean! Clean! because he knows what is going to happen. Olsen has such a mournful expression while he has one hand over his nose that the ref takes pity on him and gives him two free throws. Man, I get tired of holding my hand up when they make a stupid call! Another time, one of their little guys got past Norman for the millionth time and while he was going up for a layup I cracked him good. I mean I don't think he had any feeling in his arm for 15 minutes. This, I admit, could have been called an actual foul. But it is so rare when these stupid refs call a foul that is really a foul that I thought for a second that I would get away with it, even though their guy blew the layup and for an alibi clutched his arm like it was busted. What an actor. But there was a delayed whistle and that was No. 4. Hetzel yanked me while the guy was choking on two foul shots and chewed me out, but before that the crowd gave me quite a hand, standing up, when I trotted off the floor. I really hustled and got about 10 rebounds, though I put in only two buckets from the floor and missed a foul shot. The rims are very tight and the ball has a tendency to go in and out again.

But when I'm not in, the team goes to pieces, and in the third quarter Long Beach led 40–36. Then from somewhere out under the rocks Hetzel found a sophomore named Dan Kluttz—ain't that a name?—and this kid did all right. He is a big rangey kid about 6'5" and he took Haley's passes and stuffed in about 8 points and we slid ahead 46–44 with about 3 minutes to go. Then Long Beach put on a full-court press with three guys climbing all over Burkhart when he took the ball downcourt and he panicked and gave the ball away twice and with a minute to go it was 48–all. So Hetzel calls time and I go in for Cantwell who has been having a great game with two big points. In the huddle Hetzel tells us to slow down, make sure of our passes and feed to Norman and not foul.

Well, wouldn't you know the first thing that happens is, I'm clear at the top of the key, Burkhart throws me a pass—the first pass he has thrown in three years of basketball—and I see Norman is covered. So I fake Unger out of his pants, come down when he is going up and go up when he is coming down. I put the ball up and it goes Swish, but while I'm coming down again I hit him. Now, if I go up I have to come down, right? That is what they have been teaching us in physics all year. But the ref calls a rare one—a charge after the shot—and Unger gets a free throw. The worst thing is it's No. 5 for me and I'm out. What am I supposed to do? I said to the ref while he was taking the ball downcourt. Stay up in the air? I got to come down for God's sake. While I'm informing him of these facts Hetzel is screaming from the bench and Haley grabs my arm and tells me to shut up or there'll be a technical. I was all ready to poke him, the ref I mean.

Anyway, I'm out on fouls, Unger sinks it and Hetzel is not too pleased because except for Haley he's got no defense. But somehow we kept the one-point lead because Burkhart developed a hot hand after two months and Norman managed to stuff a few of their guys under the basket. So we beat them by 2 but with decent refereeing we would have by 20.

I forgot to say that one time there was a loose ball at midcourt with Burkhart and one of their guys scrambling for it on the floor and I casually pushed Unger into the pile-up by mistake and it was called a foul on *him*. Har-de-harhar.

At home later I wasn't in too good of a mood and when Terry yapped something at me I might have given her a kind of push. She starts to holler and then whacko! The Old Man came down on my left arm. What a *rap*. With his knuckles. Man, he is fast when he wants to move. I still feel it. Did he ever crack you like that? If he had hit my right arm a shot like that I would be writing this with my teeth. Then he made me go upstairs and hit the books, which frankly I don't find too inspiring lately.

Well, in spite of all our troubles, the team is 7–1, but next comes Jericho with an 11–0 record and they are *tough*. I suppose even at Michigan you heard about their center, Cleary, who is 6'9" and was All-County as a Junior. He was also All-County tackle and weighs 235, so you got to *know* he's tough.

Regards,
The Ex-King

Jan. 27

Dear Brudder,

Did we get plastered, I mean smashed! It was partly psychology and partly that Jericho is some ball club. In the pregame warmup they came out in these cool white silk warmup suits with red stripes and Navy collars with Lions written across them in red. Each player has his name on the back of his jacket. The game uniforms are white with red stripes and the players' names and numbers are on the back in red. And they have red-and-white striped knee socks, making them all look 7 feet tall. They look like a million bucks just standing still, and they really move when they chuck around their red-and-white warmup ball. In a layup drill about four of them dunked, including Cleary of course, who nearly takes the rim off, and Williams, a 6'2" Negro who jumps like he was 11 feet tall.

We completely went bust from the opening tapoff. Cleary outjumped Norman by 50 feet and batted the ball to Agostino, who passed to Williams who was racing downcourt and it was the fastest two points you ever saw. Burkhart took the ball upcourt, fired it up and somehow sank it. They brought it down, fed to Cleary and he bulled past Norman and stuffed it in. He also got fouled in the process because he has a neat trick of delaying the shot until you think you can stop him and suddenly you are hitting him somewhere. So Norman sadly stuck his hand up.

Then Burkhart took it down, couldn't get off a shot and flipped to Norman. He was completely smothered by Cleary and Agostino and put up a bad shot. Williams jumped a hundred feet in the air with his legs in a high spreadeagle to discourage anybody coming within ten feet of him, came down, fired a long pass to Mazurek and Mazurek put in a layup. So far we had been playing two minutes almost and I hadn't touched the ball yet.

After that, Cleary was all over the place, blocking shots, sinking chippies, drawing fouls with his great move, passing off to Agostino and Williams and not letting Norman get off a decent shot. I was 2 for 8 on long jumpers and 4 for 5 on foul shots. We were outrebounded, mainly by Cleary, outfoxed and outgunned. At the half they led us 42–20, with Cleary scoring 24. In the second half Hetzel tried all kinds of defenses but this guy simply cannot be stopped. That is some ball club. They finally won it 79–43. Nobody said a word on the way home on the bus.

The Press picked *this* one right.

Cordially,
Larry

Feb. 25

Jeff,

Sorry not to have written before this but the old folks have been on my back about studying and there hasn't been much to write about. Things have been generally rotten with the team. Dissension, low morale, everybody dogging it. After we got plastered by Jericho we slipped by Keith 54–50 in overtime. They are a terrible ball club but everybody on Northside has become a prima donna. Nobody passed the ball, the defense was ragged and it seemed nobody cared. At half, with them leading 20–19 Hetzel never said a word to us in the locker room, just let us stew. After the game was finally over Haley told me he was so disgusted he would positively never pass the ball to Burkhart or Norman again, and I assume Norman and Burkhart have sworn similar oaths about each other and Haley. I swore I was never going to pass to Burkhart, I might pass to Norman because I am going to have to play with him next year, and I would pass to Haley exactly the same number of times he passed to me. I swore I would not set picks for anybody but Haley because he is good about setting picks so you can get off a shot, but he is the only guy on the team that will do it.

Compared to our next 3 games, though, the one with Keith was a jewel. We went on a beautiful losing steak—to Molinas, Bay Shore and Hartsdale. I am beginning to feel sorry for Hetzel because he is desperate trying to pull the team together. There is no horseplay in practice and he looks like he didn't sleep in a year. He sometimes puts in Kluttz for Norman, but who is going to pass to a sophomore? He put in Rancom for Burkhart but Rancom is a terrible outside shot. He put in Cantwell for Haley, but Cantwell doesn't like to shoot, though he is no ball hog, and we lose Haley's scoring power.

Hetzel is giving us pep talks one day and calling us gutless the next. He is one disturbed mentor, I kid you not. Since the Jericho thing everything that was wrong with the team has popped out like straw out of a rotten burlap bag. Nobody says Nice shot when you stick it in, or pats you on the pants for encouragement (always excepting Cantwell) or anything. We are like a bunch of zombies out there.

You didn't do me any good by making the Dean's list. I was informed about it by the parents, naturally. So I said, Yeah, but can he touch the rim? That went over like a lead balloon. Nothing ever *reaches* you, does it, the old man screamed at me. He is not too pleased at how the team is going after our good start. I hope this will help you see things in perspective, he says to me. Not everything in this world revolves around sticking a ball in some hoop! Oh boy.

We are 5 and 4 in the league, 8 and 5 over all. If we blow the next one, against Keith again, we won't be in the tournament, because only the first three teams are eligible. Personally, I will be glad when it's all over.

Regards,
Larry

Mar. 2

Dear Jeff,

Somehow we squeaked by Keith, before empty stands, 65–62. In the first half we tried the new offense, with Norman passing off mainly to Haley and it worked OK. Once in a while Haley would pass to me and I would pass back to him on a give and go and it worked pretty good. I had a hot hand finally and scored 20, 16 from the floor. In the second half we went back to the old system and they stopped Norman cold. With them ahead in the third quarter we went back to the new offense and Haley went crazy, hitting from all over. He made

our last 8 points. Saunders went in for Norman at center and
crashed the boards pretty good.

We finished third in the league with 6–4. Long Beach won
it and Molinas was second. Anyway we are in the tournament.
Jericho, which won their league easy, is seeded No. 1.

Thank you for the kind words in your letter. I will try to
stay cool.

Cordially,
Larry

Mar. 3

Jeff,

You will never believe this. Today in practice Hetzel started
out by giving us what he calls an attitude talk. It is like a
dignified chewing out. He said we weren't playing like a team
and that we would lose in the first round against Glenville if
we didn't "get on the ball," as he put it. He is a great
phrasemaker. He bawled out Haley for missing some practices, Burkhart for chucking, Rancom for throwing the ball
away too much, Norman for not hustling on defense and me
for not being a team player. That is a laugh, since I am the
only guy who passes and the only one besides Haley who will
set a pick, but what can you do? Then he goes to the
blackboard and gives us a *new* offense—new beyond the other
new one, I mean. This one has me instead of Haley faking and
cutting for the basket and getting the ball from Norman—so
suddenly it is me who is the team scorer. There are all kinds of
variations, depending on how they sag and if they play zone or
man-for-man, but I am the guy supposed to get the ball under
the hoop. I don't know if he is trying to punish Haley or fool
the opposition or what.

So then we try it out in practice. At first it didn't go too smooth, but finally we got the moves right and I had a great streak against the second string. After practice Hetzel calls me to one side and says, You think you can take the pressure, Larry? I pointed out to him I just stuck in 30 points. Yes, he says, but in front of a tournament crowd, against some tough defenses and while a couple of guys are hanging onto your arms? Watch me, I told him. Actually, I am not that confident, but I figured he needed some reassurance and God knows he looks awful from worry, so that was my good deed for the day.

They were pretty glum in the locker room. You would think I had sold them out or something, but I guess that is to be expected when you are thrust into the role of hero suddenly.

We have two more practices before Glenville Sat. night.

Warmest regards,
Larry

Mar. 6

Jeff baby,

The new offense worked like a charm. The King stuck in a fat 27 points to lead both teams in scoring and we licked them 74–68. Norman put in 14, mostly on tap-ins, and Haley put in 12, mainly on passes from me in the fourth quarter when they were swarming all over me and I couldn't get a shot off. My arms and ribs are mighty sore and now I realize some of the walloping Norman has been getting when he tries to shoot from close in.

It is great being high scorer. Everybody congratulated me, even Hetzel. When I came out with about 10 seconds to play in the fourth quarter, what a roar went up from our side, everybody standing up, even their fans. I was asked to two parties after the game but I was so bushed I just said goodnight and slogged home. Terry met me at the door with a bow and

said, Hail to the King when I came in. In the game following
ours, Jericho murdered Molinas 82–53.

Tues. night we play St. Paul's in the semis. They won their
league without losing a game so you know they *got* to be
tough.

Cordially,

L.

Mar. 10

Jeffrey,

I'm enclosing a newspaper story of the game because my
version might be a little hysterical. St. Paul's has guys 6'9",
6'7", two 6'5"s, and can they jump! They did a dunking drill
in the warmup. One guy dunks, the next tomahawks, the next
stuffs it through the basket with one hand and catches it with
the other when it comes through. We didn't shoot, we just
stood around with our mouths open watching them perform.
The crowd went nuts and I bet there wasn't a person in the
gym who didn't think they would win by 20. Including our
varsity.

They ran up a 12–0 lead right away before Burkhart puts
in a long-range missile and we steadied down a little. Their
guys were big but we found when we put a press on them, they
took steps or threw the ball away. I hit a streak finally and we
were only 2 behind at half. I don't know what their coach fed
them in the locker room, but they came out *mean*. They
crashed the boards, they gunned from outside and stuffed us
when we got near the basket. They threw a few elbows and we
threw a few. It was 54–44 for them at the end of the third
quarter. Then Norman got hot on tap-ins and their 6'9" guy,
Majekowski, picks up his fourth foul. Then Burkhart takes the
ball down, fires it to Norman at the low post and Norman

throws to me while I am cutting for the basket. I see Majekowski on my right ready to slap the ball when I put it up, so I fake the shot, come down, go way up and put the ball in. I managed to make him hit me, so it's No. 5 for him and he's out. I stick in the free throw and we're a point behind with 20 seconds to go.

Manners comes in, bad knee and all, to help with our full-court press. They get the ball downcourt and we put three guys on the man with the ball and Manners steals it! There's 6 seconds left. Hetzel calls time so he can give us the play and send in Cantwell for Manners. He tells Rancom to throw it to Burkhart or Cantwell, whoever was free, and for that party to throw to Norman at the top of the key. I was to be at halfcourt and cut for the basket as a decoy and Norman was to fling it to Haley, who was to start down right, then cut sharp left for the left corner. Haley was to put it up, no matter what. St. Paul's couldn't crowd us too much for fear of fouling, which made things easier.

From out of bounds Rancom finally got a pass off to Cantwell who saw Norman was covered and flung a long one to Haley who wasn't ready for it. He leaped and twisted, juggled the ball a few times and I almost died. Then he shot from 25 feet out, almost without aiming. The ball hit the backboard and the rim and fell out—but from somewhere Burkhart came running like a streak and jumped 50 feet in the air and tapped it in. You should have seen us jumping up and down, Haley hugging Burkhart and Cantwell slapping Norman on the back and Rancom dancing with Kluttz and the whole bench going crazy.

There was about a second left, so St. Paul's threw the ball in glumly and their guy couldn't even launch a full-court heave before the buzzer sounded. The fans swarmed onto the floor whooping and hollering and we had to run to escape with our lives.

I scored 24 for the team high and was asked to 4 parties—
two on the way to the bus, because Burkhart and I are the
team heroes, him for the last-second bucket and me for the
entire game. I am skipping them all because my chest is
burning and my legs are dead. But after the Jericho game I
promised myself a big blast whether we win or not. I forgot to
say Jericho made the final by licking Wampahonsset 84–51,
Cleary scoring 39.

At home the Old Man raved about the way Norman and
Haley played and Burkhart's clutch basket. I wonder what the
hell game he was looking at.

Yours,

L.

Mar. 11

Jeff,

I am BMOC around here all right, the girls turning around
to stare at me when I pass, the men teachers talking about the
tournament and the Jericho game instead of filling our heads
with facts, and I got an A from Miss Kearns the Soc teacher,
along with a cheery smile, on a test I didn't answer half the
questions on, and I wouldn't be surprised if *those* answers
were kind of shaky. In cafeteria there is always a big noisy
mob around Haley, Norman, Manners, Burkhart and me, and
they are slapping us on the back and bringing us milk and
asking how many each of us are going to score against Jericho
and how we are going to stop Cleary. That is a sobering
thought.

The crowd was so big at practice today that Hetzel threw
them all out of the gym on the assumption they were bothering
us. I scored something like 42 against the second string, but

who's counting. We also practiced presses, freezing, foul shooting and different defenses. We have one more practice before J-Day.

Regards,
Larry

Mar. 14

Dear Jeff,

Yesterday I sent you a clipping from the Press that came out the day before the Jericho game where Hetzel said I was the most promising Junior shooter he ever coached. Burn it. We played them Saturday night and I played *rotten*. The whole thing is like some kind of nightmare.

The game was played at the Molinas gym which is the biggest in the county and you had to be there at 5 p.m. to get a seat it was so packed. Everybody had the jitters coming over on the bus, nobody clowning around, stealing hats or anything. Kluttz was chewing his nails and Norman yelled at Haley to shut up, he was chewing his gum so loud. The principal and the men's dean came with us, presumably to give our morale a goose. About 8 busloads of Northside students were already there when we arrived which made us even more nervous.

In the locker room Hetzel saw we were tight so he reminded us we beat a tough team in the semis, the team that won't be beaten can't be beaten and such golden words as that, and forget the crowd, he says. You could hear them screaming inside the locker room. So we ran out on the court and you never saw such an electric atmosphere with the crowd standing up and shrieking, waving signs Beat Northside, and We're No. 1, and No You Ain't, and Stomp the Lions, and organized rah-rahing—If you don't *believe* it, we'll yell a little *louder*.

There are about six dozen cheerleaders in red and white and orange and blue scampering all over the floor, shaking their calabashes and doing splits and the Jericho Lion is doing cartwheels and acting comical by chasing people. In the middle of all this we're trying to find the basket in a layup drill. I might mention that this is the first time a Northside team ever got this far in a county tournament and our supporters are as nervous as we are. It is a spooky feeling.

Then Jericho sprints out, led by Mazurek, the captain, and trailed by Cleary, the county high scorer. The yell that went up and the stamping and the whistles would scare you. Suddenly these red and white uniforms are flashing all over the place with snappy ball-handling and dunks and double axes and tomahawks. We got two guys who can dunk and it is pretty tame stuff compared to the Lions, believe you me.

The starters are introduced—me last—and you should have heard the roar that went up, as big as the roar for Cleary. Manners and Mazurek chat with the refs, we grab hands in the huddle and this, as they say before an amphibious landing, is *it*.

Norman for some strange reason manages to outjump Cleary. The ball goes to Haley, he passes to Burkhart, and Swish. Jericho is hardly rattled, though. They bring the ball down, Cleary cuts behind Norman and while I'm stepping in front of him to stop a drive he passes to Williams under the basket and it's up and in.

Now comes the worst part. I had a bad first quarter, blowing chippies and getting shots blocked. Our guys dutifully passed to me when I was open but either Jericho blocked the shot or I got tight. I guess I was 0 for 6 and the only guys scoring for us are Norman and Haley. A couple of times I was held while shooting but it wasn't called and the more I missed, the more confidence oozed out of me.

With about a minute to go in the first quarter, it's 16–12 for them and Hetzel pulls me out. There wasn't much sound when I came off the floor but I imagine a lot of nudging went on among the fans. Hetzel didn't start me in the second quarter, when they led 20–14. While the game is going on he says to me on the bench, Listen, Larry, you're not doing us any good with your shooting and our problem is stopping Cleary. I'm going to send you back in, he says, and I want you to forget about shooting. Be the first man downcourt on defense and stick with Cleary. Keep him from getting the ball. Play him tight.

So while Haley is taking a foul shot, in I go, to assorted boos, and try to stick with Cleary. It ain't easy, because he is big and fast and rough. The first time he tries to get a shot off from the top of the key I foul him and he sinks a couple. A great beginning. Some of the fans are hollering, Put Cantwell in! We score and they buzz downcourt again. I stay close to Cleary so he can't get the ball, Mazurek misses, Haley gets the rebound and we score. The pattern is the same through the quarter, with me taking 20 steps to Cleary's one and sticking on his back. But at half I have three fouls against me and we're behind 36–29. I am dying from running, jumping and moving my arms around like a windmill.

In the locker room I am chewing on some of Muth's oranges and Hetzel is explaining some offensive and defensive errors and I don't hear a single word.

Jericho gets a big hand when they come out but the one we get is bigger. At least they have not run us off the court yet. This time Cleary gets the tap. He bats it to Williams and Williams throws to Mazurek who throws to Cleary who stops suddenly near the foul line and I'm all over his back. So the whistle toots and it's a push—foul No. 4 on me and I get yanked. I come out and the silence is worse than boos. Cantwell goes in as Cleary is sinking two and we take the ball down and Haley scores on a baseline drive. It's also a foul on Cleary—No. 3. We stay even with them for the next minute and I'm urging Hetzel to stick me in because I might as well foul out as sit on the bench.

He pulls Cantwell out and once again I'm dogging Cleary wherever he goes, in front of him, in back of him, around to the side, jumping up and getting faked and recovering and waving my arms in front of his face. Little by little we catch up —two on a tap-in by Norman, two on a jumper by Haley, four on rocket blasts by Burkhart, two on a layup by Cantwell who's in to rest Norman. I'm fouled once by Williams, which I miss, and once by Cleary, which I sink. So I have one big fat point. Meanwhile Haley and Cantwell are playing good defense and rebounding good. I have to play it cautious, so I stay out of crowds, and because my shooting is cold I pass off instead of taking the shot.

At the third quarter it's them 54 and us 50, so it's still a ball game. Norman comes back in, gets outjumped by Cleary, the ball goes to Williams but Haley grabs it and they have a tussle that lands them both on the floor, tugging and twisting. Williams outjumps him on the jump ball and Cleary gets it, but Burkhart grabs it and gets flung around in a circle like a terrier. On the jump ball, Cleary bats it to Mazurek but Haley intercepts it and fires downcourt to Rancom for the bucket. They come down, taking their time, and finally Mazurek is in for a jumper and makes it. Haley shoots and misses and Norman catches it on his upraised palm, goes up with it and in. What a roar from our side.

Mazurek misses a set shot and we come down for what you might call the key basket. Burkhart flips to Haley, Haley dribbles and gives to Norman and meanwhile I have cut and am under the basket. Then while Norman is rolling to his right the whistle blows and it turns out I have made a 3-second violation, staying too long inside the key, and Jericho gets the ball. Our crowd is wild—half of them screaming it wasn't three seconds and the other half booing my stupid move. The

Jericho fans are screaming Go, Go, Go while Mazurek is taking the ball downcourt. They score six points in a row while Cleary and Williams are controlling the defensive boards, and from there the game seesaws, with Norman launching himself up and sticking the ball in and Haley sinking short jumpers.

With about two minutes to go it is 68–65 and Hetzel calls time. We flop down on the bench to rest while the subs stand up and Hetzel, red in the face, tells us we didn't come this far to lose and to get out there and score. He is talking fast and hard and slapping his fist in his hand, like he was trying to pour energy into us. Meanwhile I am so tired from galloping up and downcourt, trying to follow Cleary's fakes and jumping up to compensate for his height advantage I can hardly breathe. My chest is on fire and my legs are dead.

The next disaster is that they take the ball out of bounds while we're putting on a full-court press, the ball gets by our chasers and suddenly I'm all alone under our basket with Cleary and Williams coming at me. Williams is on my right and dribbling fast and I figure he'll fake a shot and pass to Cleary, so I charge toward him and stop so he'll have to pull up. Then when he fakes the shot I leap to my left to hit the ball, but he doesn't pass, he shoots. I make a quick lunge for the ball which I bat out of bounds, but at the same time I hit his forearm and the whistle blows. Foul on 42! the ref screams and I have to stick my hand up. That is No. 5 for me. I trod dolefully to the bench. Williams sinks them both and we are 5 behind with 55 seconds left. Haley drives in for two because they don't dare foul him. When they bring the ball down, Manners and Burkhart are leaping around so to cover their guy that he passes wild. Norman picks it off, lopes down for the layup and it is 70–69.

Three of our guys are on Mazurek as he comes downcourt but he gets the ball to Williams, who dribbles a little bit, and then they start a freeze. The seconds are ticking off while they're passing to one another just past midcourt and the fans on their side are going wild, beginning to count out loud as it gets to 10, 9, 8, 7—I am sitting there with a towel on my head, resigned to the fact that I am the goat of the game with my one lousy stinking point, and with three seconds to go, Agostino throws a pass to Williams that Burkhart deflects and before it goes out of bounds it hits Cleary on the leg. There is a big argument about whose ball it is, but we get it. We have it out of bounds at midcourt with two seconds to go.

Hetzel calls time and we have a huddle. How are we going to get a shot off from midcourt in two seconds? He talks mainly to Haley and Norman. I'm no longer active but I listen. The team grabs hands and swarms out on the floor. The Jericho players are cavorting around a little bit, because they have got a lock on the championship and the Lion is shaking his hands in the boxer's salute and their coach looks like he might have the beginning of a smile on his face. The ushers are having a hard time keeping the fans off the floor and the amplifier is blaring that the game is not over and please stay in your seats, and the noisemakers are clacking. You would think one of our guys was shooting a foul shot, they are making so much disturbance.

Haley takes the ball from the ref, fakes to Burkhart, who is covered, and to Norman, who is down by the basket and covered by Cleary and to Rancom, who is also covered. Then he leans back and fires the ball at the backboard. Cleary jumps but can't reach it. It hits high and rebounds to Norman, who is about six feet to the right of the foul line. The clock starts ticking and he sticks it up. The ball hits the support that holds the basket, goes about four feet in the air as the buzzer sounds, hits the outside rim and then you should have heard the explosion. Norman jumps 50 feet in the air, Hetzel is slamming Saunders on the back, Burkhart is screaming and running over to slap Norman on the back, our fans are jumping up and down so hard in the stands you can feel the slats crack. Their lion is looking stunned. Haley gives me a look and bends his fingers and rubs his nails on his jersey and purses his lips like he had done something great—which he had—and then the fans are on the floor, about 80 million people crushing Norman and carrying him off. Their coach pushes through the mob around Hetzel and says what a great clutch player Norman is and Cleary reaches up, kind of gloomy, to shake Norman's hand. The one nice thing that happened to me was that Williams came over, shook my hand and said, You some ballplayer, man, and ducked off with Cleary and the others. Haley came bouncing by on some shoulders and one of his girl friends tried to reach up and kiss him but he was swept away by the crowd.

The team was very jolly going back on the bus but I wasn't in a mood for fun. I skipped all parties, skipped all recaps of the game by the family and got in the sack with my aches for company. I guess for the first time since I was eight, I bawled. Some way to end the season, eh?

Larry

Mar. 8

Jeff Baby!

Things are not so bad after all. There was a big assembly this p.m. (I missed Soc and English) and the team was introduced, some cups were awarded, and I was introduced as next season's captain. I forgot to say that the day before, when I was absent, the team elected me. In the assembly Hetzel told everybody I did great in the game by holding Cleary to 14 and kept him from getting the ball, which stopped their whole attack. He also said I played great defense all season, which is why the team did as well as it did. Sometimes I wonder if I am wrong about Hetzel—now and then he almost acts like a thinking human being. Of course he did not say anything about my deceptive passes or field-goal percentage, but what the hay.

Haley got MVP and in all the speeches that went on, nobody, thank goodness, mentioned my one point against Jericho. Although you might say it was the *key* point. The Old Man is pretty delighted about the news and he gave me a buck to go up and get a hero sandwich. And who has a better right to it?

Regards,
Larry

P.S. I've decided to go out for baseball rather than track, but I intend to tell Coach Burns that if I can't pitch, the heck with it.